CW00797323

Also by Gareth E. Rees from Influx Press:

Marshland: Dreams and Nightmares
on the Edge of London

5/100

The Stone Tide

Adventures at the end of the world

Gareth E. Rees

with illustration by Vince Ray

To David
Limited edition. Rare.
Signed. Enjoy.
Gareth E Rees

Influx Press, London

Published by Influx Press
49 Green Lanes, London, N16 9BU
www.influxpress.com / @InfluxPress

First edition 2018. Printed and bound in the UK by Clays Ltd., St Ives plc.
Paperback ISBN: 978-1-910312-07-0
Hardback ISBN: 978-1-910312-28-5
Ebook ISBN: 978-1-910312-08-7

Editor: Gary Budden
Copy-editor/Proofreader: Momus Editorial
Cover art and design: Mark Hollis
Comic: Vince Ray

In memory of Mike Hughes

1974–1996

'Hastings is the gateway into an enchanted garden ... Between the hills and the sea it lies—the most romantic province in this England of ours. Scarcely a place in it seems to belong to this present: from end to end it is built up almost entirely of memories ... nowhere in our coasts shall you find a stretch of land so crowded with the ghosts of dead men and dead empires.'

Walter Higgins, *Hastings & Neighbourhood*, 1920

Contents

PART TWO - DWELLING

PART THREE - DEPARTURE

PART ONE

Arrival

'I'm gonna move to Hastings,
Go as low as high can go
We all suck on Hastings rock,
It's the hardest rock I know'

Salena Godden

I

Gull Terror

In our final days in London, Emily's granddad had a stroke. His head hit the floor and cracked like an eggshell. He was ninety-six years old. There was nothing that could be done, the doctor said. They had to let him go. But he was a farmer in his working days and he had the heart of an ox. His body refused. He hung on, ailing on a Southampton hospital bed. We had no choice but to carry on with our move. Our life was in labelled boxes, ready for loading. A younger couple with a new baby were eagerly waiting for us to leave. Our time was up.

Emily and I had bought a dilapidated Victorian terraced house in the East Sussex seaside town of Hastings. No central heating. Antiquated wiring. Damp and dry rot. Overgrown garden. Foliage in the guttering. Cracked chimney pots. It was what estate agents call a project.

At the viewing we found the owner, Angela, hunched in the corner of the living room like a frightened bird, surrounded by books, cats and mouldering furniture. She and her husband had bought the house with another couple in the early 1970s and converted it into two separate properties. Their arrival marked the end of an era. The house had been occupied for almost a century by the family of the Victorian who built it. After constructing the terrace, he'd chosen to live in this property because it had the lowest resale value. Being situated on a bend in a road, it was wedge-shaped with peculiarly angled rooms. It remained in his family until Angela's lot came along with their woodchip and plasterboard partitions.

Now both husbands were dead and only the two women remained. Unable to deal with the crumbling house, they retreated into two rooms on separate floors and gaffer-taped electric fireplaces into the surrounds. Eventually, Angela was left alone to sell the place on. When we came for the viewing it must have been heart-wrenching for her to see Emily and me in her home with our two daughters, ready to knock down what she had made, paint over all she'd known and replace her memories with our own. We should have realised she'd not go quietly.

Two days before we were due to move, a distressed Angela rang the estate agent and told them she needed more time. But things were too far gone. There was a chain of people with contracts signed and removal firms booked. There was no going back.

Emily phoned Angela. 'Are you okay? Can we help?'

'I was sitting here, looking out the window at the park,' said Angela. 'I don't know if I can leave ... all this ...'

'It'll be a family home,' said Emily. 'We'll look after it.'

'I don't know. I haven't packed any of my things yet ...'

'If you want to leave some bits and pieces behind to pick up later, that's fine.'

'I feel like I rushed into this, I—'

'Is there anyone who can help you?'

Angela explained that she had a nephew with a van who she could ask to come and shift the furniture, though she barely saw him these days. He didn't visit. Never called around like he used to, not like in the days when all the family lived here, when her husband was alive. She had been left alone to deal with this change. It had all happened so quickly. Forty years in this place and now her possessions had to be cleared in a matter of days. She wasn't prepared. But her nephew, he was a good lad. Did she mention he had a van? He could do two trips, or three if necessary. There was so much to get rid of. Perhaps if we could wait another week or two? He was very busy, always working, but his van would be ideal. A few weeks, maybe more. That would give her time to prepare. How about that?

Emily gently convinced Angela that it was out of our hands. She had no choice but to move on the completion day. But we suspected she would be there when we arrived with the removal truck. What would we do then? Haul her out by her ankles? Legalities aside, this was her home. Her life was in these walls.

The death of Emily's granddad on the morning of the move intensified the feeling that we were changing the generational guard. After a sombre drive from London, we pulled up beside the overgrown front garden, white lilies pushing through the weeds.

'Hello?'

There was no sign of Angela. No sign of life at all. It was as if nobody had lived here for decades. Light strobed through moth-eaten holes in the curtains. Cobwebs darkened the corners of walls blistered and pimpled with damp. A stink of rotten earth wafted from the cellar. Racing green Victorian paint peered from beneath a flap of 1950s wallpaper. On the plaster beneath was a handwritten signature, dated 1885. I couldn't make out the first name, but the surname was Marsden. After the final letter, the signature looped across the plaster and mutated into a cartoonish portrait of a man with a beaky nose and a bird-like body, perhaps that of a duck or herring gull. Most likely, this was the man who built our house.

Beneath his zoomorphic self-portrait were scrawled other names and dates. Tom and Margaret who visited on 21 July 1973. Anne and Dick from Cardiff. Olive Strange. Sam (aged five) and Cherie (aged seven). Hilary. Tony. Ron. Jim. Isabel. Presumably they were all friends of Angela's who had come to Hastings to muck in with the project and get a bit of sea air at the same time, wandering to the arcades, eating ice cream on the pier, running down the shingle with their trousers rolled up. What wonderful luck to know people who lived in a holiday town. Of course, they were happy to come down for the weekend and help get the house into shape. Angela only had to ask. According to the dates on the wall, the renovation started in June 1974 and ended in August 1975. When the project came to an end they made valedictory marks on the plaster and sealed them beneath wallpaper.

'It's all coming to the surface now,' I said.

The absence of those former residents and their visitors hung heavy. Above the front door, a cracked stone lintel was the house's broken heart. Its subsiding interior had the wonk of an eighteenth-century galleon. There was an oppressive gravity to the place, as if it could no longer bear the weight of its own existence. We crept up lopsided stairs, running our hands over woodchip. In one of the bedrooms a disintegrating carpet revealed a layer of newspapers dated 1989–90. I read the headlines. A story accusing Rupert Murdoch's papers of distorting the facts about the recent Gibraltar IRA killings. A commercial for a brand-new channel called Sky Movies. Afghanistan peace talks in deadlock. A smiling Colonel Gaddafi with a crowd of cheering supporters. Shopworkers defiant against the unions over Sunday trading laws. A warning about ozone depletion in the atmosphere. War, politics, television, environmental collapse. The same old news cycle, spinning in a whirlpool of time.

In the yard, a handless clock hung on the wall. A pipe jutting from a concrete wall oozed slime into a vat. Steps led to a vertical jungle of weeds and a fox den, overlooked by an ancient yew, entwined with the branches of a tree which had grown and died within it. Pushing through the nettles and briars we found sculptures strewn in the undergrowth: snake heads, an urn, an owl, two ducks, a sleeping lion. Somewhere beneath this thorny tangle was a garden that had once been landscaped, illuminated and resplendent with clay sculptures. A temple to al fresco living. Like Machu Picchu it had been hurriedly abandoned, its totems and symbols swallowed up by nature. There was a metal handrail to help the unsteady visitor but it was buckled and rusted. Not to be trusted by someone with frail bones. Angela can't have been up here for years. As we explored further, our cocker spaniel Hendrix tore through the undergrowth, crazed by the scent wafting from the fox den. Worried he'd escape into the private allotments at the back of the garden we ushered him into the yard and wheeled a tabletop in front of the steps to seal off the wilderness.

That night we lay on a mattress beneath a broken chandelier in a room the colour of dried blood. It was hard to sleep. Our frantic toing and froing had kicked up years of dust. Our chests were wheezy. Eyes gritty. Noses clogged. Damp, cold air seeped through the bedclothes and made us shiver. Outside the window, shark-faced boomerangs appeared, seagulls caught in the glare of street lamps. They circled our house all night as if we were fresh meat washed up by the tide.

When I woke the next morning, I could hear my daughters giggling next door. They seemed excited at least. Wearily, I shuffled into their room to check that they were okay, but they were both fast asleep.

My throat tightened. These weren't walls which separated our rooms. These were storage vats. Before any renovation could begin, there would have to be an exorcism.

*

The night before Emily's granddad's funeral was sickly humid. We were living in the only two rooms upstairs that weren't filled with boxes, cooking on a camping stove. Downstairs was a no-go area. The kitchen was rotten, with cork panels warped, the paint peeling and the linoleum black and rippled with damp. No oven, only a chasm full of spiders where it used to be. An adjoining bathroom was caked in grime and dead skin. The toilet had no handle, only a cord dangling from a cistern with a sign that read:

PULL IN A

DETERMINED MANNER

STRAIGHT UP

This would all have to go. Stripped. Binned. Gutted. Torn down.

Before bed I took Hendrix downstairs for a wee. I cursed and bumped my way through the jumble, then waited in the doorway of the backyard in my pants and T-shirt. He ran up and down the yard, barking furiously. In the darkness I could make out something near the vat of slime by the concrete wall. A white orb, like an eye, swung back and forth as if scanning for something. For me. I could hear clattering and clicking. The scrape of a knife. Hendrix ran up to me, tail low. Freaked out, I led him back into the house and locked the door behind us. Whatever that thing was, I didn't want to deal with it. I would not die in my pants.

I tried my best to sleep but I could not shut out the noise of whatever was in our yard. It beat something repeatedly against the side of the plastic slime vat. The noise was slow and rhythmic, the tempo of a New Orleans funeral march—BANG—BANG —BANG.

Next morning, Emily and I went to investigate. As soon I opened the door there was an eruption of clattering and a startled cry. The culprit emerged from behind the slime vat: a herring gull with its head cocked at an awkward angle. It lumbered in a circle then back to its corner, ricocheting drunkenly between the slime vat and the wall. It looked like it had suffered a stroke.

'You'll need to get it,' said Emily.

'What do you mean get it?' I stared in horror at the bird with its blank eyes and hooked beak. It was cornered. Close to death, with nothing to lose. This wasn't right. Could it be coincidence? This thing – now – in our first week here?

'It's frightened,' said Emily.

'It fears nothing,' I said. The bastard was giving me a look that I'd never seen on an animal before. An expression of sheer malevolence. I suspected that this was no ordinary herring gull but more likely a diabolical incarnation of Mr Marsden, the bird-like Victorian builder who had depicted himself on the plasterwork.

'Damn you, Marsden,' I muttered.

'I'll get you something to protect your hands,' said Emily.

Next thing I knew I was crouched low, wearing a pair of oven gloves, in a face-off with the fiend. I scuffled towards Mr Marsden, grimacing. He lumbered backwards and began scraping his beak against the kitchen wall like a gangster with a blade. We glared at each other. I tried to hide my fear but my pulsing Adam's apple gave the game away. He lurched into a run, forcing me back into a flower pot. I counter-charged but the bastard waddled behind the slime vat. For a while he thwacked his head angrily against the plastic, then he was out again, staggering in circles.

'Fuck this.' I threw down the oven gloves.

Even if I could grab the bird, I had no idea what to do next. Take it to A&E? Dump it on the road? Tear out its beating heart and offer it to the gods? We had to drive to Southampton for a funeral. If we hung about any longer we'd be late. Nature would have to take its course. I wheeled the tabletop away from the steps: an invitation to the foxes beneath the yew tree. We piled the kids into the car and took off at speed, leaving Mr Marsden looping around the yard.

When we returned the next afternoon, he was gone. All that remained was a knocked-over plant pot and a gull feather. I hoped this sacrifice was enough to placate the house. Until now, it had been a museum of other people's memories. But things had changed. The gull was in our story. The first of many. Because like it or not, we were here to stay.

We'd all just have to learn to get along.

II

On the Rocks

Shortly after my first daughter was born I developed a serious walking habit. Every lunchtime I'd close the door on the nappies and caterwauling and head across the Walthamstow marshes, Hendrix by my side, jotting down notes and taking photos of abandoned sleeping bags, crow carcasses and crumbling water filtration systems. Eventually I wrote a book about London's marshland that was well enough received to justify my daily absconding and I was not going to give up the habit now that we'd moved to the seaside. This town was where the sex magician Aleister Crowley came to die, John Logie Baird carried out his first television experiments and the Piltdown Man hoaxer lived as a child. There were new stories to be found and new reasons to get out of the house. The lower floor was effectively derelict. Storage for boxes we could not unpack until the renovation, which could take many months, had claimed the space. 'Don't expect this to be quick,' warned Emily. There were walls to knock down, tradespeople to call for quotes, specialists to come and assess the damage. It meant we had to huddle in a makeshift upstairs kitchen full of decayed furnishings, heating our supermarket ready meals on a camping stove. We threw out the stair carpets and all the curtains to get rid of the musty smell but even with the windows propped open the air was fungal. A layer of grime coated every surface, as if someone had been using the house to cook pots of human fat. Emily spent an hour scrubbing dead skin from the bath, retching and heaving.

'I wonder if any of the dead skin is from someone who is now dead,' I said, watching from the doorway.

'Don't,' said Emily.

'Imagine, the final piece of you that survives on this earth – a black ring on a bathtub.'

'You're not helping.'

Quite frankly, I couldn't wait to get out with the dog. The sea, the sea, the sea was the place to be. As soon as I got the opportunity, I escaped to the bottom of our road, where an embankment carried the railway line above an underpass which led into Morrisons' car park, then Queens Road, a scruffy Victorian street lined with bridalwear shops, nail parlours and mini-markets displaying rows of luminescent bongs. I hadn't realised that bongs were such an essential impulse purchase. Folk liked their weed here, clearly. They liked their fags and booze too. Outside the Priory Meadow shopping centre, rows of pensioners smoked on benches. A man pushed a buggy, can of lager in his hand, a three-year-old girl trailing behind. She kept getting in the way of oncoming pedestrians. 'Bastards,' the man seethed under his breath. Then he turned to his daughter, 'Just tell them all to piss off.'

After London, the street lamps seemed absurdly tall. Their gargantuan bulbs glared at me as I circled the town centre where French students tossed coins at a busker in exchange for 'Here Comes the Sun' and teenagers giggled at the raffish temporary tattoo vendor. I strolled up Robertson Street until I came to a road that separated the town from the promenade. I waited to cross by a lamp post covered with wilted flowers, Stella cans and the words 'Gone But Not Forgotten'. A man in his forties stared out from a photo. Cars whished past unheedingly.

On the promenade, I leaned against railings where danger signs warned 'Falling Debris' and a poster advertised a concert by The Upbeat Beatles.

COME AND PARTY
LIKE IT'S 1963!

Hastings Pier was a charred skeleton. The remains of a campaign banner, flapping from the rusted gantry, bore the word 'SAVE'. Information boards on the hoardings told the story of a renovation which had not yet commenced. On the walls of the visitors' centre, artworks blended sepia photos of the pier in its heyday with colour shots of what it might look like when the works were completed. Edwardians strolled beside happy families from the future while hot air balloons and jet planes jostled for supremacy in the sky.

Steps led me to the beach. It was low tide. The shingle gave way to a slab of sand, shimmering like raw steak, peppered with shells. The air shifted and warped. Heat, possibly, rising from the earth, or something else. Mesmerised, I lost all sense of the town behind me. There was only sand, sea, rocks, sky. A gust of salt air whipped into my nostrils. It carried a memory. Or not even a memory, but the very sensation of a moment long forgotten, as if the past twenty years had never happened and I'd crossed a time-space dimension to the West Sands of St Andrews, on the coast of Fife, 900 miles north, in 1996. It was the beach where they filmed *Chariots of Fire*, a long curving paleness against the wide muddy blue of the North Sea, stretching towards the cathedral and castle. My best friend Mike was a little ahead, in jogging bottoms and a T-shirt, despite the chill, turning back to me and laughing. 'Come on,' he said, 'you fat bastard.'

He'd challenged me to a run that morning, teasing me about my nascent beer belly. In my years at Sheffield University I'd done little more than booze and read. By the time I came up to St Andrews to study for a Masters, Mike was in training for the army. They made him do things like haul a backpack of rocks up a Munro without any sleep while being attacked by ninjas, or so he told me. He could be full of shit. But I couldn't deny the evidence on the beach as he accelerated away from me with surprising speed. Faster. Stronger. Unstoppable.

Lungs heaving, I crumpled onto the sand and watched him run towards his destiny.

That castle, looming.

*

There was a castle in Dover, where Mike and I first met at school in 1985 and later became best friends. We'd pass it on the way into town to go underage drinking on Saturday evenings, wearing ridiculous sports jackets we'd plundered from charity shops to make us look older. There was a castle in St Andrews too, from which Mike would fall. And there was one here in Hastings, though it was little more than a few crooked teeth on the jaw of West Hill's cliffs. On the vertiginous rocks beneath the ruin, teenagers huddled in folds of sandstone and looked toward France. Like Mike, they liked to climb, to live on the edge. Kids these days, same as kids those days. Some joker had graffitied an eye onto a bulge in the rock, giving West Hill the appearance of a beached leviathan. It watched me dolefully as I shambled along Pelham Beach, unused to the effort of walking on shingle, that constant falling away, the fizz of water percolating, a thousand micro-rivers changing course beneath my step. I tried to focus on the stones, forcing the apparition of Mike back from whence it came, not allowing the tide to take me into that deep history. Until this moment, it hadn't occurred to me that I'd retained such a powerful connection between the coast and what happened to Mike. Or perhaps this was happening now because of the imminence of my fortieth birthday, the gloom of the house we'd bought and the uncertainty of my place here. No friends. No personal history. No link to the locale but only to the sulphurous algae and churn of waves I'd known in St Andrews two decades ago. Whatever the reason, I wanted to dismiss the memory and embrace my new life. Look forward. See what was there before my eyes.

Up ahead a man in a high-visibility jacket swung a metal detector over wavy lines of kelp. A girl and her boyfriend smoked on a pebble ridge. Out on the wet sand, the lean silhouette of a lugworm fisherman hunched over his pump, a dog barking in circles around his bucket. I came to a crooked outfall pipe jutting out from the beach, gushing lime green freshwater into the sea. Beyond was a long line of hollows in the shingle where someone had walked earlier. I followed it, placing my feet in the pits their feet left behind. There was something forlorn about the way the trail meandered. For me, these prints were as poignant as prehistoric footprints exposed on Norfolk shorelines by storm tides. After all, what's the difference between an 850,000-year-old human footprint and one that's five minutes old? In the grand scheme of things, we are all fellow ancients, sharing the blink of an eye.

I cut up from the beach, over the miniature railway line, past the go-karts, trampolines, funfair and amusement arcade. Elvis stared out from the side of a slot machine. Next to him Sooty, Soo and Sweep were trapped in a glass box, playing synth-pop cover versions for a pound a go to feed their crack habits. Soo's voice sounded hoarse. After each song finished, a prize dropped through a slot. It felt a bit desperate.

Through a smog of hot dog and candyfloss fumes I drifted onto Rock-a-Nore Road, where tourists waved gulls away from polystyrene pots of cockles and snapped photos of the eighteenth-century net shops—huts for fishing equipment, tall and black lacquered. A Kinks track blasted from the Lord Nelson, where fishermen unwound after work. On the pavement outside the pub, a skinny old man in a suit stood by an upturned bicycle, smoking a rollup, frantically turning the pedal so that the back wheel span. I hung nearby, watching, noting down what he was doing on my iPhone.

The road on which he operated his spinning machine was called The Bourne, a brutal slab laid over the stream which once trickled through the Old Town, dividing it in two. Perhaps this was an ex-fisherman performing a rite by the ancient waterway, mimicking the winding of a winch. He seemed nervous, jittering from foot to foot. Whenever the wheel slowed he glared at it caustically, then gave another turn. I slipped from the shadows for a closer look.

He stepped out, furious, and yelled, 'Stop copying my fucking idea!'

I backed away, guiltily slipping my iPhone into my pocket. By the time I reached the net shops, he was at his wheel again, turning, as if nothing had happened. Leaving him to it, I hurried past the Fishermen's Museum, once the community's church, to the aquarium and the car park. I kept walking as far as I could, until everything stopped. The town ended abruptly at railings festooned with warning signs. Sandstone cliffs stretched into the horizon. The walkway dropped onto a beach of weathered rock, wet slabs tilted like broken tables. The vinegar stench of seaweed. Yawning mussels and the stripped bones of a fish. A rusting anchor. Fisherman's rope. Plastic bottle.

Things returned that had been taken away.

Now there was no stopping it. Memories of that May day in 1996 came flooding back—sudden, surprising and visceral. As I stood before the Sussex shore's ragged maw, listening to gulls cry and waves churn, I was transported to the beach beneath St Andrews Castle, the tide low beneath a bleached sky, my young heart beating hard, a metallic taste in my mouth. I could see Mike lain on a broken rib of stone where the dog walker found him earlier that morning. He was curled up as if asleep, still wearing his tweed jacket, jeans and leather-soled shoes, looking so tiny between the foot of the castle and the vastness of the sea that had brought him home. There were already police on the beach. People crying. I joined my flatmates in a huddle and we stared out in silence, trying hard not to believe.

They sent Ben out to identify the body. He walked towards the rocks, surrounded by coppers, head bowed like a condemned man. Mike often crashed on someone's floor or slept over at his girlfriend's house. There was a chance he was warm and naked in her arms, sleeping off the whisky, and this was some other poor bastard for others to cry about. But we knew Mike, and we knew what we'd been up to the previous night, and how he hadn't come home. We knew what Ben would find. And Ben knew most of all, picking his way over the rock pools towards the inevitable.

That afternoon, when the police had done their probing and left us to drink, reminisce and cry, we stood on the second-floor landing, talking to friends who came with condolences. I heard the latch on the front door and looked down through the stairwell to see a hand gripping the bannister and a head of red hair hung down, like someone about to reveal a shocking secret, tortured by the imminence of his shame, footsteps slow and plodding. He wore a tweed jacket, corduroy jeans and leather shoes, just like—just like … had anybody else noticed this? No, they were all chatting drunkenly, the idiots. I tried to alert them to what was happening but I was transfixed on the pale hand sliding up. It couldn't be, but this was Mike returned. Christ knows how it was possible but this whole thing had been a mistake. A slip-up. An oversight. A joke. What a total and utter bastard. To make us think he'd gone like that. Brilliant. He had always been brilliant. As close to a genius as anyone I knew.

I got ready to welcome him at the top of the stairs, tears welling, arms outstretched. But when he got to within a few metres and lifted his face it wasn't Mike at all. It was a guy called Charlie and his hair wasn't red, but blond, and he was half a foot taller than Mike. I couldn't understand it. I knew what I had seen. For that minute, I had existed in an alternate universe where my friend was alive, having played the most fiendishly sick prank. It was as good as real, for fuck's sake, as good as real.

Charlie stretched out a hand to shake mine. 'I'm so sorry,' he said.

Not as sorry as I was.

III

The Bare Bones

Beneath the woodchip modifications, a Victorian house was waiting to be revealed. Emily and I stood on the staircase in masks, and swung mallets at the partition wall that separated the stairs from the hall. Boards exploded. Beading dangled. We were talcum-powdered with plaster dust, as white as ghosts. As splintered panels fell away we beheld an ecosystem that had flourished for forty years in the gap between wood and woodchip. Clusters of spider legs were shrouded in silk and human hair. At our touch cobweb curtains fell open to expose wooden panels, along which tiny black pods ranged like climbers on an ascent. I wondered if they were some terrible new lifeform gestating, waiting for the light.

'What's that?' I pointed at something in the debris. A

child's shoe. Sealed within the partition wall for forty years. Why was it put there? To ward off evil spirits? Emily replied that sometimes a shoe in a wall was just a shoe in a wall.

Day by day, month by month, we peeled back the flesh of the house. Beneath the brown 1970s wallpaper we found 1950s wallpaper – dazzling suns in golden circles. Beneath that, 1920s wallpaper. Then a Victorian jungle of flowers and geometric shapes. But we had to go even deeper. Dry rot had spread from floor to dado rail on the ground floor. A specialist came to sort it out. He pulled away the plaster to reveal a ribcage of Victorian laths. Exposed to light, grains of mummified matter poured from the holes, as if from a pharaoh's tomb.

Next, we tried to find the source of the musky damp air. Emily yanked up the floorboards to reveal a mess of fluff and pipes littered with bottle tops, pen lids, wrappers, fingernails. It was horrifying how much life had accumulated in these hidden spaces. Behind a water tank in the kitchen we found a box of Tampax from the 1980s.

'Wow, they're a real period piece,' I joked. But really, I was aghast. 'How can something like that stay there for so long? Who put them there? Why? And how can it be that nobody looked in that spot again for another thirty years?'

Emily told me that she didn't know but if I couldn't cope

with other people's memories, then perhaps I should move into a flat in a new-build somewhere.

'You can take the dog with you,' she said.

*

The renovation was Emily's idea. She was the practical one. I was a freelance writer cursed with poor hand-eye coordination and a pathological fear of electricity. But Emily was mechanically literate, able to see how things could be deconstructed and reconstructed. Anything she didn't know, she could learn after ten minutes on a laptop. If there was a plug to change, a computer to fix or shelves to build, Emily was the woman for the job. She could screen print, tile, dye, upcycle, sew, remake and renew. She breathed life into dead things.

When I met Emily she was recently out of university, where she had studied art history. She worked in customer services for an investment newsletter company, answering phones and taking abuse from elderly gentlemen with too much time on their hands. She let them rant about how terribly they'd been served by the latest stock recommendation, that the markets weren't working as predicted and they wanted their money back. She'd defuse their ire with breezy empathy, agree that the world was going to hell and that the best thing they could do to protect themselves was sign up to an even better newsletter for £79 a year. Emily was good at her job. But she wanted to move on to other things. She bought a book called *Web Design for Dummies* and learned how to build websites. It took her a day. Weeks later she got a job in digital marketing. Just like that. Now she wanted to build something tangible we could live in, and fill it with fabrics and furniture she created herself. She had already enjoyed interior design success with our first London home, with photographs of her work appearing in a glossy style magazine. This was what she wanted to do next. When she fixed her mind on a goal, she was unstoppable.

There was smartness in her genes. Her father was involved in the development of digital TV broadcasting in the late 1980s. He later spearheaded live field trials and walked away with an OBE for his efforts. I didn't know whether it was coincidence that we'd come to live in Hastings where, in 1923, John Logie Baird used bicycle lights, wax and glue to build the prototype of a machine that would transform the way we viewed the world. Television appropriated an idea that had been around since the nineteenth-century, when occultists sought mechanical means of manifesting spirits. A chemist named

William Crookes devised the first radiometer to measure psychic forces and later pioneered work on vacuum tubes, cathode rays and spectroscopy. Others sought to manifest not spirits but the universe itself. The Norwegian inventor Kristian Birkeland, addicted to caffeine and barbiturates, became obsessed with reproducing the Northern Lights in miniature. In the early 1900s he experimented with terrellas—scaled down magnetic models of the earth—to create an artificial aurora at each pole. But in his final drug-fevered days, stricken in bed, he sketched out a far grander vision: a chamber carved into a mountain peak would become the world's greatest vacuum chamber, with a cathode to charge the particles. Into this he would project images of the planets, stars and aurora. A devoted mass would climb the mountain every Sunday to behold the universe swirling in a cathedral of stone.

Baird had less grandiose aims. He was a serial entrepreneur whose failed ventures included a remedy for trench foot, a new form of soap, and a project for making jam in the open air while he was out in Trinidad—foiled by an attack of sugar-crazed insects. A sickly man who struggled to fend off regular bouts of cold and flu, Baird moved to Hastings to overcome a near-fatal illness. He took restorative walks between East Hill and Fairlight. The blood pumped oxygen to his brain as he huffed and puffed above the town, with ships many miles distant, a suggestion of France's coastline, Beachy Head, the spit of Dungeness and the concave ocean between: the world the lens of an eye staring into space. Suddenly, his vision was clear.

Baird carried out experiments for television in a workshop above the Queen's Arcade. One day a 12,000-volt shock threw him across the room, smashing equipment and burning his hands. When the landlord evicted him he moved back to London to continue his work. He would return to the East Sussex coast in 1946, doomed by his final illness. By this time his invention had been superseded by the Marconi Corporation's cathode ray system and TV broadcasting halted by a world war that had ravaged Europe. But as he sat on a bench by the De La Warr Pavilion in Bexhill, shivering under a blanket, the English Channel looked the same as it did when he walked the cliffs of Fairlight as a young man. As if nothing had ever happened, or that everything that would happen, already had.

*

Emily invited a stream of tradespeople into the house to pull it back to its bare bones. They erected scaffolding. They tore at the walls. They hacked at the render. They shovelled sand into a mixer. They removed wheelbarrows of rubble. They blared Radio 1's compressed pop shite from industrial-sized radios. They tried to talk to me about the works.

'Gareth, mate, do you want the pad stones for the steel exposed or embedded?'

I had no idea what any of that meant. 'Ask Emily.'

'Are you going to be moving the soil pipe or keeping it where it is?'

'God knows. Better ask Emily.'

'Do you want us to board out the kitchen?'

'She's right there,' I pointed at my wife. 'Fire away.'

After a while the questions stopped. Now the men leaned coquettishly towards Emily, nodding with amazement at her knowledge of construction methods, fondling their tool belts. Every so often they'd look at me pityingly as I shuffled about with bags of shopping and babbling children.

To make matters worse, on my fortieth birthday I bought a dinosaur. After a pit stop in The Hastings Arms, I stumbled into an antique shop in the Old Town where I beheld a three-foot-high replica of a T-rex skeleton. The man behind the counter told me there was a lot of interest in the dinosaur but if I bought now they'd deliver it for free. Above his head was a row of flying ceramic Hitlers, like those ducks people had on their walls in the 1970s. I was tempted by the Hitlers, but the dinosaur seemed precisely the sort of thing we should own. So I handed over my bank card. By the time I got home I was less sure of the appropriateness of the T-rex skeleton, bearing in mind the state of things. There was a gaping hole where a kitchen had been, protected only by tarpaulin. Boxes blocked the downstairs windows. The electricians were rewiring, so every floorboard was up, bar a central strip no wider than a shoe. I had no idea where we would store a dinosaur skeleton. The only available space was beside our mattress. When the doorbell rang, a disappointed Emily ushered in two delivery men, who carefully carried the T-rex across the walk-board to our bedroom while the electricians downed their tools.

'That's a little bit eccentric, mate,' said the chief electrician.

'It's his birthday,' Emily explained, as if I was five years old.

We sat on the mattress for a while, staring at the skeleton, my sole contribution to the house's renovation thus far. What we lacked in terms of beds, curtains and cooking equipment we had more than made up for with fake dinosaur remains. I could hear the workmen laughing outside. Fuck it. Let them judge. I didn't care. But to get back in Emily's good books I took the girls to the park across the road.

Alexandra Park was an ornate strip of Victoriana designed in the gardenesque style, with all the trimmings. Boating lake. Bandstand. Miniature railway. Streams slaloming between cedars, pines and ashes. There was a playground in the area of park right outside our house, but the girls grew bored of it so I took them grumbling up the hill to the nature reserve, where cormorants fanned their wings in glistening reservoirs and anglers sipped from flasks. Up here was what I'd dubbed the 'secret playground'. The girls loved this place. Approached from the woods it was as if we'd stumbled on a private paradise of swings, balance beams and slides. But it was an illusion. On the brow behind the playground was a road from which the park was clearly visible to passing drivers. This didn't matter to the girls. Magic was a point of view. They would always call it the secret playground. The myth was now in their DNA, transmittable down future generations.

Months earlier an oak had fallen during high winds and smashed the railings. Rather than remove the thing that almost killed their children, locals embraced it. The branches were severed and the trunk turned into a caterpillar sculpture with ropes to clamber up. While my daughters sat on the back of this beast I gazed longingly north. At the furthest reaches of the wood I heard there was an ancient waterfall which was the source of that water flowing through the park, beneath the town, and out from the pipe on Pelham Beach. A place where Sussex's most famous dinosaur, the Iguanodon, once roamed. When I got some free time it would be a worthy mission for me and the dog.

IV

The Lost World

On a sunny September day, sharpened by a sea wind, Hendrix and I walked to the uppermost reaches of Alexandra Park, and entered Coronation Wood, where spectres of light danced in the lily ponds. I followed a stream up into the gill, a ravine cut into sandstone by water which once poured from a great waterfall known as Old Roar.

Quickly, the wind stopped and the heat rose. Hendrix panted in the stream as I negotiated the slippery dips and crests of the track. The only sunlight was that which filtered through a chlorophyll canopy. Embedded in the banks were concrete blocks from which iron pipes arched across the stream. On either side were towering stacks of sandstone, thick as tabletops and furred with moss. Trees burst from the cracks and curved upwards, thirsty for light, spidery roots gripping the rock. Yellow fungus, shaped like ears, eavesdropped on me from felled trunks. Birds trilled techno riddims over the low-end buzz of insects feasting on dead wood. Gradually the ravine deepened, as if I was plunging beneath the town and back in time.

On the path ahead a middle-aged woman and her husband were clad in hiking gear. They seemed uncertain about their route, gazing anxiously left and right as if waiting for a bus.

'Is it much further?' the woman asked me.

'Not far, I don't think.'

'I have never been here before.'

'Neither have I.'

'Do you know the way?'

'I believe there's only one way,' I said.

'What do you think?' she asked her husband.

'I don't know,' he shook his head sadly.

I couldn't tell whether I was having a deeply cosmic discussion or if they were just lost. I left them looking hopelessly at their watches and never saw them again.

The air grew danker the closer I moved towards the waterfall. Little wooden bridges crossed me from one side to another, some built on supports from the era when tourists and Romantic artists flocked to the gill, drawn by its gothic gloom and ferns. As the foliage thickened I came upon a wall daubed in lovers' graffiti, with a magnificent arch above. This was the viaduct carrying St Helen's Road in an altitudinous world of tarmac and cars. The traffic noise faded as I left the bridge behind and pushed on to the falls. A viewing platform looked onto Little Roar Gill, a grotto of a rock ledges and lichen, dripping with water. Somewhere further north was Old Roar, unreachable and litter-clogged, the great falls which were once—as the name suggested—voluminous enough to roar. Those times were gone. All I could hear was trickling, as if from a toilet cistern. Then another sound. The giggling of children. Faint at first, then louder, until their shrieks and squeals echoed around me, like the disturbed spirits of the prematurely deceased. Ghosts of dark and lonely water. I looked up to see only foliage. But I knew that somewhere above the canopy was a town with roads, houses and families playing in back gardens. Daily 21st-Century life continued as normal on that lofty plateaux, but I was deep in the lair of prehistoric monsters.

One hundred and forty million years ago, I'd have stood in a river network in a Mediterranean heat. At the end of the cretaceous, Iguanodons roamed here. Their fossilised bones were first prised from the Old Roar quarry in 1873, then later by the amateur palaeontologist, Charles Dawson. In 1909, he was the site manager of a dig where he extracted fragments of an Iguanodon with assistance from his new friend, Teilhard de Chardin, a young Jesuit priest. Teilhard had come to the town the year before to train at a seminary in Hastings. He was a passionate fossil hunter who loved to search the shore for prints and bones. As he did, he felt that a universal being was taking shape in nature before his eyes. This idea germinated into a visionary book which he wrote in 1938 called *The Phenomenon of Man*. It was banned by the Catholic Church until the 1950s for its blasphemous ideas. A copy was handed to me by my boss when I got a copywriting job in London in my mid-twenties, and blew my mind. It was 1999 and I'd just started using the Internet for the first time. This scandalous tome of cosmic Catholic philosophy predicted the World Wide Web. It described how life on earth had begun with the convergence of simple carbon compounds into cells, then the organisation of those cells into increasingly complex forms, leading to the evolution of consciousness. Through human beings this consciousness had become aware of itself, allowing evolution itself to evolve, instigating what Teilhard called the psychozoic era. Like a forest fire, our ideas, cultures and technologies were spreading to form an incandescent layer of thought around the earth, known as the noosphere, in which humans could be omnipresent through telephones, televisions and—after his death —the World Wide Web, the ultimate manifestation of his vision. Each of us was a bright node of thought, interconnecting with other nodes to become a single hive mind that would evolve into ever more complex arrangements until all thought converged and we become one with God. In that instant, death—and even time itself—would cease to exist. He called this The Omega Point. It was our ultimate destination.

Such lofty notions didn't trouble Charles Dawson, who saw only his own destiny in the fossilised bones. Instead of sending the Iguanodon remains to the Hastings museum for the good of the local people, he sold them to the British Museum and pocketed the cash. Dawson was already one of my favourite local anti-heroes. He fell in love with fossil hunting a young boy growing up in St Leonards-on-Sea. At sixteen he left school to join a firm of solicitors in Uckfield, but his passion persisted. Mentored by geologist Samuel H. Beckles, Dawson amassed a hoard of fish, mammal and reptile fossils worthy enough to donate to the British Museum. Aged twenty-five he co-founded the Hastings & St Leonards Museum Association, putting himself in charge of acquiring artefacts. It was at this time that he decided his rate of discovery was not fast enough—nor epochal enough—to achieve his ambition: election to the Royal

Society. He decided to push things forward with some of his own creations.

He began with a fossil tooth, which he sent to Arthur Smith Woodward at the British Museum, explaining that it belonged to a new species of mammal from the Cretaceous period. It didn't. It was prehistoric mammal tooth from a more recent epoch which Dawson had manipulated with a wire brush then embedded in a mass of Cretaceous fossils. Next, he excavated the Lavant Caves, a series of chalk tunnels near Chichester. It was empty of anything interesting, so he sneaked in an array of delights: prehistoric worked flints, red deer antlers, Roman mosaics, human teeth and Georgian coins. There was little need of proof. This cavity could be anything he wanted it to be—and it could, possibly, have been a prehistoric habitation, Neolithic flint mine, civil war hideout or smuggler's hold. Who was to know?

Later he showed the British Museum a cast-iron Roman statue, claiming he'd bought it from a worker who found it in a slag heap near Hastings. Really, he had aged an eighteenth-century reproduction to appear Roman, using his self-taught skills in metallurgy and chemistry. Then he presented the Brighton and Hove Natural History and Philosophical Society with a mummified toad inside a piece of flint, explaining that the flint had been brought to him by workmen. No, he shook his head, he didn't know how it could have got there. Perhaps it crawled in through a tiny hole, when young. It was not for him to draw conclusions, but for society to marvel at the world beneath their feet. Yes, all this praise was flattering, said Dawson, fingering his pince-nez, but he was merely a lightning rod channelling the unseen. He had a knack of being in the right place at the right time, that was all.

On Good Friday in 1906 he stood on the deck of the SS *Manche*, a steamer travelling from Newhaven, enjoying the views of the East Sussex coastline rolling by – Beachy Head, Pevensey, Bexhill, Hastings and Rye. As the steamer passed level with the spit of Dungeness he saw something black moving quickly through the water, parallel to the vessel, but at some distance. Peering through his binoculars, he spotted a series of arched loops breaking the waves in a serpentine motion.

A giant eel, perhaps? An aquatic dinosaur?

He couldn't know for sure, for it wasn't really there. But if it had been, he was sure it would have looked like those serpents reported by sailors in far-flung oceans in times of yore. To record the marvel for his burgeoning catalogue of natural curiosities, Dawson snapped photographs with his Kodak camera until the beast 'entered the path of the sun's rays on the water' and disappeared from sight. Alas, the photos did not emerge with any clarity, only a grey smudge within a greyer blur. Even by Dawson's low standard of proof, it wasn't good enough to submit to the experts.

In 1909, Dawson returned to palaeontology with a new plan. There had been startling finds of early humans on the Continent, including Cro-Magnon man in France and Heidelberg man in Germany. The thirst for such a discovery in Britain was so great, Dawson knew that if he were to achieve such a feat he would write himself into the pages of history. A chance piece of correspondence with Sir Arthur Conan Doyle about his next novel, *The Lost World*, gave Dawson an idea about what he could do. All he required was a monkey jaw, a human skull and a very old hole in the ground. For instance, the million-year-old alluvial deposits he'd recently found by a country road in Piltdown would do very nicely.

V

The Eel with a Head the Size of an Armchair

It turns out that Charles Dawson and I shared three things in common: a love of dinosaurs, a predilection for making things up, and an encounter with a sea beast. Mine entered my life when I was sixteen years old. I'd heard a rumour that there was an eel with a head the size of an armchair in Dover harbour, not far along the coast from Dawson's sighting. It was important information because on Wednesday afternoons I'd go with the school canoe club to brave its waters. Our teacher would unload us from the minivan then take off at speed, leaving us in our wetsuits like dwarf police frogmen preparing for a grizzly day at work. Tiny on the shingle we clung to a shuddering landscape. Hovercraft rasped towards France while the great hulks of ferries drifted past the harbour wall. Cars on the A2 looped out from the cliff over queues of trucks. Gull cries mingled with beeping horns, tannoy announcements and the rattle of wheels on steel gantries. The air stank of fuel.

We dragged our battered kayaks across the shingle and pushed out into the cold, oily water. For an hour we paddled in circles, raced each other along the wash, or practised kayak rolls. Deep below, the mutant eel slithered along the seabed, snacking on fish and discarded tyres. Of course, I never saw the eel, not in the flesh. It was too canny for that, knowing how it would be feared and hunted. I imagined that it not only had a head the size of an armchair but also the shape of an armchair. You could get hammerhead sharks, so why not armchair-head eels? I didn't need to see it to know what it looked like. The eyes of the eel were situated on two armrests, like headlamps on a vintage Mini. Its mouth was a flapping seat cushion with rows of razor-sharp teeth. Its body extended almost a third of the length of the harbour, but it remained coiled most of the time to keep warm. At night, it pushed out into the Channel to seek a proper meal, perhaps a porpoise if it was lucky. In desperate times, it followed ferries in the hope of someone falling overboard.

On Saturday nights my schoolmates went drinking in The Castle pub. They had grown bristly square jaws over the summer holidays and refused to share their secret growth hormone potions with me. I was skinny, small and looked about twelve. I snuck in one night, getting someone to buy me my pint of bitter. I got through half of it, hunched in the corner, before the barman slung me out. Right in front of everyone. Nobody opted to come out to help me get booze from an offie. Not one person.

Some of them even smirked.

Humiliated, I went to the beach and stood at the water's edge, looking at the lights of the ships beneath the moon. I decided that I might commit suicide by walking into the water with pebbles in my pockets, like Virginia Woolf. The eel with a head the size of an armchair would seize the chance of an easy meal and I'd vanish into the belly of the beast forever. But after a short while I retreated up the shingle, thinking I might find a tramp who would buy me a can.

Not long after that we were at canoe club again. Rick – one of my popular schoolmates who always got into pubs – paddled far out into the middle of the harbour. Showing off, as usual. He did a kayak roll, toppling sideways into the water, until all you could see was the yellow underside of his kayak bobbing in the waves. We all waited for the big reveal. But he seemed to be struggling. When he flipped up again, there was only a torso stump sat in the kayak. The top half of his body had been bitten clean off. A long artery

The Eel
Rick
Armchair head
by Gareth Rees, 1990

wiggled and waggled from his severed midriff, hosing blood into the air for a few seconds, before it emptied and flopped into the cavity.

I don't remember what happened after that. Helicopters and people in those plastic contamination suits, most likely. But anyway, it was a great day that really should have happened.

*

No teenager thinks they are normal, but my life was weird. I lived in an MoD-funded school for the children of soldiers on the A2 where it stooped past Dover Castle towards the port. The school formed a D-shape lined with boarding houses surrounded by fields, with a clock tower and dining hall in its centre. We slept in dormitories with strict rules and early bedtimes. In the mornings, we'd be woken at 6:30 a.m. by angry sixth formers to carry out chores, then marched to a hall to eat rubbery eggs and cornflakes, followed by a tedious session in chapel. Classes like Maths and English were mixed with shooting at an indoor range, where we would don berets, lie on sandbags and fire decommissioned First World War rifles. We'd honk on clarinets, parp bugles, or bang drums at military band practice. On Saturdays, we'd bull our shoes and shine brass belts for our Sunday parade where a dyslexic Regimental Sergeant Major in a busby would inspect us and yell things like, 'You are skating on thin water, sunshine!' During a bomb alarm he once bellowed, 'Ejaculate the library!' and he wasn't joking. On weekdays, he roamed the school with a brass-tipped stick, keeping order and protecting us from the IRA. He was obsessed with security. When the occasion demanded it, he drove his Land Rover over unattended bags, leaving behind an explosion of pencils, calculators and Wham bars.

When I arrived, aged eleven, fresh from a primary school in an industrial town outside Manchester, the school was terrifying. Pupils were caned, slippered, slapped and forced to run with heavy loads as punishment. The day was engineered to eradicate any notion of free time. No personal clothes allowed. Everyone got a regulation short back 'n' sides haircut so that we all looked the same. On the rare afternoons we were permitted to walk into Dover we felt like the Midwich Cuckoos, locals staring at us in our gold-buttoned blazers.

At first I tried hard, joined in and laughed a lot. Then in my teenage years I discovered punk, goth and folk music. I read George Orwell. I twigged that something wasn't right with the jingoistic narrative. I began to detest all things military and that *Boy's Own* nonsense which was drilled into us. Running with logs on our shoulders. Stripping Bren guns. Saluting flags in a chapel marbled with names of the dead from innumerable wars of Empire. I hated the hypocrisy of the Irish situation, in which I realised I was complicit. I'd play The Pogues' 'Streets of Sorrow/Birmingham Six' loud on my tape player. By my bed I Blu-Tacked a picture of Bobby Sands' spirit rising from his starved corpse. During a parade, I was caught hiding under a bed reading plays by Sean O'Casey, but nobody really cared about my feeble ideological protests, only that a rule of attendance had been broken. I was a rebel without a clue and unpopular with my peers, who thought me a miserable death-obsessed refusenik, with my pretentious poems, apocalyptic short stories and nonsense about giant mutant eels.

My salvation was Mike. He was the most intelligent person in my year. I can't remember him ever getting anything other than an A in exams. For Mike, learning was effortless. If he revised I never saw it. He had small, neatly uniform handwriting as though his thoughts were streaming out of a printer. There was an adultness about him, from his spectacles to his penchant for waistcoats and suits. We bonded over a love of writing and books: Iain Banks's *The Wasp Factory*, Kurt Vonnegut's *Slaughterhouse-Five*,

B. S. Johnson's *Housemother Normal,* Ted Hughes's *Crow,* Virginia Woolf's *To the Lighthouse,* Laurence Sterne's *Life and Opinions of Tristram Shandy.* In his room we played guitars. He picked at the strings with finely wrinkled fingers and sang the songs of Michelle Shocked, Billy Bragg and Tracy Chapman in a soaring baritone. I'd hammer chords, mumbling half-baked poetry, for I was tone deaf. I liked music that rasped and slurred, like Tom Waits and The Fall. I was obsessed with the Bob Dylan documentary *Don't Look Back,* particularly the way Dylan improvised his myth in front of a camera as he dealt with the pressure of playing to expectant audiences. The idea that you could live your life like a fiction.

Mike really did have another life. At night, when the school slept, he put on dark clothes and slid out of his window to prowl the grounds looking for buildings to climb. It began with easy ascents to the roof of the boarding house. Then trickier feats like shinnying to the tops of rugby posts. Eventually he conquered the top of the clock tower, which must have been an unnerving climb without ropes. I wouldn't have known. I hated heights and didn't get involved. But I knew of his manoeuvres from the traffic cones he left at the peaks of his ascents for all to see the next day, sometimes with a note pinned to a wall below:

They seek him here,
they seek him there,
they seek King Cone
everywhere

Mike was a fledgling urban explorer, challenging the walls that contained us, questioning the system with fingers and toes, making a mockery of the school's architecture.

This urge to climb was to be his great undoing.

*

Sheffield University, summer 1993. Mike came to visit me in my Hall of Residence. I played him my favourite song of the moment, a thirteen-minute live version of 'Calvary Cross' by Richard and Linda Thompson, which I'd bought from a second-hand vinyl shop because that was the kind of cool retro guy I was now that I was doing English at university. It was how Mike and I dreamed ourselves to be when we were imprisoned in school. Smoking Marlboro Lights, we nodded along as Thompson sang. But he was so tired that after a few beers he fell asleep on the floor before my friends turned up to say hello. We sat with cans of Special Brew, looking down at the sleeping bag with a shock of red hair tufting out, as if planning what to do with a dead body.

After taking a gap year to yomp up foreign mountains, Mike had shocked me by getting commissioned into the army. His plan was to attend St Andrews University while undergoing training. I was outraged. This was insane, I told him, why would anyone want to do that? We'd left all that behind. We'd rejected that, hadn't we? Fuck the military. Fuck this insane flag worship. Right? Mike said it was a way of proving a point to his father, but he was unusually cagey. He told me it wouldn't change anything. Life would be an adventure. Death or glory. To prove it he suggested we hitchhike down to Dover to reunite with a few old friends, stopping off in London for some busking.

The following morning, we rasped down the M1 in a Reliant Robin with a South African who steered with his feet while rolling cigarettes, shouting over the wind as it howled through the open windows. He dropped us off in North London and we took the tube south where Mike had arranged for us to stay with someone he met while travelling. We emerged from Brixton station, blinking in the sunshine. The streets were a bustle of feet and chatter. Barbequed food smells. Drunks laughing with fags and cans. Rastas hung out on corners. Speakers blared reggae from vinyl shops and hairdressers. Outside a tumbledown house we met Mike's friend, a wiry Australian with a Trotsky beard. I can't remember his name. Only that the inside of the house was dark and dirty, piled with unwashed plates and inhabited by a gaggle of international visitors. They cooked lentil stew, asking us to contribute coins to the slot that kept the electricity going. But by the time we fell into winy sleep there was only candlelight and the tapping of bongos.

The next day we took our guitars into central London to earn a night out. On the Embankment, Mike sang Billy Bragg's 'This Guitar Says Sorry' and we tapped a skiffle beat. Then I bellowed Dylan's 'The Ballad of Frankie Lee and Judas Priest' and we hit those bar chords as hard as we could. It wasn't long before a policeman moved us on.

'Is this because busking is banned?' Mike asked, petulantly pushing his glasses higher onto his nose.

'No, it's because you're shit,' he said.

We mooched about until the coppers were gone, then tried again near the tube station. We were moved on before the end of the first song. We edged further south onto Waterloo Bridge where we were drowned out by the clatter of passing trains. It was pathetic. But at the end of the day we had over five pounds each, sympathy money more than anything – enough for a few rounds that night in a smoky Brixton pub where an Irish band gathered round a table with bodhráns, banjos and fiddles, and stomped out better music than we could ever hope to play. That tenner seemed to last all night. It was magic money. I don't know where the drinks came from but they kept flowing like the conversation. Back at the house we hit a cheap bottle of spirits that Mike's mate found in a cupboard and that was us, down and out for the count.

*

After I got my degree I left behind the crusty boozers, underpasses and high-rises of Sheffield to live with Mike and his flatmates in St Andrews on the coast of Fife. There were five of them on the second floor of Castlegate, a corner building on a terrace overlooking a rocky beach at the foot of the castle. As I pulled up in my cranky Peugeot 205, Mike opened the door, threw open his arms and cried, 'Gareth, you've arrived.' We set to, drinking our way through a decadent, dark winter. In the spaces between parties I began a terrible novel:

The Castle

By Gareth Rees, October 1995

'Who are you?'

The wind whips the cry to me from the roadside as I cling to the stonework of the castle, a fourteenth-century ruin rising out of ocean-battered rock on the east coast of Scotland. I'm in a crazy shag embrace, legs wrapped around the two sides of a desolate wall as if shinnying up a fat tree, arms above my head, fingers limpet like in the welts. From here I am aware both of how high I have climbed and how difficult the next stage of climbing will be.

Above me, the wall angles towards a peaked summit. This would be no problem but for this bastard-narrow ridge over which I have to pick my way before I reach the iron cockerel dancing on his axis at the pinnacle of my adventure. I'll never get there. I'm already stuck.

'Who are you?'

I can make out a woman by the railings below, some interfering so-and-so, no doubt, finding my naked arsehole intriguing. Yet her only question is, 'Who are you?'

As I shift to get a better look, I pull a piece of stone from the wall. There's a chance I might simply come away from this ancient construction and fall to my death – but screw it! I'm simply ecstatic at this handy chunk of ammunition. I hurl the stone at the woman –

I'd based this protagonist on Mike, who'd scaled the castle's southern wall one night shortly after I arrived in the town. I remember him yelling some line from *Macbeth* and looked up to see him strutting on the ruins, framed against the stars, the moon in his glasses, the breaking waves a round of applause. It was majestic, stupid and terrifying. Little did I know that he was acting out a scene from his own death.

At the beginning of 1996 I kissed a girl at a party. Her name was Katy. She was funny and wild with a Cheshire accent and black boots. We tottered back to her place and I slurred goodnight by the door. She had a boyfriend but I knew it wasn't serious. This was the best opportunity for romance I'd had in years. I plucked up the courage to phone her the next day and insist she come out with me. She hesitantly agreed. That evening we lay hungover on a grass bank outside the house, looking at the stars above the castle, and listened to the sea. For want of a better chat-up line, I told her about the eel with a head the size of an armchair in Dover harbour. I made up as many things as I could to embellish it, growing confident in telling the story now that years had passed and I was finally trying to become a proper writer, the kind that girls might admire.

Amazingly her hand was soon in mine and I felt that rush you never truly feel again, when you're a young adult falling in love, and the world is your oyster, and the night never has to end. As Katy and I walked down the street, arm in arm, my beloved eel broke through the surface of the water, beaming from gill to gill, and doffed one of its armrests to the moon.

VI

Storm Surge

It had been a long time since I'd thought about the eel with a head the size of an armchair. For years it had slumbered in the recesses of my memory. It was as if the beast had followed me up the coastline of Britain when I moved from Dover to St Andrews but then lost my scent when I moved to London. During my years living inland it had lain dormant, coiled around the ribcage of a wrecked schooner off Dungeness, awaiting my inevitable return to the coast. Now the eel with a head the size of an armchair was back. Not quite visible, but there nonetheless. I glimpsed it out of the corner of my eye whenever I walked up the rocky promontories of Hastings and looked towards the sea. Among the waves a hump, a splash, an inky darkness beneath the surface. It had re-awoken a sense of dread. Of fearful anticipation. The way

I felt that first time when Mike clambered onto the castle wall and bellowed with laughter, shortly after I arrived in St Andrews for that ill-fated year. I could sense that here in Hastings something catastrophic was awaiting me too. That I'd been lured here for reasons as yet unknown. I was not the only one to experience this magnetic pull. From the books I'd read about Hastings' history, many writers, occultists and inventors had come down here to end their days. Was I to become one of them?

In our makeshift upstairs kitchen, over a dinner of beans cooked on a camping stove and a pre-roasted Morrisons chicken, Emily asked me why I was so distracted. I didn't know what she meant by that, I said, wiping spilled orange juice from my daughter's plate and toeing the dog away from a fallen fork.

'It's like you're not here.'

'I don't know. I've been thinking about writing something again. Maybe about Charles Dawson, Teilhard de Chardin, and Aleister Crowley. They're linked to ... something weird about this town.'

'Uh-huh.' Emily disliked history. Manstory, or whatever she called it. But despite her scepticism, she'd taken time out of hammering walls and hypocritically laughing at the jokes of alpha male plasterers to build me a website where I could post my research. Each night when the girls were asleep we'd sit side by side in bed, surrounded by ceiling-high stacks of Pickfords boxes, plugged into separate laptops. She would stare at endless rows of bathroom taps with barely distinguishable stylistic differences while I lurked on occult conspiracy forums and local history portals.

'Trouble is,' I said, frantically scrubbing ketchup from my youngest daughter's face, 'for some reason I keep thinking about Mike. Funny that, after all these years. It's the smell of the sea or something ... I can't get him out of my mind. If I'd known it was going to be like this, living on the coast, I'd never have ... Then there's the fact that the world is ending. You have seen it out there, haven't you?'

The storms came before Christmas and would not go away. Days were a constant drizzle interrupted by hours of hard rain when ninety-mile-an-hour winds battered the south coast. The TV news showed people taking selfies on sea walls beneath ten-foot geysers of spray. Dogs were swept off promenades. Boat masts snapped like cocktail sticks. Railway tracks carried away in rivers of mud. Villages under water. At night, the sea cried for more. After a month of rainfall, East Hill gave in. A tower of stone broke away from the cliff on Rock-a-Nore, just beyond the Stade car park. It tottered momentarily then exploded into the sea to the screams of onlookers. Moments later, another column slid away with a roar.

The morning after, I walked Hendrix to the beach. Storm surges had vomited stones over the promenade and onto the main road. On Pelham Beach, wavy lines of kelp left by the retreating tide were entangled with the corpses of starfish, lolling clam tongues, oyster shells and smashed mussels. Amongst the organic detritus were hunks of metal. The innards of a computer. A child's shoe. Bleached bones of driftwood and tree boughs like charred human arms. Above me, herring gulls wailed an insane chorus as they circled the carnage for easy meat.

At the edge of the car park I joined a crowd of spectators at the railings by the 'Danger of Falling Rocks' signs. I could see an eighty-metre-high strip of sandstone, golden pale against the muddier brown on either side, where the cliff had broken away. There was a pile of rubble on the beach beneath. Some of the newly fallen rocks were the size of cars. I strained to look for bones in the freshly exposed sandstone—an Iguanodon or a Saxon warrior's skull. A strange shape caught my eye. A goatish head on top of a human torso in a freshly scooped hollow. More like an ancient statue than a fossil. But it was too dangerous to go onto the beach for a closer look. Instead I remained with the crowd in silent communion, watching for tremors with a mix of dread and hope. I wondered if eventually there would be a memorial bench located here:

In memory of Gareth E. Rees
He liked to come to this place
And watch the world collapse

*

Of course, this had happened before.

One October night in 1250, the moon turned red and swollen. All along the coast from Hastings to Winchelsea, shutters were tied down, animals brought indoors and fishermen returned to shore. Prayers were murmured. Within hours a gale howled and a mighty storm tide surged through Winchelsea, wrecking bridges, churches and houses. Survivors said that the English Channel appeared to burn. By morning, all but the hardiest buildings were lain to waste. No sooner had the townspeople repaired the damage than a second deluge came, in January 1252. It wrenched boats from their moorings and tore anchors from the seabed, ships spinning into the rocks. Trees launched from the earth. Steeples exploded and roofs collapsed.

In the years that followed, rapid climate change swelled the seas, forced tides further inland, accelerating the eastward pull of longshore drift and breaking up the shingle bank beneath Winchelsea. For over three more decades, the heavens wreaked havoc on East Sussex. In 1287 a storm rolled in with the combined force of all the tumult which had come before. For days and nights waves battered the coast. Chunks of Hastings' West Hill collapsed, ripping the castle in half, tumbling rocks and stonemasonry into the harbour. In the aftermath, the coast was entirely reshaped. The course of the River Rother was altered, leaving the once-coastal port of New Romney stranded inland, and turning landlocked Rye into a port. As for Winchelsea, the whole town was reduced to a pile of ruins that could only be seen at low tide. Over the following months its townsfolk watched in disbelief as the place in which they had lived, loved and played sank beneath the waves. Eventually the moon had mercy and drew the ocean's shroud over her bones. Old Winchelsea was never seen again.

Once blocked, Hastings harbour began to fill with silt and shingle. The town's days as a powerful Cinque Port were over. No more warships. No more funding from the Crown. No more tax exemptions. Hastings was left to its own devices, enduring years of isolation, piracy and poverty as it struggled to eke out a living from fish, boat-building and net-making. The no man's land that had once been the harbour was a place for locals to graze their livestock in peace beneath the overgrown remnants of William the Conqueror's castle.

In the eighteenth-century a craze for sea bathing turned Hastings into a hot spot and a property boom began. The Old Town was crammed with houses and considered a dirty disreputable place, so development spread to the west of the castle. A man named James Burton began constructing a new town for wealthy holidaymakers, known as St Leonards-on-Sea. The materials for construction were hewed from local quarries, along with the fossilised bones of ancient monsters. A new workforce began to squat on the silt of the dead harbour. First, shacks and upturned boats, then proper houses. A development steered by the wealthy shipping merchant family, the Breeds. When officials challenged the status of this community, they countered with a symbol of defiance, raising an American flag. Henceforth it became known as the America Ground, even after it was eventually acquired by the Crown and a new town centre built upon it in 1850.

I could make out the ghost of the old harbour on my walks whenever I looked down from St Mary's Terrace, on the highest ridge of West Hill. The town was a circular sprawl of Victorian buildings in a bowl between West Hill and the elevation known as the White Rock. In ancient times, water would have once fed into this harbour from the valley that descended from Old Roar Gill, running past my house to the Priory Meadow shopping centre, which was once marshland at the edge of the harbour. The river was still there, culverted beneath Harold Place, running underground between Debenhams, Wetherspoon's and Costa then out to the sea via the outfall pipe on the beach.

Overlooking this was what was left of West Hill after the cataclysm of 1287, a steep promontory, zig-zagged with pastel-coloured Victorian terraces, bearing the castle ruins on the brunt of its seaward cliff. Behind the castle, a lush green parkland sloped towards the lichen-speckled roofs of the Old Town on the other side of the hill, a quaint relic of yesteryear clustered with net shops, Tudor houses, fishing boats and churches. The greenery of West Hill was striated by pathways lined with memorial benches:

Pat and Wynne Wells 1920–2008 remembered with love.

In Loving Memory of Doris Green, Sadly Missed by Family and Friends.

In Loving Memory of Our Mum Olive Martin 1921–2006 Who loved Hastings.

In Loving memory of my dear wife Florence Lansell.

In Loving memory of Flo and Alf Longman: Down memories path we will walk with you forever.

Vincent James Penny beloved Husband and Father: A quiet sleep and a sweet dream when the long trick's over.

Walking past the benches, reading the inscriptions, I was reminded of that cemetery where we buried Mike on a cruelly sunny day in 1996. After driving in convoy from St Andrews to Edinburgh I read his eulogy in a church with his family looking on and his coffin at my side. We'd spoken together at so many debates when we were teenagers that I instinctively half-turned towards his body as I said:

'Mike loved the absurd, the fantastic, the strange. He turned everything into an adventure. If the bare facts were not exciting enough, they would be by the time they came burbling from his mouth.

'He would tell you some nonsense about needing confidence and bravado to live in this world, but it wasn't that which inspired his stories. It was a generosity of spirit that led him to touch so many lives, to persuade and encourage them, to be their friends.

'That is why there are so many people here now.

'That is why I came up to St Andrews in the first place.

'That is why I loved him.'

After the service, we filed towards the cemetery where we carried his body from the hearse to the sound of a bagpiper playing on a hillock. He was the latest slot in a row of marble on a manicured lawn on the outskirts of the city. Rectangles of soil marked out where his neighbours would soon be laid. There were flowers, photos and trinkets on recent graves but older rows were sparse where time had scarred over the wounds of grief. Being the shortest of the pallbearers, the casket hovered a few inches above my shoulder, my forefinger pressed up against the wood, as if I was spinning a basketball. When we rested him by the pit for his final descent I broke down in tears. This was worse than seeing him lying on the rocks beneath the castle. At least that ragged shore was where we lived and played. This cemetery was on the city's ring road. A place where only the dead dwelled.

Hastings' West Hill, on the other hand, was a cemetery in the land of the living, with wooden stones. The memorial benches were aligned on public footpaths, more a function of town planning than actual places the deceased would have sat to take in the view. If they were genuine spots of significance they would have been situated where walkers, lovers and loners abandoned the path to sit on the grass, clamber over rocks and talk, kiss, declare their love, end the relationship, reveal the secret. Memories are made in these moments of transgression.

There were more inscriptions on the cliff by the castle, overlooking the seafront. Every inch of exposed sandstone carved with names and initials. Unlike the benches, these were a precise location where someone sat and recorded the moment in stone. These rocks were a library LP of educational field trips, marriage proposals, inaugural joints, first kisses and family holidays. I ran my fingers over the text:

> LEAH AND SHANE ... Sexy... SARA... Lenka... KRISTIAN... Peace... Elliott... PERLA... ZOE... Joy Larkin 1930...

Many of the markings were indecipherable, worn smooth by feet and buttocks, overlaid with new inscriptions. I could see writing upon writing. Memories upon memories. Generation upon generation. People kept coming in crashing cycles of birth and death, rubbing each other out, endlessly forgetting.

Down below the dangling legs of tourists, the cliff had been reinforced to stop erosion and landslip. Red walls built into the rock. Caves sealed with mosaics of brick. West Hill was a temple of memory which Hastings was shoring up by every means possible. The town was determined to hang onto itself. Stop it all slipping away.

'If Mike is somewhere above us, basking in his own glory,' I said in the conclusion of my eulogy, 'he would like us to learn something from the energy with which he lived. And if he isn't, then he lives stronger still in all our hearts.'

I said this with all the optimistic gusto of youth before I learned that hearts are weak and memories ephemeral. West Hill offered people something more enduring: a means of preserving their legacies in stone. But even that was not enough. Long after those who scrawled the names of loved ones on rock and wood were dead, and their children's children died, their inscriptions would remain, detached from any human connection, until the cliffs finally crumbled, taking a jumble of meaningless words into the sea.

VII

Pissing on the Ridge

After a year in Hastings we were still cooking on a camping stove. In a desperate attempt to restore our dilapidated kitchen, Emily and I left the kids and dog with my parents in Wiltshire and headed back to Hastings to get the job done. It was dark by the time we pulled into town, and we were hungry, so we parked the car by the Stade and went to The Dolphin pub. A plate of rock and chips and a couple of pints later we were in the Royal Standard, drinking another round, marvelling at the wonder of being in a pub without a bag of wet wipes and children pulling at our arms, demanding crisps. All the crisps were ours now. All the chips. All the cider. All the ale. We filled our veins with it. Eventually, we decided that we absolutely must go home so we could get up first thing and start painting the kitchen. Staggering past

The Jenny Lind we heard a voodoo rockabilly band called Vince Ray's Loser Machine make a fantastic racket. Inside, revellers cheered, danced and waved their glasses in the air.

'Just the one,' we agreed, and inside we jigged to the tunes with a young couple who were necking cheap plonk. I felt jubilant enough to buy a few bottles. This was like the old days, when Emily and I were first going out. Years fell away from our eyes and I swear she was glowing. Misinterpreting our inebriation as happiness, our new friends made the mistake of inviting us to their flat, which had a well-stocked fridge and a spiral staircase to a roof terrace. We plundered their wine and jabbered about God knows what. I tried to hug the woman, crunching my face into her bosom, while Emily shouted nonsense at the man at an excruciating volume. Soon the couple were hiding behind their breakfast bar, guarding the fridge and loudly suggesting taxi numbers. The last thing I remember was falling down the spiral steps on my arse and Emily howling with laughter as we were hurled from the property.

We awoke in our bedroom the day after, surrounded by boxes, layered with plaster dust. We were bruised and sick. Even before our binge I'd been feeling unwell. Something had been nagging me since I left London. A throbbing lower back. Intermittent pain in the testicles. An incessant urge to wee. It was so bad this morning it felt as if my gonads were filled with molten magma, shooting jets of fire towards my kidneys. I could hear Emily spewing liquidised chips and cava into the toilet next door. It was hopeless. There would be no DIY today. The painting was off. The best we could do was to switch on a laptop and watch TV with the curtains closed. But all through the day we were tormented by rustling and scratching from the chimney breast, with intermittent thuds descending incrementally down the wall.

'What the hell!' Emily hissed. 'There's something in the chimney!'

I pulled the duvet over my head. 'Ignore it and maybe it'll go away.'

The following morning, we ventured downstairs. The rustling had descended to the chimney breast above the fireplace in our living room where scaffolding cast hieroglyphic shadows on our sheet-shrouded furniture. Little parps and hoots echoed in the flue as florets of soot coughed from the duct. We sat on the sofa and watched in fearful amazement as the scratching intensified and a dirty cloud began to billow. Eventually there was a soft crump. Something heavy fell into the grate then flopped onto the floor. A black mass writhed and squeaked. We watched in horror as a creature unfurled itself, fanning its matted wings, neck craning. It staggered left, then right, yellow eyes frantic, leaving webbed prints in the wood.

'Get it out!' I yelled.

'You get it out!' yelled Emily.

I opened the front door. 'Grab a broom!'

'You grab a broom!'

'No, you!'

With a sigh, Emily ran to the cellar door to find the weapon, then came around behind the juvenile gull, shaking itself to a ragged whiteness, gaining confidence as it minced back and forth, coughing and squawking. Sliding the broom roughly on the floor to make a noise, she ushered it onto the doorstep where it hopped and flapped in a dash across the road to the park. Emily slammed the door and that was that. In silence, we stared into the hall, a mass of sagging woodchip, wooden planks and the scribblings of Victorian builders. Beyond was the gutted shell of the kitchen, a repository of all our failures. For the first time since we got married it felt like we had stalled. Like the future was empty and decrepit.

'This was all *your* idea,' I said. 'You can do what you like. I'm going back to bed.'

*

The hangover passed, yet the pain in my pelvis worsened. I was no medical expert, but there seemed to be a pulse in my perineum and there could be nothing good about that. I checked for lumps in my balls but everything seemed lumpy suddenly. My testes felt like those knobbly rubber chew toys we bought for the dog. Had they always been this way? Whatever the case, they hurt the more I walked but I wasn't about to give up the walking habit. If I wanted to write another book it was the only way to find the plot. In this town stories were written into the benches. Carved in the rock. Whispered in pubs. Printed in the mud. Washed up on the shore. I could smell them in the salt air. Hear them pounding on the shingle. Stories of sorcery, shipwreck and tragedy. Stories of fraudsters, inventors and dreamers. Stories of environmental catastrophe and prehistoric extinctions. Whatever my fears, I had to sort this problem out, even if it meant going to the doctor's surgery, one of the worst places on earth. So that is what I did.

When I was thirty years old I went to a GP with a similar kind of pain in a similar area of my body. He asked a few questions about my lifestyle then booked me in for sexual health tests. The subtext was: *hey, roving young buck, with all your carousing, get thee to a clinic*. But aged forty-one, things were very different. When men pass the age of forty there's an automatic shift in the algorithm on the medical computer system. After forty, when the doctor types in your symptoms – no matter what the complaint, whether it's a headache or an ingrown toenail – the following will appear:

FULL RECTAL EXAMINATION

This time the doctor asked no questions. Instead he sighed, reached for his surgical gloves and said: 'Please lie down on your side and tuck your knees in to your chest.' Before I could register what was about to happen, it was happening. It's not as if I expected the doctor to make a speech or give me five minutes alone to gather my thoughts, but this was brutally sudden. First cold gel, then what felt like a slithering octopus.

So began a peculiar journey in which I was the topography, the doctor the traveller, the destination my prostate gland and the map an anatomical diagram of the male human. It struck me that I knew very little about my internal geography. I could vaguely locate most of my major organs, if pushed, but I'd no experience of the *territory*. Now a man's finger was pressed on my prostate gland, as if angrily ringing a doorbell.

'Is this painful?' he asked.

It was impossible to answer. I didn't feel pain, nor a lack of pain. I had transcended these binary concepts. This was more existential than painful. Until this moment, the prostate had been nothing more than an idea. A concept talked about by old men and people who keep old men alive. Now it was very real, a fiery meat peninsula, bristling with nerves, recoiling at the intrusion of the doctor's rubber-clad finger. My prostate was like that first Incan who beheld a conquistador on a horse coming over the hill's brow: sheer bewilderment, then terror. A realisation that nothing would ever be the same. In that moment, the world he knew was lost.

As I pulled up my trousers, the doctor washed his hands and asked, 'What do you do?'

'I'm a writer.'

'Do you sit down a lot?'

'Yes, but I walk a lot. Every day.'

He squinted at his computer screen. 'Have you been under any stress lately?'

'A year ago, I got into debt and had to leave London and now my wife and I are living in a building site with two young children and a dog,' I said. 'Other than that, no.'

I leaned forward and caught a glimpse of my medical notes. I could make out the words 'ACTIVE IMAGINATION' in block capitals on the screen.

'Are you really worried about this?' he asked.

'Yes.'

'Then I'll arrange for some tests.'

Four weeks later, I was sent to Conquest Hospital, a convenient mile away from the cemetery on The Ridge, a wind-blown upland behind Hastings. In the nineteenth-century it was lined with grand Victorian villas, their inhabitants drawn by the invigorating healing air and majestic views of the sea. But by the end of the twentieth-century most had been demolished, replaced with new-build estates.

On the day of my appointment, I raced there in my car with a bladder full of water, as instructed on the forms, so they could measure something known as a *flow rate*. Once seated in the urology department I realised my appointment would be delayed. It was pandemonium. Nurses ran down the corridor, muttering something about a problem with a catheter insertion. I could hear an old man howling beyond the curtains. His sister, a spindly woman in her seventies with nut-brown dyed hair, was seated a few chairs away. 'Something's gone wrong,' she clutched the nurse, 'hasn't it?'

I felt terrible for her, and even more so for her brother. But I urgently needed to unleash several gallons of urine. I broke into a sweat, eyeing the toilet sign. A nurse dashed into the office opposite to make loud cancellation calls. As the kerfuffle dragged on, water continued to flow into my bladder until it began to throb. Finally, scraping curtain rings heralded the emergence of a bed containing the catheter patient, alive but moaning, one hand reaching up to God. He was raced down the corridor by a phalanx of nurses and porters, his arthritic sister giving chase.

Calm descended upon the urology unit. An Irish nurse came up to me. 'Are you waiting?'

I nodded, doubled over with pain.

'I expect you're desperate for the loo,' she said. 'Come with me.'

She ushered me into a small room then up to a funnel with a mechanical contraption at its base and a bucket underneath.

'You'll be doing your doings in there,' she said, leaving the room. 'Wait till I give the say-so.'

I heard her heavy shoes clop away, then rustling beyond the wall of the room. A service hatch flipped open and her grinning face appeared in it, like some demented 1970s dinner party hostess.

'Ready when you are!' Her head disappeared from the hatch.

The moment I relaxed my bladder, piss gushed into the

funnel in bursts followed by streams followed by bursts followed by streams followed by bursts. It simply would not stop. As soon as I thought I was done there was another surge. It was as if Old Roar Gill had re-emerged after all these years through my stricken urethra. The bucket was filling up fast, with a beery head of foam frothing dangerously towards the rim. *Dear God*. Finally, the flow became a trickle, then drops, then one final surge, and it was over.

It was many, many minutes later before I trotted sheepishly around the corner and entered the room where the nurse sat, monitoring a spidery graph.

'That was a lot of the old huffing and puffing there,' she said.

I sat down. 'Is that bad?'

'Look at this,' she pointed at the graph. 'Normally you'd expect the curve to go quickly up, then come down with a long tail.'

I nodded.

'But yours,' she said, 'yours just goes up and down, up and down, up and down, with little peaks and little troughs.'

'That's not normal?' I asked.

'Not at all!' she said, cheerily. 'Lie yourself down here.'

I lay on the bed while she smeared oil on my pubis and

pressed down hard with an ultrasound device. After a while she sighed.

'Your bladder's not emptying properly, I can see that for a starter. You might have a narrowing of the urethra or something. Prostate disease maybe.'

'Oh God.'

'Never mind. I'm sure it'll all get sorted in the end,' her face darkened suddenly, 'one way or another. What tests have you got next?'

'Blood, then semen.'

'Oh, semen, righto,' she said. 'You'll enjoy that.'

VIII

Driving Mr Wicked

Aleister Crowley also came to The Ridge with trouble in his nether regions. But the notorious Great Beast couldn't masturbate his way out of it. In his *Book of the Law,* communed to him in Cairo by an entity named Aiwass, Crowley proclaimed the dawn of the Age of Horus, a new aeon in which humans would evolve their consciousness to become Promethean masters of their destiny. To unleash the spiritual energy required for our transformation, Crowley developed a ritualistic blend of wanking, bisexuality and drug consumption known as 'sex magick'. His efforts failed. By the 1940s he was in poor health, his asthma alleviated only by the ten grains of heroin he injected every day.

'I feel lonely like a frightened child,' he wrote, 'so much to do and my physical instrument untrusty.'

Crowley moved to Netherwood, a gabled Victorian guest house on The Ridge, owned by Vernon Symonds, playwright and actor, and his wife Kathleen Symonds, nicknamed 'Johnny'. In advance of his arrival a telegram told them to expect a consignment of frozen meat. On the big day, an ambulance rumbled up the drive. The door opened and Crowley stepped out in wide knickerbockers and silver-buckled shoes, clutching a pile of parcels.

'Well, there you are, that's the frozen meat,' laughed Vernon Symonds.

Gone was Crowley's infamous paunchiness. He was thin and yellow-skinned. Frail. Wisps of white hair rose like horns on either side of his head and an elfish beard pointed south from his chin. He chose room number 13, with an ivy-shrouded window looking out from the top floor. It was a simple room with a wardrobe, bookshelf and writing table. At night, he stayed up scribing letters to thinkers on the occult scene and injecting heroin. In the morning, he strolled along The Ridge, pausing to take in the view of the sea, palms turned towards the sun, a gold coin in his mouth as a talisman. When he felt up to it, Crowley called on his friend, a grocer named Mr Watson, to take him out for drives or escort him to Hastings Chess Club. These decisions were often based on the throwing of I-Ching sticks. A matter of destiny.

However, on this unfortunate day in October, Vernon Symonds could not get hold of Mr Watson when Mr Crowley requested a driver, so instead he asked a young woman by the name of Peg Stamford if she could assist. Peg waited in the foyer for her passenger to appear, impatiently twirling her car keys. This was tiresome. She should never have agreed to drive the old man but she wished to please Mr Symonds, who had theatrical connections in London. Everyone said Peg looked like Rita Hayworth and could act just as well. She just needed a break. Anything to get out of Hastings.

In 1942, she had joined the Women's Auxiliary Air Force and drove lorries from the base in Biggin Hill, carrying laundry, coal, airmen, bombs and the coffins of dead soldiers. She took to it like a duck to water. The only thing she never got used to was the grey woolly underwear they made her wear. Awful, truly awful. But not as awful as returning home after the excitement of the war to her father's dull lectures about the financial benefits of marriage, her mother's vacant stare, and an endlessly ticking clock. Daddy meant well, but if she had learned anything about men after life in an airbase, it was that they were mainly hot air and cock.

Presently, a goateed figure wheezed down the stairs in a tweed jacket, red cape and plus fours, clutching two flat sticks. *Dear God,* Peg thought. *Would you look at the state of it!*

The old man looked her up and down. 'Where's Watson? Watson usually drives me. I want Watson to drive me.'

'He's on deliveries,' said Peg. 'You can wait until later if you like.'

Crowley shook his head in exasperation. 'No, no. The stalks have spoken. I have only this window of opportunity. You'll have to do.'

Peg prayed that the old man would sit in the back of the car, but he flopped into the passenger seat, swirled his cape onto his knees and rested the sticks upon it. His hands were curiously small and yellow.

'Can you drive this thing, then?' huffed Crowley.

'Do you mean a three-speed motor car with a four-cylinder engine? Oh, I've handled bigger beasts than this, Mr Crowley, believe me. Bigger beasts even than you.'

Peg hit the accelerator and they roared onto The Ridge, plunging down Elphinstone Road towards the town and the castle, cragged over a wintry sea.

After brooding a while, the old man said, 'You haven't you know.'

'Haven't what?'

'Handled a bigger beast. I have rampaged with the wildest fuckstresses in living memory ...'

'Oh.'

'... and almost tore their bottoms off.'

'You must be very proud.'

'It's not about pride.'

'It sounds very much like it's about pride.'

'It's about man's will.'

'Well, I am not a man,' Peg declared. 'So I will not.'

Crowley's eyes narrowed. 'Miss, do you know who I am? Do you have any notion of what I am capable?' He waggled his fingers at her ears.

Peg hit the brakes. Crowley lurched forward with a grunt as the car swerved to a stop at the side of the road. For a moment Peg worried that he'd snapped in two.

'Look here, Mr Crowley. I am happy to do this favour for Mr and Mrs Symonds. But any more of your magic tricks or bottom-tearing talk, and I shall drive you back to Netherwood without another breath. Is that understood?'

The old man shrugged.

'Then it's settled. So where would you like to go?'

Crowley fondled his sticks and sniffed the air. He stuck out his tongue to reveal a gold coin, slimy with saliva, then withdrew it, lodging it between his gum and cheek.

'Bexhill-on-Sea.'

'As you wish.'

As Peg hit the coastal road out of town, Crowley gazed

out at the bomb-damaged houses and abandoned gun posts on the shore, his lips moving ever so slightly, as if incanting something, or rehearsing a speech. As they approached Bexhill-on-Sea he began to harrumph and grunt like a broken engine. After a couple of minutes, she could bear it no longer.

'Please—stop—please—or I will drive us into the sea, I swear.'

'No, *you* can stop,' said Crowley. 'Here will do nicely.'

The car pulled into a concrete bay beneath the modernist concrete wall of the De La Warr Pavilion. Peg turned off the ignition. 'I'd like to make it clear that I stopped because this is a sensible place to park. Not because of your hypnotic powers.'

'You never can tell,' said Crowley.

Unwilling to wait like a taxi driver, Peg followed Crowley as he shambled onto the forecourt beneath the pavilion's cantilevered balconies where shrubs rustled in an unseasonably mild October wind. On the promenade, he seemed unable to get his bearings. He walked in one direction, finger in the air, then turned back on himself, cape billowing behind him. He did this over and over until he grew breathless. Eventually Peg stopped following. She leaned against a railing, lit a Pall Mall and observed him with contempt.

'For goodness' sake,' she cried. 'You're like a trapped goat. Decide!'

There were a few figures on the beach clutching onto their hats. Peg couldn't understand why British people persisted in seaside hat-wearing. It was idiotic. Utterly idiotic. A world war, millions of deaths and still they worried about being seen in the right headwear. Crowley watched them like a hawk. Occasionally he made as if to approach one of them but, as he drew closer, thought the better of it. Eventually something caught his gaze and held it—a figure sat on a bench looking out to sea. After a moment's contemplation, Crowley started towards the figure with determined strides. As he passed Peg he muttered: 'Follow me if you wish, and prepare to be amazed.'

'What does that mean?'

Crowley lifted his cloak up to his chin. 'Now you see me … ' He quickly covered the rest of his head with his cloak. 'Now you don't. Watch. Or, rather, *try* to watch.'

The old man began to creep on tiptoes towards the figure on the bench, lifting the cloak high above him with clawed hands, like a pterodactyl. The seated man was oblivious, gaze fixed on the horizon. When he was a few yards away from the bench, Crowley pulled the cloak tight around him so that he was entirely covered from head to toe, and inched slowly in front of the man until his crotch was directly in front of his face.

Peg sighed and hurried towards the pair.

'I'm so sorry, sir,' she said to the seated figure, a spectacled man in his fifties wearing a thick scarf, his legs covered in a blanket. 'This gentleman is a little unwell in the head.'

'You can see me?' Crowley asked Peg.

'Unfortunately, yes,' said Peg.

'Aha! But *he* cannot!' declared Crowley.

'I can see you well enough,' said the seated man in a Scottish accent without bothering to look up.

Crowley's face fell. 'Admittedly the effects of invisibility are short-lived, but effective enough. Mr John Logie Baird, I presume.'

The man started in surprise. 'Yes, that's correct.'

'Do you know who I am?'

Baird shook his head.

'I am Aleister Crowley.'

'You don't look like Aleister Crowley.'

'Ah, well, appearances can be deceptive. Would an imposter have known that you were here, in this spot, on this day, at this precise time, without being informed so? And could he achieve such a feat purely through his powers of divination? Ha ha, no sir, no he would not. Explain that!'

Baird looked wearily at Peg. 'Is he Aleister Crowley?'

'Apparently so,' said Peg, leaning against the back of the bench.

'Then I'll accept the fact.'

Peg vaguely remembered hearing something about John Logie Baird and his television broadcasts from London when she must have been thirteen or fourteen, before the war put a stop to it all. She considered asking him if there would one day be a place in television for an ambitious young woman who looked like Rita Hayworth. But huddled in his blanket he seemed a man who had lost his place in the world. The fight had gone out of him.

Crowley was incensed at Baird's indifference. 'Ho ho, well then, as you're so preoccupied, Mr Baird, I won't dilly dally and simply say what needs to be said, as I have come all this way and—' he glared at Peg, '—wasted a lot of energy.'

'Energy is never lost,' said Baird. 'Merely transferred.'

Crowley scowled. 'You stole it. Didn't you?'

'I beg your pardon?'

'You know very well what I mean. This television of yours ... or rather not yours ... not yours at all ... was to be mankind's inheritance.'

'Pish.'

'You, sir, have initiated the world into your own

cataclysmic and—and—*amateurish* cult. You know nothing of what you have unleashed.'

'My word. You live up to your reputation as a windbag, Crowley.' Baird smiled uneasily. 'Is this a prepared speech? Come to think of it, how did you know to find me here today?'

'Aha! I did not expect you to understand! You haven't the capacity! You haven't the *skills*!' Delighted at his own invective, Crowley clapped his tiny hands until they began to blur. 'Unbeknown to you, this technology was being cultivated in secret by adepts, like Promethean fire, for the liberation of mankind.'

'An interesting interpretation,' mumbled Baird, looking around the promenade as if for help.

'Oh, interesting is not the word! Not even close! If only your greedy little mind could imagine such a thing—to see across dimensions, to commune with the spirits, to wield influence in the universe! But you, Mr Baird ... you stole the work of visionaries far greater than you, and passed it off as your own, you thief!'

'Steady,' said Peg half-heartedly, feeling she was duty-bound to step in. 'Can't you see this man is ill?'

'No, I will not be steady, young lady, I will be swayed and buffeted by my ire, like a ship in a tempest, until he goes green with nausea.'

'It's out of my hands,' said Baird quietly. 'Take your complaint to the British Broadcasting Company.'

'You heard the gentleman,' said Peg. 'Out of his hands. Now let's go.'

'No,' barked Crowley, 'no we shan't until I've said my piece. I have spent my life fighting against society's most stubborn prejudices. I sacrificed everything. But you, sir, shilled the power of second sight to the British Broadcasting Company for a handful of gold. In this single act of treachery, you have condemned us to a most tawdry and compromised epoch, damn you!'

'Absolute nonsense,' said Baird.

'When it all starts up again, I would like to be on the television,' said Peg. 'It sounds a hoot.'

Smiling, Baird gestured at Peg. 'See?'

Crowley's face flushed. His white horns of hair looked stark against the redness. 'You damned entrepreneurs. You stumble upon scraps of magical wisdom then strip away every iota of spiritual meaning. Much like the noble coca leaf, chewed by the natives of the Andes ...'

Oh dear God, thought Peg, lighting another Pall Mall.

'... when consumed raw, it allows men to run up mountains, but when processed into cocaine it ensnares those same men in the grip of addiction! This is your legacy,

Baird! Rather than effect our release, you have secured our enslavement. The public will laud you for it, but make no mistake—they are morons!' Crowley bellowed the word again at the top of his voice. 'MORONS!'

'Right,' snapped Peg. This was embarrassing. 'You're coming back with me.' She reached out for his arm.

'I will not submit to the age of enslavement!' yelled Crowley, pushing her roughly.

At this, Baird cast aside his blanket and struggled to his feet. 'I can take your jealous rage, Crowley. But leave the young lady alone. She is but a child.'

'Excuse me!' said Peg. 'I am perfectly capable of—'

'Oh my, Mr Baird,' Crowley cackled. 'Suddenly you're quite the picture of health, quite the knight in shining armour. All the more fun to bowl you off your steed!' Crowley raised his palms toward Baird and made quick pushing gestures, as if to force balls of air at the inventor.

'Have you quite finished?' asked Baird.

Crowley grabbed Baird's scarf, pulling him close, until their noses were almost touching. He spoke in a terse staccato. 'I—was—there.'

'What are you talking about?'

'I was there, on the East Hill, the very same day as you … it was to be *my* discovery, *my* epoch, not *yours*.'

The inventor looked genuinely surprised. 'I ... '

'Oh, you ridiculous old fools.' Peg mimicked a childish whine. 'It's your epoch, no it's my epoch, no your epoch, no my epoch—hell's bells. I will outlive the both of you. Perhaps it's my epoch.'

They were interrupted by a voice in the distance. 'I say, what's going on? Leave him alone at once!' A middle-aged woman ambled towards them, holding onto her hat in the wind, looking like a total imbecile, Peg thought. Crowley saw her coming, but didn't let go of Baird. Instead he pulled Baird's scarf even tighter and snarled:

'I—know—what—you—did.'

'Fie!' gasped Baird. As he said it there was a loud crack across the sea, as if the horizon had split earth from sky. Peg almost jumped out of her skin. A gust of wind howled around them with great ferocity, whipping Baird's discarded blanket down the promenade like a dancing ghost. The light dimmed as a peninsula of purple cloud rose quickly over Beachy Head and blocked out the sun. Two terns flew backwards above them, shrieking. Peg saw a sudden flash of fear in Crowley's eyes. But Baird's eyes, they were burning. He seemed to expand without getting bigger, and rise taller as if levitating, without his feet leaving the floor. He wrenched Crowley's hands from his neck and spoke, his voice no longer weak but a deep boom:

'Nihil est verum, omnia licet!'

He pushed Crowley across the promenade with astonishing force, sending the old man skittering over the slabs and into the promenade wall. Immediately, the wind dropped. Baird crumpled, as if all the air was suddenly let out of him, and sat on the bench with his head bowed until the woman reached him.

'John!' She cradled him tight to her bosom. 'Are you all right John?' She glared at Peg. 'Your grandfather should be ashamed of himself!'

Over by the wall, Crowley writhed and groaned, his cape spread across the ground around him, as if theatrical blood was spilling from his body.

'Indeed,' nodded Peg. 'I'm going to bloody kill him.'

*

On the drive back to Netherwood rain began to fall. Heavy drops spattered on the roof of the Ford Anglia. The coin in Crowley's mouth ticked against his teeth in time to the windscreen wipers. Crowley seemed smaller in his suit, his neck more turkey-like than Peg remembered on the drive out. He was in a lot of pain and trying not to show it but his hands were shaking terribly. She could tell this sort of thing had happened to him before.

'Well?' she said, finally. 'How did you think our day out went?'

'Bewilderingly,' said Crowley. 'Let's hope things improve in my next incarnation.'

'Before you go dying and leaving my world a much-improved place,' said Peg, 'it's worth knowing something. And I don't mind telling you this. In fact, I really must insist upon it.'

'Spit it out then, woman.'

'I have driven the dead bodies of soldiers and missiles packed with explosives that might have torn me to shreds. But you are, without a shadow of a doubt, the most awful load I have ever transported.'

'Never mind.' Crowley sighed and looked out of the window. 'It's not the end of the world.'

IX

Smoked Cats

On a rare night out, Emily and I sat in The Stag beneath a display cabinet of smoke-dried Tudor cats, thinking of things to say that didn't involve the children, my pelvic agony or the house we'd bought. As each week passed the building grew shabbier and more malevolent. The kitchen might have been finished at last, but the living room remained a sagging mess with a demolished partition wall that threated to pull everything into the sod. Since the electricians had replaced the Edwardian wiring every light switch dangled from a hole punched through to the laths, showing spaces between rooms that could not be entered but blasted out grave-cold air as we passed. Each day I wrote at my computer in the same room in which we'd found the 1989 newspapers. When I walked to and from my desk, the disintegrating carpet coughed dust, got into my lungs, clogged my nose with dead matter. But these complaints weren't for a night in the pub. They were to be repressed beneath smiles and alcohol.

Besides, there was already too much to think about with this occult puzzle I was beginning to put together for the Hastings book. For want of something better to say, I told Emily about my John Logie Baird and Aleister Crowley theory. That both men had come to this coastline in their final year of existence. That both had dedicated their lives to endowing humanity with new, advanced modes of perception. But while Baird became enshrined as a local hero, Crowley was blamed for all the town's woes and the crazy occultists who came to the town after his death. People like Alex Sanders, 'King of the Witches', initiated into witchcraft by his grandmother through ritual sex acts, who became a leading light in the Wicca religion, and ended his days in St Leonards-on-Sea. It was alleged that he once used the power of masturbation to will into being a spiritual baby called Michael, who would occasionally take over Sanders' body and act like an unspeakable prick at parties.

'Well,' sighed Emily, when I'd finished. 'This all sounds very you.'

'What do you mean by that?'

She hugged my arm unconvincingly. 'I don't know. You've been a bit weird yourself lately.'

Oh God. I knew what that was all about and really it wasn't how it looked. Earlier that evening she had caught me squatting over my eldest daughter's *Frozen* official merchandise hairdryer, using it to blow cold air up my nether regions. It was something I'd read on the Internet about preventing bacterial infection in the perineum. Anything to end my recurring pain was worth a try and Emily didn't own a hairdryer.

'I've got a lot on my mind,' I said.

To change the subject I asked the landlord—a shaggy-haired, piratical-looking fellow who was a member of the Hastings Shanty Singers—about his take on the smoked cat corpses in the cabinet above our heads. He explained that the witch Hannah Clarke allegedly lived in the building during the sixteenth-century. At night, she'd fly over East Hill on her broomstick, searching the coastline for French invaders. As legend had it, she sealed the cats into the brickwork as a charm to ward off the plague. He explained that the more likely story was that the cats crawled into the chimney for warmth, after which someone unwittingly lit a fire and smoked them to death.

'I've actually bought another one since,' he said. I was impressed. Two smoked Tudor cats are just two smoked Tudor cats. But three smoked Tudor cats are a *collection*.

A bluegrass band was setting up in the corner with double bass, guitars, accordion, harmonica and banjo. At the table adjacent to ours was a lean kid in his early twenties with tousled hair, goatee and a black sleeveless T-shirt that showed off his tattoos. Between sips of red wine he puffed an e-cigarette. He was deep in conversation with a man in his early fifties. Flat cap. Twinkly eyes and ruddy Dylan Thomas cheeks. They were an odd couple. Friends? Father and son? The older man leaned in close to the rock kid and touch his arm tenderly, words slurring from the corner of his mouth.

'Sometimes ... have you ever just ... gone for it, you know ... ha ha ... thought, what the hell ...?'

'I live life how it comes, man,' replied the kid. Puff, puff, puff went his fake cigarette.

A couple in goth clobber arrived, greeting the kid as they sat at the table. They seemed bemused by the presence of the drunk man in the flat cap. I realised suddenly that the two men didn't know each other at all. They had only met that night. As the bluegrass music rattled into motion, the friends spoke with heads bowed close, leaving the older man out of the conversation. Desperate, he turned to Emily, 'Isn't he gorgeous?' He touched the young rock kid's arm again.

Emily smiled. 'Well, if you think so, that's what matters.'

The man explained that he'd been drinking at home and popped out to get an Indian takeaway. On his way back, the younger man had stopped him to ask him directions to The Stag. Smitten, he had followed him to the pub. He pointed to a bag of curry going cold at his feet.

'If he won't have me tonight, I'll put something in his drink!' He cackled loud enough for the kid to hear.

The kid shook his head, laughing. 'No way man.'

'Hey, I'm alright, aren't I, though? … right? … I'm fairly good looking? Right?' He turned to us again, mugging for laughs, but his eyes were sad.

This painful charade continued well into our second drink. When the younger man went out to have a real cigarette, the older man followed. At their return the goth couple raised their eyebrows and mouthed, '*Whaaaaaat … are … you … dooooooing?*'

The rock kid looked hassled suddenly, worried that it had gone too far.

'Why won't you come back with me?' the older man pleaded.

'Because my type has tits and a vagina,' the kid said. 'Sorry.'

Despite the chugging guitars and harmonica wail, I could hear a snap as the older man's heart broke. Or it might have been a beer mat falling. I couldn't tell. He grabbed his bag of cold curry with one hand, and touched his amour's face with the other.

'I never have anyone to go out with,' he mumbled. Then he staggered from the pub. The door creaked shut. For a few minutes I could see him outside the window, shivering in the cold, looking up and down the street, defeated. His isolation was unbearable.

'Poor guy,' said Emily.

I slugged my pint and looked up at the smoked Tudor cats. Life was hard. The best you could hope for was a little warmth now and then, even if the attempt killed you.

*

I remember now. Unusually, it wasn't Mike who told me the story, but his friend Mark. It happened the year before I arrived in St Andrews. He and Mike decided to go trekking in the Cairngorms. They took a small tent, camping gear and stove, but the going was harder than expected and they were forced to set up a makeshift camp on the mountainside, drinking whisky from hipflasks as night came down cold and wet. Mark's flimsy summer sleeping bag was woefully inadequate. As the temperature plummeted, Mark began to shiver, breathing in short sharp bursts as heat drained from his body. Panic set in. Mike instantly recognised the early symptoms of hypothermia. He hauled out the spare clothes and towel from the rucksack and sealed Mark into his bag to keep out the cold air. He boiled water, making sugary tea which he forced his friend to drink. They spent a long night in the pitch darkness with no hope of contact or escape. Mike talked and talked to stop Mark zoning out and falling unconscious. He sang songs and told jokes. He climbed into Mark's sleeping bag and cuddled close. The two of them fused, a human zygote, tiny in the womb of the Scottish landscape, alone together until first light.

In the morning, they were able to make it down the hill to safety. By the following day, they were ruddy cheeked and belligerently drunk in a Chinese restaurant in St Andrews yelling, 'We're alive! We're alive!'

For all his posturing, Mike wasn't so interested in telling this true story of how he saved a life. He preferred to tell me his story about how he was trekking up a mountain—I can't remember where, perhaps Mount Kinabalu in Borneo, or somewhere in the French Alps. He'd entered a hut to get out of the cold weather. There was already an older man in there, sat by the stove drinking a mug of tea. They got talking about climbing. The man was an experienced mountaineer who had done K2. Coincidentally, Aleister Crowley had also led an expedition up K2 in 1902, carrying a small library of poetry books in his pack and turning back after 20,000 feet, stricken with malaria and snow-blindness.

Mike asked the man what he was doing on this relatively unchallenging route. The man shook his head sadly. 'I'm up here because I like mountains, but my climbing days are over ... since the tragedy.'

When Mike probed him for an explanation, the man replied that it was hard to talk about, but he'd been climbing with his best friend. They were ascending a steep incline when rock-fall swept him over a ledge, leaving him dangling by a rope, while his partner was trapped on the line on the rock above him. 'I was left hanging,' he said, 'and there was nothing I could do.' He couldn't climb up his own rope, but neither could his partner pull him up. The man shook his head sadly. 'It was a terrible situation. We were like that for an hour. Me in mid-air, my best friend safe on the rock but joined to me by that damned rope. The only way he was going to get back off that mountain was if he cut me loose.' The man's eyes were so sad, Mike remembered, weathered and wrinkled on such a young face.

'So, what did you do?' Mike asked the climber.

The climber turned to him. 'I got out my knife,' he said. 'And I cut the rope.'

And with that, the climber vanished.

Mike was left alone in the cabin, the wind whistling, terrified out of his wits.

'That's bollocks, Mike,' I laughed. 'Total bollocks.'

'Truth,' he said.

We were in the same Chinese he took Mark to after the Cairngorms fiasco. It was his favourite restaurant. Apart from the all-night bakery with its macaroni pies, I can't remember him going anywhere else. Back then there were meagre culinary pickings in St Andrews. We were usually too skint to go out, especially when we could spend the money on wine, but on this occasion Mike had brandished his credit card and insisted that both of us should go and eat as much crispy aromatic duck as possible. He was recklessly generous like that. To hell with caution. The future was another universe.

There was a peculiar atmosphere in the restaurant that evening. It was less rowdy than normal; the lights were low and we were speaking with a candle between us.

'Have you noticed how everyone in here is a couple?' I said.

Mike laughed. 'I've just realised ... it's the fourteenth of February.'

'Happy Valentine's,' I said, raising my glass.

It was almost exactly three months before the end. Before the night on the castle. How young and innocent we were in that moment. How beautiful life is when you have no comprehension of your place on the map of time. Ahead of Mike and I was a wide-open frontier land where nothing had been decided and anything was possible. But as it turned out, only I got to travel there.

Twenty years on there seemed much more of this world behind me than in front of me. I wandered a crumbling landscape busy with ghosts, where every object spoke of what had passed and all lines led back into history. Flowers taped to lamp posts, inscribed benches on paths and promenades, blue plaques on houses. They kept me constantly aware of other people's triumphs and failures, the fleeting nature of life and the many ways to perish. If society kept up this compulsion to memorialise then soon every road would become a procession of shrines. Every house a biography. Every cliff-edge a monument to the fallen. Every castle a tombstone. Every pub a cat mausoleum.

'Gareth, what's up?' said a woman's voice. 'You look upset.'

It was Emily, coming out of the toilet in The Stag, smiling uncertainly.

Last orders had come and gone. The pub was almost empty.

It was *time*.

'You were right,' I said. 'I'm not myself at the moment.'

X

The Black Arches

On a bright autumn weekday morning, I hauled my daughters to school through the park and past Blacklands Church. On one side of its tower, the clock was stopped dead on midnight. On the other, the clock face told the correct time. This chronological duality unsettled me. As usual, the lollipop lady was at the junction, saying something about the weather. 'It's going to be a cold one today,' she grimaced. 'Sure will be,' I said, not really caring about the weather at all. When it was chilly she wore a fluorescent woolly hat, which was funny because her real hair was a golden bob that almost glowed, as if she was born to do lollipopping for a living, although it might be any one of a number of jobs she did throughout the day. Proofreader. Astronomer. Author. She was only there from 8:40 until 8:55

in the morning, waiting with a grin as we approached.

We pushed through the usual array of parents. The girl in high boots who was always on the phone, the two women with pushchairs who stopped on the corner by the road sign and discussed deep interpersonal relationship issues as if it wasn't 8:50 in the bloody morning, and the Alfred Hitchcock lookalike who waited in his hatchback, engine running, back windows covered in obnoxious stickers that said things like HONK IF YOU'RE HORNY, with a comedy cat's rear-end sticking out of the boot, soggy and blackened by exhaust fumes. There was the tall man who always wore shorts even when it was snowing and the short woman with an underbite who barked at her three kids and the Malaysian guy who always nodded hello to me but I could never remember what it was that made us nodding acquaintances in the first place. Every morning, the same people in a remix. Same melody, different arrangement.

After the girls were safely in school I marched up the West Hill where I passed by the memorial benches, taking photos of those I'd missed. Eventually I stopped beside a curiously toy-like pentagonal lighthouse, overlooking the Old Town. Beneath my feet, deep inside the hill, were the St Clements Caves, a network of tunnels in which carved nooks cradled mysterious sculptures, including one that some claimed was a Baphomet statue, a goat-headed idol revered by Aleister Crowley. True or not, it didn't surprise me. There was no escaping the Great Beast in Hastings.

In the final weeks of Crowley's life his doctor, William Brown Thomson, threatened to end his heroin prescription. Crowley was furious. He declared, 'If you do I shall die – and I shall take you with me.' On 2 December, 1947, the Great Beast passed away. A day later Dr Thomson was found dead in his bath. Thanks to his chilling invocation of the doctor's demise, Crowley's legend took root. It was said that he'd not only cursed Thompson but the whole town. That if you lived in Hastings you could never leave. Try it, and you'd always come back, unless you found a stone with a hole on the beach and took it with you everywhere you went.

The curse gained traction as Hastings & St Leonards' popularity as a tourist destination waned. Owners of empty guest houses were given government subsidies for taking in those with financial or psychological difficulties from other parts of England. As major mental institutions closed in the 1970s, their patients were relocated in Hastings & St Leonards. Many came voluntarily, fleeing to a cheap place of last resort. The town became one of the most deprived areas in Britain and a national suicide blackspot. The end of the road.

After the Great Beast's death, occultists began to drift to this part of the coast, including Alex Sanders, who founded the Alexandrian version of Wicca, died in St Leonards and was cremated on The Ridge. George Hay, founder of The Science Fiction Foundation and editor of *The Necronomicon* anthology, ended his days in the Old Town. Another resident was Eric John Dingwall, the psychic investigator who scrutinised the work of mediums and exposed the spirit photographer William Hope as a fraud. In 1954, he married Dr Norah Margaret Davis and later moved to St Leonards. When she died unexpectedly, he fell into the arms of the occult, attempting to contact Margaret through a medium. After this, he reported that his clock began behaving 'curiously' and objects would fall from shelves or float across the room.

Year after year they came—magicians, addicts and dreamers—drawn by majestic views, salt air, ley lines and cheap housing. In 2013, St Leonards resident Kevin Carlyon, high priest of British white witches, declared it the occult capital of the UK. Vulnerable people were being lured into Crowleyist black magic cults, he said, like the Ordo Templi Orientis (O.T.O.) whose Shemish Lodge was based in the town. Peaches Geldof spent her summers in Hastings as a child, and had O.T.O. tattooed on her arm. When she died of a heroin overdose the tabloids speculated on her black magic connections. Rumours went that Crowley was a MI5 agent and that the O.T.O. was a front for the secret services. They said Peaches was killed for her knowledge about high-level paedophile rings.

This was typical. Everything linked to Crowley's legacy swirled in a witch's brew of misinformation and invention. But I couldn't resist these stories. They were what I loved to write. That was why I was up on West Hill that day. I was out searching for things to put in a book. Something to give me a sense of control, away from subsiding walls and the demands of children. It was pathetic really. But the thoughts of Mike and mummified cats in The Stag had given me an idea. If this town was a nexus of hotlines to the past, why not find out how those lines connected with each other? Why not seek out the ghosts at the other end?

Where I stood was a case in point. Built into the side of West Hill, just beneath the lighthouse, was Harpsichord House, an odd wooden-slatted building with its second floor shaped as a wedge lodged into the rock, creating a bridge over the footpath. This was once the home of Rollo Ahmed. Born in British Guyana at the end of the nineteenth-century, he journeyed into deep South American jungle where the he witnessed the magic rituals of Amerindian tribes and learned about their natural medicines and psychedelics. Arriving in England, he passed himself off as Egyptian to shill herbal remedies before entering the London black magic scene where he befriended Aleister Crowley and wrote *The Black Art*, a history of the occult. By the 1950s he was holding rituals in Harpsichord House, wearing a purple cloak, silk scarf and beret, the sounds of tribal jazz rumbling from a gramophone as incense curled around jungle idols on the mantelpiece.

Pausing in the shadows beneath his home, I tried to make out the dates carved into the stone … 1974 … 1967 … There was a square metal hatch in the rock, gouged with holes, as if someone was desperate to break in. Down the footpath was a steep Victorian terrace where guitarist John Martyn lived in the 1970s, another lifelong follower of Crowley. At the bottom, St Clements Church was squat among Tudor facades and a garden in memory of the White Swan Hotel, obliterated by a German bomb, killing its Sunday afternoon drinkers. I crossed The Bourne, a culverted stream which had become a busy road, onto All Saints Street, a Tudor relic with overhangs and wonky beams.

Looming above the Old Town was a slope of brambles on the upper flank of East Hill known as Mount Idle. At its crest was an exposed seam of sandstone in which were visible three lancet-shaped forms. It looked like a church

OMNISCIENT
OMNIPOTENT
ITNOTGAOTU
SACRED
TO THE MEMORY OF
WILLIAM EDWARDS
WHO DIED 29TH MARCH 1842
AGED 85 YEARS
ALSO ANN
SECOND WIFE OF THE ABOVE
WHO DIED 30TH APRIL 1813
AGED 45 YEARS
FEAR GOD AND KEEP HIS
COMMANDMENTS FOR THAT
IS THE WHOLE DUTY OF MAN
ERECTED BY THE BRETHREN OF THE DERWENT LODGE
FREE MASONS IN GRATEFUL REMEMBRANCE OF HIS ZEALOUS
SERVICES FOR A PERIOD OF FORTY YEARS. A.L. 5843

or the entrance to a Gothic tunnel system built into the promontory. These were the Black Arches, carved by a man named John Coussens in the eighteenth-century. In my first months in Hastings I'd been fooled into thinking they were a three-dimensional structure. Once I noticed them, I became obsessed. What were they? What were they doing up there?

Now that it was late autumn, the vegetation was clear enough for me to visit them. My ascent began in the graveyard of All Saints Church, where I paused at the 1842 headstone of William Edwards, freemason, on which was carved an All-Seeing Eye with a hexagram, square and compass, and the inscription: OMNISCIENT, OMNIPOTENT, OMNIPRESENT.

From here I ascended a path, wild with nettles, to the highest ridge of East Hill, and worked my way towards the sea. The arches appeared almost by surprise. Up close they were less precise than they seemed below, crude simulacra carved into rock, painted black and daubed in graffiti. A stolen fire exit sign was propped against the central arch, its arrow pointing down as if it was an escape hatch from the apocalypse. Lager cans and fag butts were strewn around. I put my eye up against a crack, forehead cold against the stone, but I couldn't see anything. As always, I felt trapped on the outside of things. I had an unbearable urge to push myself deep into the hill, as if it was simply a matter of will, as if the answer to the riddle of existence was inside.

What was Coussens trying to say? There were plenty of reasons a person might want to alter the landscape, be it for mischief, art, coded communication or the desire for legacy. Perhaps he saw God in the hills. Perhaps he wanted to open the doors to another realm, beyond that which could be seen with the naked eye. Perhaps this was his form of *television*, a spirit manifestation machine like the one which barbiturate-addicted Kristian Birkeland dreamed of carving into a mountain. Perhaps it was the result of a drunken bet. Perhaps Coussens would wait for a traveller to ask about 'that strange little church' then suggest they scramble up Mount Idle to get a closer look, guffawing as he watched them go.

What larks!

Perhaps he used the arches to lure tourists up the hill, where he'd crack their skulls and cast their bodies off the cliff edge to appease those sea devils who threatened him with damnation.

Perhaps.

On my website, I posted a plea for information about the Black Arches. A few weeks later I received an email from the Rt Hon. Earl de Mychel Wayne Quinnell, whose wife was a direct descendant of John Coussens. He told me, 'John Coussens created the hoaxes, the Black Arches and the Minnis Rock ... there has never been any written information on this character. It has been passed down from one generation to the other.'

What the hell was the Minnis Rock? I googled it. There was no precise location, but an aerial photograph of small caves beneath a road I recognised. I was dumbfounded. On my walks to the Black Arches I'd passed near the Minnis Rock many times and never realised it was there. This I had to see.

I was supposed to pick the girls up from school, but the discovery was too exciting, so I mumbled something to Emily about vital research and marched to the Old Town. I took my usual path to Mount Idle but turned off at a tributary in the long grass. And there it was! The Minnis Rock, hidden from the road by foliage, a six-foot-high seam of sandstone rising from mud like the upper half of a human skull. There were three carved entrances, like the Black Arches, but they led into three chambers, with holes carved in the partition walls. When I stood inside, the holes formed the shape of a lizard eye staring back at me. The surface of the Minnis Rock was grooved with markings, including a carefully scribed date: 1727. This cannot have been the work of their alleged creator, John Coussens, for he would have been too young. On the Internet I'd seen a sixteenth-century drawing by a

Dutch artist which showed the caves being used as a sheep shelter long before he was even born.

So who carved that date?

*

At the dawn of the nineteenth-century a poor old woman called Hannah Weller lived in a shack near the Minnis Rock. She had far outlived every soul who knew her as a smart, playful young woman. To the folk of the Old Town she was naught but a grumpy hag whom they suspected of sorcery, for oftentimes pigs and sheep refused to pass by her dwelling.

'Please, ma'am, let them by!' the drovers begged. Hannah would throw up her hands in despair at their idiocy and the animals would suddenly start moving again. The drovers thought this gesture the lifting of the spell so they went home and told their family yet more stories about the witch they'd seen do magic with their own eyes.

In particular, she terrified one William Crump, a signalman working at the lookout station on Fairlight Down. Every week he walked into Hastings to run errands, avoiding Hannah, who was old beyond human possibility, uglier than sin, and from whom a single stare could jolt his heart out of rhythm.

His boss was Commander James Anthony Gardner, who thought black magic a load of bunkum and Crump a fool. One morning, Gardner had purchased eggs in the market but needed to attend to other business in town, so he gave the eggs to signalman Crump to take back to the station.

Crump dutifully stashed them beneath straw at the bottom of a basket with a yessir, will do sir, you can count on me sir. But instead of attending to further matters, Gardner changed his mind and headed back towards Fairlight, letting Crump follow with the eggs.

On his way, Commander Gardner passed Hannah Weller carrying a ragged bundle of clothes.

'Ah, Hannah, good day,' he said with forced breeziness.

'Sir,' she murmured.

'I wonder if you'd be so kind as to do me a favour?' asked Gardner. 'A fellow named Mr Crump—you can't miss him in his frock coat—will be travelling this way shortly with a wicker basket. Will you give him a message?'

Hannah didn't like the sound of it, but she shrugged in agreement.

'Please tell Mr Crump that he should be careful of the eggs at the bottom of his basket and make haste. Be sure to tell him, Hannah. It's very important. Oh, and don't tell him you've seen me.' With that, Gardner headed up the hill, smiling fiendishly.

Moments later Crump waddled into view around the bulge of the Minnis Rock. Catching sight of Hannah, he hesitated, then started in a wide arc to avoid her. Determinedly, Hannah cut towards him, tripping and cursing over rivets of grass. Crump tried to accelerate, but with the eggs so fragile, and not wishing to disappoint Gardner, he could do little more than mince. Soon Hannah stood in his way and said, 'Mr Crump?'

Oh, dear Lord she knew his name. What sorcery!

Hannah tried to remember Gardner's words, 'Um, you should be careful of them eggs in yer basket, you know, and be quick about it and not loiter by the way.'

Crump was aghast. He looked down at the straw, which completely covered the eggs, and knew there could be no way she would know there were eggs concealed therein, except that she had the power of second sight, given to her by congress with the Devil or some such awfulness.

'Thank you,' was all he could think to say, terrified she would cast a spell on him. 'Good morning to you.'

Hannah nodded meekly, then trundled past Crump, while he strode in the opposite direction. After some yards, he saw a footprint in the mud, made by one of Hannah's clogs. One sure way to know if she was truly a witch was to unsheath his knife and drive it into the mark she left.

As he did so, he turned around to look and Hannah was staring back at him at the very same time!

It was all the evidence he needed. Trembling, Crump rose to his feet, knife still in his hand. 'You ...'

Worried he'd come at her in a rage, Hannah barked, 'Be gone! Be gone with you!' as if shooing away a herring gull. It worked. Crump turned and ran as fast as he could to Fairlight, the eggs cracking in his basket. In his published recollections, Gardner explains that Crump 'told his whole woeful story to the midshipman with many illustrations, which the midshipman believed to be as true as holy writ'.

Standing at the Minnis Rock, Hannah Weller wiped a tear from her eye. She had been used by Gardner. 'Hannah, oh Hannah,' she murmured, 'you should have known better than to trust a man of the ruling class.'

She stared into the caves. The number 1727, engraved in the rock, caught her eye, as it always did. That was the year she was born, a cataclysm which drained every drop of blood from her poor mother's body and killed her stone dead.

Shortly before her father followed his wife to heaven and left Hannah to fend for herself like a feral cat, he told her that he had carved that date on the rock in remembrance, 'So as nobody should ever forget there was love here once.'

Foolish man. She hoped one day the ground would open

to swallow the caves into the fiery depths, and all of Sussex with it. If that were a curse, let the Devil make it so, and to hell with everyone.

*

Nobody knew why the Minnis Rock was there. In 1892, a historian named Byng Gattie claimed that it had been carved as a chapel for local seafarers. The same applied to the Black Arches, he said, which were but abandoned after the designer died on the job. This claim absolutely infuriated the celebrated local archaeologist, Charles Dawson. In a newspaper article, he retorted that a sorely mistaken Mr Gattie had discovered a modern antique, carved by Mr John Coussens at the end of the previous century. At the time he was scribing this rebuke, Dawson was embarking upon his campaign of archaeological manipulations. No doubt he was miffed that he hadn't first had the idea to excavate these caves. With his fictionalisation skills, undoubtedly he would have found something to make them significant, whether there was anything there or not.

Like me, he felt an irresistible urge to fill in the gaps.

XI

Arthur Conan Doyle and the Monkey Man

The Dawsons rather enjoyed their lunch at the home of Sir Arthur Conan Doyle. The author was in an ebullient mood, regaling Charles and his wife Helene with tales of his experiments into telepathy with the scientist William Crookes. He was becoming increasingly convinced that it was possible to channel the spirits of the dead from the other side. It would only be a matter of time before a breakthrough. He was considering going public with his beliefs. What did they think?

'I'm all for causing a stir!' cried Dawson, rather drunkenly. 'Shake awake the sleeping masses! That Crowley chap has not done too badly from his esoteric proclamations.'

At this, Conan Doyle's expression dimmed. 'That rogue? He deems both my novels and spiritualism to be beneath him. I was asked to join his Golden Dawn organisation over a decade ago and I turned them down.'

'All for the better. In my view, it is better to forge your own path,' replied Dawson.

'My next work will do precisely that,' said Conan Doyle. He told them of his plans for something he called *The Lost World,* an epic journey through a prehistoric plateau in South America.

He didn't know whether it was the tone of the table conversation, or his belly full of beef, but that night Charles Dawson had a strange dream in which he walked through a dense fog. Disorientated, he drifted from the path onto a newly ploughed field, boggy underfoot. As the fog thickened he was forced to a standstill. It was as if he had departed this earth and entered another world. He was startled to see a humanoid shape moving through the alabaster soup. As it came closer the fog parted to reveal a five-foot-high creature with a bulbous cranium, long, simian arms and chimpanzee teeth. Dawson was awed. There was so much he wanted to ask this apparition. But before he could speak he was woken by the alarm clock.

Over breakfast he explained the dream to Helene.

'It is a sign that I should pursue my instincts regarding Piltdown,' he said, toast crumbs falling from his moustache.

'For that was as close to an apeman as I've ever envisioned, albeit in my mind's eye. I am on the correct path, I am sure of it.'

'Sir Conan Doyle has filled your head with stories,' said Helene, tapping her boiled egg with a spoon.

'Ha ha! On the contrary, dear, the situation may well be the reverse. Much of what he knows about palaeontology has come from our correspondence. This book he is writing, the one about ape men and dinosaurs, I dare say it's a product of his fossil-hunting, an endeavour in which I have aided him greatly.'

'Perhaps you should write your own book and pip him to the post.'

'I have no need to write anything as flimsy as a book,' smiled Dawson, 'the Weald is my novel, and I write a new chapter with every dig.'

With that he stood up, bowed to his wife, and left for work on his bicycle, whistling Caruso's 'La Donna E Mobile'.

Arriving in Uckfield, he entered his office, carefully shutting the door behind him. Spread out across this desk – as well as numerous small tables and makeshift platforms – were dozens of vessels filled with brown liquid. Fragments of human bone bobbed inside, slowly staining in the solution. A shelf was stacked with trays of teeth, mandibles, flints, vertebrae chunks, pelvis, ribs, and all manner of prehistoric bric-a-brac. A fossilised elephant's femur was propped against the wall. Beside it, an open steel chest was piled with modern tools: files, hacksaws, chisels and hammers.

Dawson opened the window to release the chemical stench which had accrued overnight. From a locked drawer he removed a two-hundred-year-old jawbone. It was an orangutan's jaw, but not for much longer, not once he'd finished with it.

He paused, as if to respect the moment. For he knew how famous this jaw would become, once discovered. The venerable Mr Conan Doyle was not the only one capable of creating apemen. Novels were one way of finding fame and fortune, but Dawson could write history with bones.

Clipping on his pince-nez, he peered hard at the jaw.

'Now, to work.'

Slowly, carefully, he began to file down the teeth.

*

'Charles?'

A voice outside Dawson's door. In panic, he looked at his clock. Almost six-thirty. What on earth would somebody want at this time?

'I say, Charles, are you there?'

The door handle rattled. There was no time to conceal the chemical solution. The solicitor stood quickly, intending to put the elephant femur on a high shelf, but the door swung open before he could move from the spot.

In the doorway stood Sir Arthur Conan Doyle, hat in his hands, cane pointed directly at him like a shotgun.

'Sir Arthur!' Dawson bellowed, overly loud, forcing a grin.

Conan Doyle's moustache bristled as he opened his mouth to say something, but then his eyes fixed on the leg bone in Dawson's hands.

'Ah, this?' With a guffaw, Dawson lurched forward, mimicking a defensive stroke, 'In idle moments I like to practise my cricket.'

'I see,' said Conan Doyle.

'To what do I owe the pleasure?' Dawson forgot for a moment that the bone wasn't really a cricket bat. He tried to lean against it casually but the femur was too short, so he ended up bent sideways like a child doing the little teapot song. Rather than correct himself, he remained leaning, as if it were completely natural.

'And the smell?' asked Conan Doyle.

'The smell?'

'The smell,' replied Doyle, pointing his cane at the vessels of liquid. 'Bi-chromate of potash, I presume?'

Dawson blanched. How could he know?

Conan Doyle smiled. 'Look here, I apologise for turning up announced. I was passing by and it occurred to me suddenly that you might still be at your work. It's rather urgent and regarding this piece of cranium you discovered in Piltdown. You say it might be very old.'

'As old as the deposits themselves,' said Dawson, attempting to prop the elephant femur under the desk behind him. He noticed Conan Doyle's gaze scanning the trays of bone fragments, one of which contained the orangutan jawbone. 'I have been digging the pits with my friend Teilhard and we have found a second piece of that same skull. With a bit of luck, there is more.'

'Human?'

'Perhaps older.'

'Ape?'

'Possibly somewhere in between.'

Conan Doyle tapped his fingers on the door frame, breathing deeply. For a fleeting second he wondered whether he'd made a mistake about Dawson's forgeries. But like his famous detective, Conan Doyle was convinced of his deductions. Besides, he had to think what a discovery of a real apeman would do for sales of *The Lost World*.

'I have had some further thoughts about my forthcoming novel.' Conan Doyle stepped fully into the office and closed the door. 'I believe you might be able to help me with a little … publicity … an offer to which I am sure you will be amenable, bearing in mind my suspicions about your clandestine activities. Suspicions which I have no doubt, are correct.' He jabbed his cane at the various tools, bones and jars of liquid around the room, 'Exhibit A, Exhibit B, Exhibit C, Exhibit D, Exhibit E. And so on and so forth. All the evidence required. Case closed. Elementary, my dear Dawson.'

Mortified, Dawson gripped the elephant femur tightly. For a moment he considered slamming it with force on the author's cranium. He had enough abrasive chemicals in the office to turn the author into a fossil and bury him in Piltdown. He could later 'discover' Conan Doyle with a monkey's jaw wedged onto his face in an eternal gibbering grin.

'Oh, and there's no need to put that leg bone away, Dawson,' said the author. 'It may come in useful.'

*

In autumn 1912, *The Lost World* was serialised in *The Strand* magazine, telling its tale of Professor Challenger's run-in with apemen and dinosaurs in South America. 'If you are clever and know your business,' said one of the characters, 'you can fake a bone as easily as you can a photograph.' That November, sales were given a considerable boost by the amazing news about the real-life apeman found on British shores. An article in the *Manchester Guardian* proclaimed: 'The Earliest Man: Remarkable Discovery in Sussex'. The Piltdown man, unearthed by Charles Dawson and surrounded with carved tools including an elephant's femur, was the missing link. Just what the British scientific community craved. Dawson's years of staining, filing, scouring and ageing were over. His creation was alive.

Four years later, he died of septicaemia. It would be another forty years before his fraud was proven. By which point Dawson himself was nothing more than a pile of bones.

XII

The Spirit Molecule

The problem with writing about dead people from history was that they infected my sense of the present, making me aware of ghosts in every corner of town, from the memorial benches and plaques to the very recesses of our house where the stains of past lives were engrained. In particular, it began to bother me that I knew exactly where Angela's late husband used to sleep. The dining room had been the bedroom when we first viewed the house, and there was a tobacco stain on the cornice directly above where he must have sat smoking in bed every night. The entire ceiling was sepia but in this one small spot it was an intense carcinogenic brown. I was bothered because I was sick of sharing my home with the deceased. But mostly I was bothered because I'd been given the job of painting the cornice white. Emily knew I was slapdash in these matters, but this didn't require finesse, only the persistent application of stain blocker and undercoat. But no matter how many layers I applied, the next day the stain seeped through. As soon as my day's writing was done and the kids were in bed, back up the ladder I would go, paintbrush clenched in my teeth like a dagger, to do battle with the effluence from a dead man's lung.

It was around that time Emily called me to the cellar to show me the beast. I hated the cellar. I hated all the grubby places beneath the floorboards, but the cellar especially. It smelled of corpses.

'It goes all the way back,' she announced as I reached the bottom of the steps. 'You can pretty much trace the footprint of the house. And look.' She thrust towards me a plaster model of a reptile, some kind of caiman or crocodile, crudely made, with multicoloured eyes and bared teeth.

'Ours?'

'No,' Emily said. 'Definitely not. I guess it belongs to us now.'

I looked at the markings on the belly of the caiman. A date, faintly scratched … 1943 … 1948 … or even 1993. It was hard to make out. I felt sick at the thought of this thing that wasn't ours. Then again, I'd come to realise that none of this was ours. Not really. A house is an accumulation of lives. It permits you to dwell among its walls for as long as those walls stand. But you will never own it. Instead the house owns you. It takes your money and makes you work hard to protect it until you either leave or die. Then it waits for the next soul to come along.

'There's also this.' Emily pulled back a stack of chipboard. Etched into the cellar wall in giant spidery letters was the word:

A house of skins. Dead skin in the bathroom. Peeling wallpaper skin. The mutated brown skin of that damned cornice. After decades of pipe smoke, free radicals had altered its cell structure, making it forever brown and impossible to paint. If it wasn't for Emily's love of period features I'd have set fire to it and danced beneath, whooping. But I had to keep going. We'd been in the house over a year and not yet reclaimed a single room. Chimney pots loomed in the hallway. Floorboards missing where the wiring needed a second fix. Holes punched in the laths where light switches had been hacked out by electricians. Scaffolding blocked out the sun. There was a lot of work to be done. Always work to be done. More work, and yet the house was becoming less with all the stripping, not more.

If it wasn't the renovation, it was our daughters. Keeping them clean, reading them stories, feeding them, dealing with tantrums, taking them to school, changing their sheets. Emily and I spoke in functional terms as we tottered past each other on the way to the next task, clutching wet wipes, hammers and coffee mugs. At some point in the last ten years our chemistry had changed. We'd gone from lovers to mortgage partners to unpaid hoteliers in the service of sociopathic midget egomaniacs. To come through this with the fizz of desire still in our veins, our love had to be stronger and more persistent than a tobacco stain on a cornice. But day by day it was fading beneath the layers.

We decided to get help to move things along. Alejandro and Marcela were a couple who had come to Hastings from Chile. Like many coastal drifters, they were on a quest for spiritual enlightenment, working as decorators to save up to build an eco-home and live off the grid, growing vegetables and harvesting ambient electricity from the air using a Tesla machine.

In 1882, Nikola Tesla strolled through a park in Budapest at sunset when he became gripped, suddenly, by a vision of an electrical machine in mid-air before him. It was so clear, he later claimed, it had the solidity of metal and stone. Quickly, he drew a diagram in some sand to capture the vision before it faded. He returned home where he lay on his couch and focussed hard on what he had imagined. From an opaque blur, new pieces of the puzzle emerged. As the vision intensified he left behind his prostrate body and journeyed deep into the structure itself for a closer look at the details. After a series of these astral sessions, he slowly constructed plans for what would become the first alternating current electricity supply system, triumphing over his rival, Thomas Edison. Since the age of seven Tesla had reported out-of-body experiences like these. As an adult, he harnessed this ability to get inspiration for his inventions, mental-travelling through new cities and countries, picturing a future transformed by miraculous technologies. His ultimate dream was to bring wireless electricity to humankind using the ionosphere as a conductor. High-voltage towers would saturate the air with electricity that could be tapped from anywhere in the world. Through this atmospheric soup, humans could send messages in real time. To prove it he built a 142-foot mast on his Colorado laboratory roof, topped with a copper sphere, and wired it to a high-voltage coil. As night fell he fired up the tower and the sky over Colorado Springs crackled with lightning bolts. An impressed J.P. Morgan became an investor and Tesla's dream was almost realised, until rival inventor Guglielmo Marconi developed a simple wireless telegraph signal. Investment in Tesla's vision dried up and his prototype power station was never built. But his ideas lived on in YouTube videos where enthusiasts explained the principles and offered homespun techniques for siphoning energy from the air.

As well as planning to escape the grid with their Tesla-inspired ambient electricity generator, Alejandro and Marcela were busy mashing up bamboo root to extract dimethyltryptamine (DMT), a chemical known as the spirit molecule. Traditionally processed from the Amazonian ayahuasca plant, DMT is a psychedelic substance that exists in almost every living thing. In humans, it is excreted by the pineal gland. For millennia, mystics have believed the pineal to be a gateway to the soul. It is the third eye, the Eye of Horus, the all-seeing eye of the Illuminati, the bottu on a Hindu's forehead, the brow chakra of yoga adepts. In 2014 scientists studying cardiac arrest survivors proved that awareness continues several minutes after clinical death, a period in which the pineal floods the brain with a mega dose of DMT. Subjects talked of warped time, bright lights, separation from their bodies and encounters with godlike entities. Advocates like Terrence McKenna believed that it opened channels of communication between humans, rocks, plants and the hyper-dimensional consciousness of the universe.

My interest was piqued. I couldn't shake the memories of Mike since I moved to Hastings. It wasn't that I'd forgotten about him during my years in London. Only that his memory didn't dwell in the city. Not for me anyway. But in Hastings he had returned to me unannounced in the crash of surf and salty sea spray, the horizon's camber and the icy whip of sea wind. It was less a memory, more of a visceral sensation, as if decades of passing time were meaningless and everything that happened to me by the sea in 1996 was happening here, now, causing the same discombobulation of my nervous system. Every time I stood on the West Hill beside the castle I was haunted by the thought that he went through an experience of such magnitude, helpless, alone and without his friends, and yet I must have been only metres away from him when he slipped. Even if it was only for a millisecond, what did he think in that moment of transmutation between the physical world and whatever came next?

Now here was an opportunity to understand what he might have experienced on his final trip. When smoked through a vaporiser, DMT stimulates the pineal gland to spurt forth its juice, delivering an extreme psychedelic experience for ten minutes before returning the tripper to normal. Alejandro said it gave him a sense of clarity and purpose. For Marcela, it helped her see the souls of plants and trees. They insisted that a revolution in human consciousness was possible, if only more people could experience DMT. As a writer, I would appreciate the magic and help spread the word, so they were happy to give it to me for free.

Months later, when the living room was decorated and my Tyrannosaurus skeleton was shifted into place beneath the cursed brown cornice, I was initiated.

*

While Emily and Marcela talked on the sofa, Alejandro added a crumbly substance to a vaporiser, flicked on the switch, then handed it to me. After the second drag my hands started to change colour. Purple, yellow and green blood coursed through my veins. After the third draw there was a sickly, drowning moment as if I was being pulled deep underwater, then the air cleared and I could see everything in motion, from the grooves in the floorboards to the curtain folds, pulsing and bulging, straining for transformation. The visuals were similar to those I'd experienced taking mushrooms in Oaxaca—heightened perception of textures and colours, eddies in time-flow and a shedding of the anxious ego, leaving me still and centred. It wasn't the trip I had anticipated but I was aware that I was holding myself back, peering through a portal at an unknown landscape but too afraid to venture further.

We drank some gin and tried again later, sat by my speakers, listening to arabesque techno. I could hear symphonies of space between each beat, elongated tones that slowly revealed their microscopic melodies, an epic concert in what must have been only ten minutes. Looking at my clasped hands, I saw an eye staring back at me, then an eye within that eye, then a multitude of eyes turning in a dense spiralling galaxy. A dimension opened up, but all I could do was stare into it.

'You have to let go,' said Alejandro. 'You will feel scared, like you are dying, but nothing will happen to you. When you know it, you will make a choice.'

Another gin. I lay prostrate on some cushions beneath the

stained section of cornice. Alejandro held the vaporiser to my lips and I took one hit, two hits, three hits, four hits, then everything began to fade. I remember the nozzle in my mouth, smoke cascading into my throat, and Alejandro gently encouraging me to breathe, his voice falling away as if down an elongating tunnel. 'He's going!' I heard him say to Marcela.

I went.

Above me, the decorative ceiling rose began to whirl, then unplugged and dropped down, opening a portal. One by one, invisible dimensional walls fell away, as if time-space was unpacking itself around me. I was lifted from my body and moved slowly through a translucent primordial soup, pink and wriggling with helix strands, towards a rotating brainstem with jellyfish tentacles, around which flitted humanoid figures with bulbous crania and long arms. This journey accelerated as I was flipped through a series of membranes, multiple worlds flickering before me like the fast-forward on an old VHS tape, so quick I couldn't latch onto them or understand what I was seeing. It was like watching other people's lives flashing before me. Then it braked. I became aware of my body—or rather, a body. I looked down to see that I was sat as if on a throne, thighs covered in scales of silver and gold. Feathers burst from my shoulders and crowned my head. My arms, long and clawed, gripped onto two stone armrests. I was a statue, high up, with my back flat against something hard, looking out over a vast plain of pyramids. I began to elongate. First my legs plunged downwards, becoming two gleaming metallic columns, striped white and gold. Next my spine clicked and my head rose quickly on a long, laddering neck, while a saurian jaw pushed from my face. I was something that was not me. I felt no fear. No love. No amazement. No introspection. Nothing you could describe as personality. Only a sense of divine right. A ferocious knowing. This might have lasted a second or minutes or hours, I don't know, then dimensions began unfolding and flipping like a Rolodex, at even greater speed than before. The gold and silver scales peeled away from my thighs, showing my jeans beneath. The ceiling rose spun back into place. The fairground ride slowed to a stop and I lay on the cushions, perfectly still and crushingly tired.

Marcela, Emily and Alejandro were watching me from the sofa, laughing.

'How long was I gone?'

'Ten minutes maybe.'

I went to the kitchen and poured myself a drink. By the time I got back in the room, the trip seemed like a dream.

And not my own dream either. More like something which might have raced through the mind of Aleister Crowley on his deathbed. Within minutes of wakening many details fell away but not the vision of the pyramids, nor the entity I became – be it statue, pharaoh, the god Horus or some alien overlord. It was impossible to describe in the aftermath. I had a desperate urge to speak with Emily, to hug her and tell her I loved her, but the three of them were hunched together, chatting and laughing, their backs to me, as if I wasn't really there.

'You see?' said Mike, sitting down beside me. 'It's not so bad, the death thing.'

I looked at him closely. At university, I used to marvel at the premature cragginess of Mike's face and the gravity of his timbre, but now I could see that he was young, barely out of childhood. I'd grown old while he remained as fresh as that last moment I spoke to him on the castle battlements.

'It's not death I'm frightened of,' I said, 'it's the moment before, the split second – '

'The after negates the before,' said Mike, rather flippantly I thought, and not in the way he would have actually said it. More likely it would have been something like, 'You wuss, Rees.'

None of this was as surprising as you might think. In my

twenties, I often conjured up Mike's spirit to share the latest situation in which I found myself. It was fascinating to imagine what he thought about life as it continued without him. My first job in radio, my first published comedy script, the thrill of my first years in London, the inebriated DJ sets, blearily ecstatic morning walks home from clubs with new friends he'd never met, travels to South America, that vision of Machu Picchu at sunrise on the Inca Trail, he was there for that, I made certain. I'd give him a tour of my new flat, show him the sights of London or explain the wonders of the Internet. I imagined him watching me and Emily at our wedding – me in a black lamé suit and a cowboy hat, she in a turquoise Matthew Williamson dress – and laughing uproariously in that way he did, head tilted back like Basil Brush.

'Look at what's happening,' I'd say, 'would you ever have believed it?' And he'd wipe a tear of joy away from his face and say, 'You've arrived, Gareth, you've truly arrived, and you look like a dick.'

But as my thirties progressed and I struggled to raise children and deal with job crises, mortgages, debts and tax, he seemed too young to bother with such matters. Marriage was too complex to explain in pithy terms he'd understand. There was less for him to guffaw at. All I could imagine was his blinking stare as he waited for a gag that never came. His disappointment at what I'd become.

But what did he know? In my funeral speech, I had praised the way Mike had lived a life full of adventure. It no longer seemed that way. He was only twenty-one for Christ's sake. I'd known him alive for ten years but my relationship with his memory had been ongoing for twenty. I was double the age he was when he died. Old enough to be his father. I had more in common with Mike's parents and was closer to the age they were when the tragedy happened. As a father, I finally had a capacity to understand at least a fragment of their unspeakable pain, which I never appreciated at the time, so rapt was I in my selfish grief. I remember how his dad's hair went white almost overnight and his mum's eyes on the day of the funeral. Those eyes. His sister's brave face, trying to hold them all together.

What a selfish fucking idiot he'd been. Five As at A level, and for what? These were nothing more than a barometer of the educational privilege he wasted. He'd left everyone behind to struggle without him. He knew nothing about having a family, or growing old, or worrying about children, or watching the ice caps melt and the seas rise. He was a child and I was his angry father.

'But that night on the castle, you didn't stop me, did you,

"father"?' said Mike, sarcastically miming inverted commas with his translucent fingers.

'No.'

'Why not?'

'I was young and stupid, like you.'

'You didn't wonder where I was?' said Mike. 'Where I'd gone?'

'I was drunk. I went home.'

'What kind of father are you?'

'A bad one.'

'What kind of friend?'

'No better.'

'For that matter, what kind of *human being*?'

'I don't know.'

'You only care about yourself.'

'I wish it hadn't happened,' I said. 'But I can't rewrite the past.'

Mike smiled. 'Can't you?'

XIII

The Battle of Carlisle

There was a time in London, in the early days, many moons ago, when Emily and I went to pubs and parties with our mutual friends. Before we'd leave the flat she would try on several ludicrously mismatched clothing combinations, snarling with distaste at the image of herself in the mirror, and complain that she wasn't keen, couldn't be bothered, and eventually plump for a crazy multicolour stripe-and-pattern getup that didn't make any sense at all but always looked cool on her, a coating of chaos she wore well. Within an hour of arriving she'd be the life and soul, a jabbering, jive-talking whirlwind of energy at the centre of things, throwing out words like 'shiznit' and 'badda-bing', taking the piss out of her friends and ballroom dancing to electronic music with me as the sun came up and the hosts eyed us sleepily. Sometimes we wouldn't talk to each other for the entire night but always we felt the security of our connection. We were a couple. A unit. Emily and Gareth. Gareth and Emily. Always full of beans and last to leave, hand in hand, drunken weirdos who deserved each other.

But that was then.

It had been a long time since we went to social occasions with friends we could laugh at and gossip about. One of us had to stay at home and babysit. Our old friends were scattered around the country and we were too busy to get to know new people in Hastings. Besides, when Emily said she couldn't be bothered these days, she meant it and I couldn't persuade her otherwise. So here I was on a Saturday night, sat alone on Pelham Beach behind the outfall pipe with a can of lager, watching the lights on a distant tanker, thinking about the U-boat that once lay here, another victim of Hastings' uncanny magnetic force.

On tow from France to Scapa Flow in May 1919, U-118 broke loose and rolled toward the Sussex shoreline. French gunships gave chase, trying to break it up with heavy shelling, but as the submarine moved closer to Hastings, they were forced to turn back. It settled on the beach, drawing crowds for many months. The coastguards took control of the vessel and assigned two officers to the job of assessing the situation below deck. Soon they fell ill. They'd inhaled chlorine released from a reaction between the damaged batteries and seawater, mixed with gasses from rotting food.

Five months later, they were dead. What had been the summer's tourist attraction was now enemy number one. They dismantled it in October. Most of it went for scrap, while some of the keel was left under the beach.

I wondered if anyone missed the ugly old U-boat when it was gone, thinking that the town had become somehow less without it.

*

It was Ellen who told Alf the story about his daddy's last day above the sea.

She said a You Boat from the Great War fired its guns—*blam, blam, blam*—and Daddy went down in the belly of Chip, right to the bottom of the ocean.

Daddy had been a fireman on boats that went to America with passengers. Funny, a fireman on a boat, surrounded by all that water. Ellen said that the fire was from the coal they burned to move the engine and it could easily go wrong and that was why Daddy was in deep doo-doo when the You Boat came—*blam blam blam*—and sent him down in the belly of Chip.

Or perhaps the You Boat *was* Chip. Alf was never sure. It happened when he was four. Now he was six and a quarter years old. He couldn't remember much about Daddy's face, only his smell and the way he made Mummy laugh.

Ellen was eleven, tall, with freckles on her nose. One night she sat Alf by the stove and read him *The Tale of Peter Rabbit,* then tucked him up in bed. Later there came a terrible wind. Alf woke up to bangs as bin lids flippity-flopped on the road outside. It wasn't even morning time yet when Ellen's friends, Minnie and Hazel, came to the door babbling with excitement about the thing that was coming to the beach – 'Get up, get up!' – there wasn't time to explain they said.

Ellen shoved Alf into his coat and they ran to the promenade.

The sun wasn't up but the sky was paling. Grown-ups held their hats against the wind and pointed at the sea. Teenagers cheered at the waterfront, feet in the foam.

Alf gasped. A sea monster rolled in the waves, black and shiny, as big and long as Hastings Pier. There was a fin on its back and antennae sticking out.

The beast ducked down and up, down and up, spluttering spray from its blowholes. Ellen, Minnie and Hazel danced and sang, 'It's coming, it's coming, the monster is coming.'

By sunrise almost all the townspeople were out of their

lazy beds and staring at the monster, half in the sea, half on land, rocking back and forth as the water swelled and shrank around it. The grind of shingle beneath its weight was a billion gnashing elephant teeth. Bigger boys and girls ran up close but a man in uniform shouted to get back.

Even though it was gianter than a street of houses, Alf wasn't scared. He felt sorry for the monster, out in the storm all night, cold and wet. The grown-ups around him kept saying something about a You Boat. It was You Boat this and You Boat that, and murmurings about the war.

That's when Alf realised who this might be.

'Chip!'

It made total sense. A You Boat came for Daddy—*blam blam blam*—then Daddy went down in the belly of Chip. This must be Chip bringing Daddy home. He had a belly so big it might hold hundreds of sailors like Daddy inside it.

'It's a submarine, you know,' said Ellen. Alf didn't care what it was called, only that it was the most wonderful thing he had seen in his whole life and it had come to sort things out.

They skipped school at lot that May. If they got to the beach before the crowds, Alf could go up to Chip and touch his skin. It was hard like iron and cold, even in the sunshine. Alf hoped he wasn't dead. But he could hear happy gurgling, gasps of air like big sighs. Sometimes Chip would trump and they could smell rotten cabbages come out of his bum hole.

More and more people came to see the You Boat. It was like a festival. The air was full of chat and smells of food. Cockle-sellers came and sweet-sellers too. Sometimes a man with a trumpet played. Everybody was happy around Chip, with their summer hats and white dresses. There wasn't anywhere better in the world now that Alf had Ellen and Chip to look after him. They sat on picnic blankets and watched Alf as he splashed in the sea with his bucket, bringing seawater up the shingle which he'd pour on Chip's skin. 'There, there, all clean now.'

Chip gurgled with pleasure. 'Oh, dear Alf,' he said in his boomy voice. 'You and I are the best of holiday friends.'

But after August there weren't so many picnickers. As summer died, folk got grumbly about Chip. Stone-throwing became a popular game the naughty boys and girls played after sundown, when Alf was in bed. He could hear it echo down the street and through his window, the sound of stones hurting poor Chip—*clang, clang, clang*! Mummy in the next room would cry, 'Oh God make it stop!' and, 'Why oh why!'

One day in September there was a rope around Chip and men in overalls on his back who pressed tools with jagged silver wheels into Chip's flesh. *Whirrrrrrrrr* went their machine. *Whirrrrrrrrrrrrrrrrrr*. Sparks flew. Chip screamed. It was so high-pitched that Alf had to cover his ears in case his brain exploded.

Alf broke into sobs. 'They'll hurt Daddy.'

'That's just stupid,' said Ellen.

'No, you're stupid,' he said. And she was. They all were. And he wasn't going to listen to them any more ever never, never again.

That night Alf got out of bed when Ellen was asleep. Down the steps he went, onto the street. Finding his way was a piece of cake—he did it every day—out the door, turn right, straight down the shopping street, onto the promenade, down the steps. And there was Chip, snoring gently. The men had left their ladders so it was easy for Alf to climb up onto his back. There were gaping holes all over him. Wires and tubes dangled. Cigarette butts everywhere. Horrible. They wouldn't be doing this if they knew how special Chip was, really truly they wouldn't.

Alf sat for a while at the edge of a hole, watching the light of a distant fishing boat bobbing, thinking about Ellen and how much trouble he would be in. Then he heard something from deep down inside Chip. Hissing. Gurgling. Water from a hose. A fireman perhaps. A fireman who loved him.

'Hello?' cried Alf.

'Hello?' a voice came back, strange yet familiar.

Daddy!

With a whoop of joy, Alf went down into the belly of Chip.

*

As I furiously tapped the submarine story into my iPhone, the light fizzled to black on the horizon and shadowy figures began to stalk the beach around me, clutching joints and sniggering. From where I sat, the buckled outfall pipe looked like a remnant of that old U-boat's torpedo tube trying to crawl out from under the shingle and return to sea. I could hear little Alf's voice holler from somewhere inside as he hunted in vain for the source of his grief and found only toxic fumes.

Poor Alf.

On the road behind I could hear a rise in hubbub outside The Carlisle pub. In the 1960s and 1970s, it was popular with bikers and rockers and therefore a target for mod hate. In 1981, a 300-strong mob of skinheads surrounded and stoned the pub before going on the rampage across the seafront in a fury of speed and lager. Now it was the premier local hangout for hard rock and metal fans. That night I was going to an event there commemorating 100 years since the publication of the *Ragged-Trousered Philanthropists* by Robert Tressell, real name Robert Noonan. Written when he lived in Hastings, his novel describes Edwardian working-class life in a fictionalised version of the town called Mugsborough. The protagonist is a painter and decorator called Owen, a socialist who tries to convince his co-workers to fight back against their exploitation under capitalism during a particularly complex Victorian house renovation. Noonan died before his book found a publisher willing to take it on. While it found fans in the likes of George Orwell, the book remained an obscure underground classic. But in Hastings it had become enshrined in the town's radical history.

Outside The Carlisle, a bicycle festooned in coloured light bulbs blared tinny techno music. A young man in a woolly hat with ear-flaps harangued a man in a wheelchair, while a woman yelled that he was disgrace. Inside the pub, between the illuminated jukebox and the regulars hunched at the bar, trestle tables were piled with copies of *The Ragged-Trousered Philanthropists*, books about *The Ragged-Trousered Philanthropists* and a new abridged version of *The Ragged-Trousered Philanthropists* for people who couldn't be bothered to read the whole of *The Ragged-Trousered Philanthropists*. There were other sympathetic tomes by George Orwell and

Mark Fisher, with intermingled socialist and communist pamphlets strewn below posters of *The Ragged-Trousered Philanthropists* event that was about to take place.

I milled with my pint as local singers took to the stage with guitars, including the mesmeric Hastings blues guitarist King Size Slim. His fingers chewed up the fretboard and he stomped and howled, twisting Delta standards into gnarly new shapes. As the booze flowed, the crowd grew bigger and rowdier. I was there to see a performance by The Poet, an old friend of mine from my London days when I used to DJ in Filthy McNasty's in Islington. Back in those days I was paid in beer to be a human jukebox every weekend in a pub which ebbed and flowed with artists, writers, musicians, gangsters, drunkards and eccentrics. The Poet was a raconteur, loud and brassy. She performed her honest, dirty diatribes at the pub's spoken word nights. They spoke of a life tumbling in and out of bars, sexual encounters and comedowns in rundown flats. Once I joined The Poet on a drinking session which ended up in Clerkenwell, where she decided to visit her friend, a famous British rock star, who lived in a flat in Exmouth Market. In the living room, addicts were slumped against the wall among glistering asteroids of tinfoil. But The Rock Star welcomed us into a warmly-lit bedroom cluttered with books and musical instruments.

As he and The Poet caught up, I drunkenly knocked over one of his beer bottles. Sensing I was about to be slung out, I picked up a guitar and launched into Bob Dylan's 'One More Cup of Coffee'. He took the bait, taking up his other guitar and strumming along, weaving a melody into my tuneless singing. It was the first time I'd played guitar with anyone since I busked with Mike on the Embankment nine years previously. Whereas Mike seemed then like he would live forever, like the world was something he could bend to his will, The Rock Star had an air of doom about him and was most famous of all for not being dead yet, contrary to everyone's expectations. Funny who makes it, and who doesn't. During our weird duet, all I could think about was, 'How did I get here?' and, 'What do you think about this, then, eh, Mike?' Then I sat down, knocked over another bottle of beer, and was told to leave anyway.

After my daughters were born I stopped bumping into The Poet. Sometimes I'd hear her on the radio sounding hoarse, and wonder what she'd been up to the night before. It was good to know she was still out there, leading from the front, fighting the good fight, drinking and loving. My London had receded into a small area of Hackney where I spent my time changing nappies and wandering the marshes by the River Lea, exiled within the city. Now I was a writer too, my children were growing up fast and our paths had crossed again in The Poet's home town.

The Poet moved to Hastings as a very young child, growing up as the only kid of colour in her class at a time when the town was facing economic woes. Her poems tell of chips and seagulls and drinking vodka beneath the pier. None of which were bad things in her view. Young life was magical and the town was a place where someone could grow strong. She and her Jamaican mother had moved here when her Irish father, a jazz musician, abandoned the family, never to return. But growing up in Hastings she learned to laugh more than to cry. It was the making of her and she never forgot it.

That night in The Carlisle, The Poet was on home turf, but looked uncharacteristically vulnerable on the low stage, peering into the lights. The crowd had been whipped into a frenzy by poet and rabble-rouser, Attila the Stockbroker. It was 10 p.m. and they were roaring drunk, refusing to pipe down. The Poet did her best to speak over the chatter. One old soak didn't like the look of a woman alone on a stage with a poetry book, and began to heckle from the back. She shifted from foot to foot, eyes flickering as if struggling to lock onto the audience. There was applause only from a handful of enthusiasts at the front. The Poet moved on to her second poem. The heckler yelled, 'What's happened to this place? This is The Carlisle, for fuck's sake.' With that, she launched into one of her dirtiest poems, riffing on a line about licking a tramp's cock, repeating it over and over, until it became a hip-grinding mantra. People began to laugh. One by one the room fell to listening. The heckler yelled again, but this time the crowd bristled and he was told to shut up.

'Fuck off!' he said.

Now he was being bundled out of the pub by the security guy and The Poet was in full flow, going through her most raucous, eye-popping poems. The pub was hooked, finally. This was her home town after all and boozers were her bread and butter. Sometimes a woman had to fight to be in her rightful place.

After all, this was also the home town of the proto-suffragette Barbara Leigh Smith, later known as Madame Bodichon, who wrote for the *Hastings & St Leonards News* in the early 1800s under the pen name Esculapius. In one polemic she declared, 'Let your blue stocking daughter, your political wife, your artistic sister, and eccentric cousin, pursue their paths unmolested—you will never make ideals of them; you will only make your home the scene of suppressed energies and useless powers.' In 1850, she ventured to Europe with her friend, Bessie Raynor Parkes, travelling without husbands or chaperones, wearing heavy boots, blue-tinted spectacles and skirts that showed off their ankles. Every step was a radical act. She returned with a passion for suffrage and spiritualism, attending séances and befriending local Pre-Raphaelite artists like Dante Gabriel Rossetti. This evening Madame Bodichon's spirit stared ferociously through a Poet's eyes on the stage in The Carlisle, in a town where the séance was ongoing, if you knew where to look.

After The Poet's defeat of the heckler we chatted outside, where people filled the fresh air with smoke and talk, while valedictory speeches were made inside. Beers became more beers and soon I was babbling away to a man with curly hair and excited eyes. He was born in Hastings but left to become a student. Now he was back to open a business. Blearily, he listened to me talking about my walks up East Hill. About the Black Arches, the Minnis Rock and why I suspected Hastings to be an occult nexus, a place used by dreamers to manifest their visions, be it Victorian feminism, fake churches, toads in flint, or television.

To my surprise the man nodded and beckoned me close. 'There's a cave on East Hill, on the Ecclesbourne side.'

'Uh-huh, I know of it.'

'No,' he said. 'Not the famous one where the hermit lived.

This cave … it's small … you have to crawl into it …'

He looked me up and down, as if to judge my worthiness, then whispered: 'At the very end of that cave is a Ouija board. It's only been seen … ever … by three people. That's right, only three. The first one killed himself. The second one went mad. And the only reason I can tell you this is that the third one made it out alive to tell the story.'

I got out my iPhone and wrote the following into the notepad:

Minnis rock, black arches.

Ouija board. East Hill.

The answer is in the magic cave.

The next day, I searched for Ouija boards on the Internet to see if there was some link to Hastings.

I soon found one.

As I should have known, it involved Aleister Crowley.

Between 1944 and 1946 John Jacob Williamson was a radio instructor at RAF Cranwell. Off-duty, he lectured colleagues about a revolutionary new form of metaphysics. There were fundamental laws that united all things, he said. They were the hidden skeleton of creation, giving the universe form and movement. While most religions taught that God was separate from humanity, we were all part of 'the Absolute' and the Absolute was everything. If we learned how to work in harmony with those fundamental laws, humankind could raise its consciousness beyond the limits of our imagination.

After the atomic dust settled on Nagasaki, Williamson warned that this transformation might only become possible after an ecological or nuclear cataclysm. In the meantime, we must develop those tools through which we might unleash our true potential. These included psychic investigation, extra-dimensional travel, aura analysis and interplanetary studies.

Williamson published his theories as *The Cranwell Lectures* and used them to found an organisation called the British Society of Metaphysicians. In 1947 they established their headquarters at Archers Court, Hastings, north of The Ridge, only four months before Aleister Crowley died there. At first, they ran the headquarters as a boarding house in the summer season. A place for those seeking esoteric knowledge to learn dowsing, mediumship, aura reading and automatic writing. They launched a publishing arm to release books about neometaphysics and a mail order business known as The Metaphysical Research Group, selling esoteric hardware including Aura Goggles, a crystal-gazing kit and an automatic writing planchette.

They also produced a version of the classic Ouija board, an elegant cream board decorated with woodcuts of holy symbols coloured in red ink. The letters were arranged in a traditional arch format, but punctuation marks were added to give spirits the opportunity for more nuanced expression.

The Society of Metaphysicians continued its work through the decades, promoting esoteric texts through the mail, including a copy of Aleister Crowley's translation of the *I Ching* and his book *Seven Seven Seven*. With a bit more digging I found that the links between the Great Beast and the British Society of Metaphysicians didn't end there. I visited the forum of the website, Lasthal—home of the Aleister Crowley Society—where a member described a leaflet for 'Frontiers of the Mind', a video in which John J. Williamson reveals 'the startling psychic battle between forces of light and dark which culminated in the death of the notorious black magician Aleister Crowley'. Another member wrote that he'd been told about an occult battle between Crowley and the founder of an esoteric organisation in Hastings by a ninety-year-old woman with a vast collection of Crowley's letters. However, considering the infamous curse, she was reluctant to talk about the whole unpleasant business.

After releasing Ouija boards and other exploratory tools into the world for more than half a century, John Jacob

Williamson died in 2012. The Metaphysical Society was run primarily as an active archive. Or at least that is what they said in public. Williamson never got to witness the environmental cataclysm that might bring about his vision of a harmonious new dawn for humanity.

But I did.

I saw the whole thing.

PART TWO

Dwelling

'One need not be a chamber to be haunted,
One need not be a house;
The brain has corridors surpassing
Material place.'

Emily Dickinson

XIV

The Dead Shore

In the early hours of the morning, at 1.38 a.m. precisely, a duck in Alexandra Park broke into a guttural, mocking laugh. *Mwa ha ha ha ha ha—wack wack wack—wah ha ha ha—wack wack wack.* I sat bolt upright in bed and checked my clock. This had happened at the exact same time for the past four nights in a row. There was something deeply sinister about a duck quacking at night. Ducks were for daytime frolics, muddy banks and laughing children. Quacks at night suggested malevolent deeds were afoot. I went to our curtain-less window and peered out into the blackness of the park, looking for signs of movement, half expecting to see the bird on the street below, looking up at me with beady eyes. But nothing.

I had been feeling anxious of late that my investigations

into the town were disturbing malevolent forces. Whether they were extant supernatural beings or figments of my subconscious, I could not tell. It was as if something diabolical was leaching through the fabric of reality, threatening to tear everything apart. Voices of children in Old Roar Gill. Ectoplasmic slime oozing from our garden wall. Animal effigies in our cellar. The leviathan eye on West Hill cliff. Ducks laughing at night.

It was all a bit unnerving.

They say that sea air is good for your health. Clearly that doesn't apply to people with past experiences of coastal trauma. Really, I suppose, the problems had started from the day we moved, when Emily's grandfather died, when I got into a fight with a seagull who may have built this house in a previous incarnation, shortly before a doctor put his hand up my rectum and Mike reappeared in my thoughts as if he'd never been away.

That was two years ago. Hard to believe when I looked at the state of this place. Our home had become stuck in time. If anything, it was going backwards. There were still Pickfords boxes pressed against the top windows, coated in dust. The ceiling of the subsiding hall wall was propped up by something called a *dead shore*, a skeletal structure of beams, girders and plates that stopped us being pulled into the earth. Every time we came through the front door we were watched by the bird-like self-portrait of Mr Marsden on the wall. At night, his gull relatives congregated at our chimney and shrieked like pterodactyls, streaking our roof in shit. Nature was re-wilding us. The garden, a forest of thorns. The old yew tree presiding at the back had grown at a ferocious rate, spreading its gigantic afro into the sky, blocking out the light, casting our interior into perpetual gloom. Bramble canes arched over the yard, gripping the wall of the kitchen, as if trying to pull the house closer. We made futile attempts to hack back the vegetation but each time it grew back thicker, faster.

At the very least we wanted to make sure the girls didn't drown in the pond, so we drained it, only to discover it was a rectangular concrete pit. Emily thought it might be the foundations of a bomb shelter. To me it looked like an Egyptian sarcophagus. The pond had been filled naturally by a subterranean stream running through the hill behind the terrace, carrying trace memories of the river that once poured from Old Roar Gill into the old harbour, still keening to reach the sea. Our neighbours warned that this stream changed course regularly, occasionally flooding backyards and cellars. Some houses on our road had a permanent flow of water below their living rooms.

Ours could be next. Water is a notorious conduit for spirits, which might explain the voices in my wall. The secreted artefacts. The crazed avian intruders. The trickling sounds I heard, day and night, even when the boiler was off and I'd checked that no taps were running. Water, water, everywhere. Moisture steamed up through the floorboard slats into our damp cellar. Spilled into slimy depressions in the backyard. And now there was this duck, somewhere out on the pond, cackling in the night. *Mwa ha ha ha ha ha—wack wack wack—wah ha ha ha—wack wack*!

'Do you hear it?' I hissed at Emily.

'It's a duck,' she murmured.

'Yes, but what's it doing?'

'Go to sleep. The kids will be up at six.'

'It's weird, don't you think, that it does this at the same time every night ...?'

'No.'

'... like a demonic rooster!'

'It's all in your imagination, Gareth.'

Emily put a pillow over her head and turned over, which I took to mean that she wasn't interested in any more chat. I lingered by the window for a while, staring beyond the park to the lights of houses along St Mary's Terrace on the brow of West Hill, leading to the castle on the precipice.

'I know what the duck is laughing at,' said Mike into my ear, suddenly. 'The duck is laughing at you, Rees, standing there in your middle-aged pyjamas with your gorgeous wife you're not spooning. It's laughing at you worrying about ducks at night. Look at yourself!'

'It's not the duck. Truth be told, I'm scared, Mike. Scared that this pain in my balls is going to kill me. And equally scared that it won't. That I'm going to be around long enough to witness the end of the world. Did we ever think that was possible? Back when a hole in the ozone layer was about the worst of it? Did we ever consider that there might be a time in our lives when we saw the end of civilisation as we knew it?'

'Ah ... um ... well ... there wasn't a time like that in my life, if you think about it.' He smiled and pushed his glasses higher on his nose for comic effect. 'I have missed this particular sinking ship.'

I remembered that there was a Hugh Grant-ishness about Mike, with his centre parting and his well-spoken bumbling charm. He would play up to it too, in those years when Grant was a front-page tabloid sex symbol, riffing on lines from *Four Weddings and a Funeral* to reinforce this link in the minds of women he wanted to impress.

'I've always believed there were laws ... governing time and space ...' I said slowly, careful to organise my thoughts. 'Humans could use our ingenuity to harness them and transcend all this crap ... or at least evolve our way out of it ... become something else, something greater. That's what Crowley and Williamson believed. That's what Teilhard de Chardin saw in the noosphere. Even John Coussens saw the entrance to the house of God in a seam of rock on East Hill. And they were all here at some point, Mike, in this town, walking these broken cliffs. Hastings is a crucible for this line of thinking. But what if these men – and they're all men, and men of financial means too, these so-called visionaries – what if they were nothing but charlatans? Power freaks? A bunch of Dawsons seeking fame and gratification? Heroes of their own making? After all, what did they achieve? And for what purpose? Things have not got better. To me the world feels like chaos. Like everything is falling apart. Our human destiny – it just doesn't exist.'

'There's only one law,' said Mike, after a moment, 'and that is that you shouldn't be such a big girl.'

'God that's so sexist.' But it's exactly what he would have said. This was the trouble with talking to a twenty-one-year old from the mid-1990s. We didn't see things eye-to-eye any more. He hadn't lived enough. The truth of that, and my part in it, was heartbreaking.

*

Around the time of the laughing duck, Emily and I started receiving mail addressed to Angela. We assumed this was because her redirection service had finally stopped. But the materials were often wrinkled and weathered, as if they'd been circulating in the system for years. A faded postcard from someone called June depicted a walk in East Anglia across a landscape that 'was so flat and wide it was like a yellow sky'. A crumpled postcard from someone called Cathy, with an illustration depicting the wizard Merlin, described a visit to Wales:

'Merlin was a born in a cave outside Caernarvon!' Cathy wrote excitedly. 'The name comes from "Caer Myrddin" which means "Merlin's fortress". It was built by Edward I, who also built Winchelsea down your way. Did you know that? Next time you should come!'

Soon letters began to arrive for other names too. A birthday card addressed to someone called Frankie, c/o Rachael Fitzgerald. We knew that in 1971, Angela and her husband Charles bought the house from Mr Marsden's daughter with their friends Cynthia and Martyn. We were the third owners of the house since it was built. So who the hell were the Fitzgeralds?

'But this is a strange one,' said Emily, handing me a shiny postcard from a local Baptist church. It had been pushed through the door with no stamp, addressed to Rose and Arnold Marsden. The front of the card depicted the sunset on an ocean with the text: 'The Light of the World is Jesus'. On the back was some printed copy about the benefits of good Bible teaching and handy parking at the church. But scrawled in red pen in the margin was this:

'We looked through your window—like what you are doing!!!!'

'Do we need to worry about this?' said Emily.

I nodded gravely. 'That's a lot of exclamation marks.'

But really, I was worried. These odd disturbances and interlocutions seemed related somehow to each other, to what I was writing, and to my own past. Or could it be that strange things were occurring because I was consciously seeking out connections, digging around for a story and, in the process, conjuring up entities over which I had no control? Either way, history was eating into my present. A creeping melancholy evinced by my burgeoning collection of memorial bench photographs, which I'd arrange on the kitchen table and stare at intently, as if concentrating hard enough would unleash a transformational gnostic message from beyond death's veil. In particular, I was obsessed with a crinkled printout of my favourite photo of Aleister Crowley bathing in a spring on his K2 expedition in 1902. I stuck it on my study wall. His pale, wiry frame and bolshy expression reminded me of Mike, or what I could remember of Mike. They both shared that compulsion to climb, to ascend new heights, to push themselves as far as they could and to hell with what other people thought.

Sometimes I dreamed of escape to territories further afield than Hastings, where I could walk myself free from these obsessions, but the pain in my pelvis had become so bad I was struggling with the daily trek. Fire in my testes. Stabs in my bladder. A throb in my perineum. These agonies came and went, and it was not as if I was crippled or unable to work, but I needed to know what was happening inside me and put a stop to it. My daily walking was essential. It was how I got my ideas and my sense of place. Without walking I was the blinking curser on a blank computer screen. A writer without a story. A father with nothing to tell his daughters. A husband who talked of taxes and efficient methods of dishwasher stacking while enduring a constant, silent worry about bacteria gnawing him to death from the genitals upwards.

I kept going back to the GP, complaining about the pain, until he suggested a pile of tests that had nothing to do with bladders and testicles. They involved all kinds of uncomfortable questions about my personal life and habits which I didn't answer very accurately. In a small, overheated room in the medical centre a kindly therapist told me I had a Vitamin B1 deficiency sometimes associated with alcohol abuse. Kind of insulting, but there you go. I was a mild-to-occasionally-severe drinker. I knew people who were far worse. Or used to, anyway. She told me that in very rare cases this could lead to something known as *confabulatory hypermnesia,* a condition in which people invent fictitious events to fill gaps in their life, confusing memory with imagination. I said that I'd never been sure of the difference. To truly remember an experience, don't you need imagination? What other tool do you have for going back in time? How factual can any memory be once excavated and reassembled? A told truth is only a version of itself. So, I went back to the doctor again and insisted this time that he put theory to one side and look directly inside my organs. He threw up his hands in despair and sent me to The Ridge for an ultrasound scan.

It was early Friday evening and Conquest Hospital was quiet, the lights blue and dimmed, as if on emergency power. Clutching an appointment sheet, I wandered the corridors looking for the radiology department. I hung about near a room that looked like an execution chamber, desks with vintage computers surrounding a bulbous white central pod containing a reclining chair. There was nobody around but for a janitor with a mop. I tried to speak to him but he shuffled hurriedly through door marked 'STAFF ONLY'. Eventually I caught the attention of a passing nurse. She seemed surprised I was there. After looking at my piece of paper she sent me to a small room at the bottom of a long corridor where a tired-looking radiologist welcomed me in.

'Only two hours to go,' she sighed when I asked if it was nearly home time. It was all I could think to say. Given the circumstances, small talk was out of the question. I lay on the bed with my trousers down. She pressed a cold ultrasound probe to my bollocks. Her face paled with light cast from the flickering image of my testicles in the monitor. She held the probe in position for what seemed an excessively long time, tapping on the keyboard and squinting at the screen. I tried to read her expression for signs of concern, much in the way I scan the faces of air stewards for signs of panic during turbulent flights. What was holding her attention? What could she see? Then, without a twitch, she moved the probe to another position and began tapping the keys again.

'Are you alright?' she said. 'You seem very uncomfortable.'

'It's … I'm not … it's the …'

'Does it hurt?'

'No.'

'Okay.'

Click, click, click, went her mouse.

Against my better judgement, I looked at the monitor. It was hard to see properly from an acute angle, but I could make out what looked like a planet as portrayed by a dodgy 1960s live TV feed, shimmering in black and white, rippled with valleys and pitted with craters. Those two glands had helped seed two children, both of whom I'd seen in their embryonic form on a similar screen. But now my testicles were redundant. Dying worlds in no need of exploring and which nobody would miss. Yet here was this radiologist, forced to spend her Friday night watching the worst television programme ever: a journey through my scrotum's inner space.

A few weeks later I was back on The Ridge, sat in front of the urology consultant for my results. He was a suave silver fox who'd sauntered in an hour late without explanation, causing uproar in the waiting room. Apparently, he'd done this many times before. Trouble with the Audi or too much traffic on the road from Rye. When I sat down he leaned back casually in his chair and explained that I had chronic prostatitis and there was absolutely nothing he – or anyone else – could possibly do about it.

'Is that definite?' I said. 'It seems like something more—'

'Let's talk pain control,' he said.

'Okay but—'

'Do you shower or bath?'

'Shower.'

'Baths will be better for you. Every night, have a hot bath and a Scotch.'

I anticipated further advice. Some medicinal specifics, perhaps. But he only smiled, hands cupped behind his head.

'That's it?'

'Not a bad way to live,' he said. 'What is it you do?'

'I'm a writer.'

'Ah.' He nodded, as if it all now made sense. 'What do you write about?'

'I'm writing a book about the Sussex coast—its history and landscape—or I was—but I keep—I keep getting distracted—this is why I'm so keen to—'

'Have you been to Winchelsea? Or Rye?'

'Yes, I'm planning to write a chapter about both—probably—the walking is hard because—'

'Oh, very good. In my spare time, I like to fly my plane over that part of the coast. It's rather magical. And let me tell you something strange—you might like this—you know how clouds tend to hug the coastline, where the sea air meets the land? Well over Winchelsea and Rye, they hug the outline of the coastline that used to be there. I find that fascinating.'

'It is. Very.'

We shook hands and I left the building.

At home I googled prostatitis. An inflammation of the prostate causing pain in the pelvic area. Bacterial prostatitis was curable by antibiotics. But it seemed that nobody could agree on what caused or cured the chronic version. In one study published in the *Urology* journal, researchers found high levels of cytokines in sufferers. These are proteins that regulate immunity and inflammation. Their presence suggested that the prostate pain was reaction to an infection that had occurred a long time ago. In which case, my body was being haunted by a bacterial ghost.

XV

Mad John

After my discovery that there might be phantoms in my balls, I started to get terrible visions. Not the inter-dimensional sort I experienced that night on DMT when I travelled to Ancient Egypt through the ceiling rose of our house, but speculative leaps into a nightmarish future, only seconds from the here and now. My daughters went quiet in the bath as I went to find towels. In my mind's eye, I saw one of them holding the other's head down under the water until the bubbles stopped. It was only a brief flicker across my frontal lobes, but enough to send me dashing down the hall. 'What's wrong, Daddy?' they said.

I didn't know. What the hell *was* wrong?

At the toilet having a piss, I watched in horror as chunks of prostate gushed into the bowl. On a walk, Hendrix leapt off the pavement and was crushed under the wheels of an approaching truck, his leash tangling in the axle, dragging me screaming behind him. One second I was on West Hill, the next I was falling, smashing off the rocks until I was a ragged fish spine floating on the tide. A firework at night was Dungeness erupting. On the beach, I stopped to admire the view and a sinkhole swallowed me whole. Emily opened her mouth to speak and the words came out: 'I don't love you any more.'

I couldn't stop these visions and they were taking their toll. It was like that moment after a bad dream, where you become aware that its events didn't really happen, yet your heart continues to ache with grief, fear and despair. For that moment, you exist in two realities at once, imaginary and real, like a quantum particle.

Reminders of the apocalypse were everywhere: my TV sucked radiated energy from Dungeness, planes burned up the sky, cars choked the air, container ships on the horizon – full of plastic things we didn't really need – leaked oil into the ocean. The extreme weather didn't help. After the mildest winter on record, this summer was particularly hot. Saharan hot. Railway lines melted and warped. Tarmac bubbled on the road. When rains came, they came hard, filling cracks, splitting stone, splintering beams, opening everything up to more sun. And so it continued. The heat was an axe, chopping everything to pieces before flash floods sluiced the debris down the drain. The TV news was an endless cycle of HEATWAVE! and FLOOD! and TRANSPORT CHAOS! But what did it matter? Hastings was the end of the line and I'd not yet found a holey stone to lift Crowley's curse, so I wasn't going anywhere. May as well hang around, eating ice cream as the world turned to stew. It seemed pointless to bother with recycling the tubs afterwards. A bit late for all that.

Hendrix got huffy in the heat. His black hair soaked up the sun. Regardless, I'd drag him up East Hill, that promontory which was gaining in magnetic power, drawing me to its heights in sunshine, wind and rain. I couldn't help myself. It was a compulsion. Always I began at All Saints Street, where I bowed to the All-Seeing Eye that glared from the pyramid on the Masonic headstone in the churchyard. Then I'd puff up the slope to the Minnis Rock and check if it had been inhabited lately. Sometimes I'd find burned ashes in one of the chambers. Magic rituals, perhaps, teens taking drugs, or the chilly homeless. Afterwards I'd ascend the ridge of Mount Idle, above the Black Arches, and gaze across the Old Town, trying to conjure up what it was that John Coussens was thinking—if anything at all—about what lay within the rock.

I'd walk over contours created by golf course landscapers or Neolithic settlers, I never could tell, to the scrubby patch of land called St George's Churchyard on the highest crest of the cliffs, where I'd stand among the memorial benches and look over the widest sea to the very ends of the earth.

On a particularly warm day I decided to give Hendrix a splash in the sea. Pelham Beach was off-limits for dogs in the summer, but they were permitted on the shore by St Leonards, so I took him over the hill known as White Rock, the most westerly of three promontories that furcated the town like the toes of an Iguanodon foot, down to Warrior Square Gardens on St Leonards seafront. Its lawns were empty but for a woman doing boxercise and three heroin addicts wearing inappropriate anoraks.

On the promenade, the modernist apartment block Marine Court was a grounded ocean liner left by the tide. Below it, the silhouettes of children stalked rock pools with little nets. Tourists drifted away from the beach but there were still rows of sunburned legs jutting from chairs outside the promenade cafés. A gang of German exchange students cajoled each other into hurdling over the rails while an elderly couple stood bemused before a vertical stack of groyne timbers festooned with padlocks – a sculpture called *My Heart Belongs to Hastings*. In the children's play area, a wooden sea serpent rose from the concrete in a series of loops, much like the one Charles Dawson claimed to see in the Channel a few miles from this spot. Was this some kind of homage? Or was I was now hallucinating serpents too?

Ahead was the double-decker promenade built in the 1930s by Sydney Little, 'the king of concrete', who transformed this part of town from a dirty tramway into a futurescape of curvaceous white slabs and chrome. Tourists strolled on the upper walkway, catching the sun, while I entered the lower alley with viewing balconies curved over the shingle. Its wall was a fusion of concrete and broken bottles which Little salvaged from a rubbish tip, separating them into emeralds, oranges, greens and crimsons. Each section was characterised by different colour and pattern formations—circles, stripes, clusters and spirals. One panel seemed a chaos of smashed glass until I looked closer and forms emerged, like in a Magic Eye picture. Numbers and letters … A … C … 6 … 6 … 6 … did they mean something?

I could make out the bottoms of wine bottles with markings of the manufacturers. Running my fingertips over them, the glass was no longer an abstract fragment, but a bottle touched by real hands that brought succour to real, beating hearts. I could smell tannin and hear the hullaballoo of drinkers as they laughed, argued and spilled their secrets a century ago. The last piss-up before being shipped out to the Great War. A homecoming banquet soured by absences. Then the good-time drinking. the raucous dance parties of the post-war prosperity jazz years, followed by the fearful, consolatory boozing of the General Strike. The smashed dreams of the 1929 crash. The remnants of a spoiled party flung onto the rubbish heap for Sydney Little to salvage. All of this was encoded into the promenade's structure, much like the names carved into park benches or the sandstone of West Hill. In Hastings, memory is a raw material.

A victim to Aeolian forces, Sydney Little's 'bottle alley' was crumbling, its once-pristine curves resembling the chewed fingernails of a neurotic, its render flaked, ceiling cratered, pillars bitten by wind and rain. Exposed girders bled oxidised orange tears down the paintwork. Puddles of piss and chips pooled in its stairwells. Thick layers of spiderweb veiled the strip lighting. I passed biro-scrawled RIPs to a teenage girl who had died. The words 'we will never forget you' inside a scrappily drawn heart. Further on, a phone number with the words 'I will suck ya cock'. The pillars were wrapped in black and white artworks from a coastal exhibition, fading and scuffed, scrawled in graffiti. One of them was an image of the pier in its heyday. In the sky above it was written: 'Curse of the Great Beast'.

Hendrix was straining at the leash, so I abandoned the alley via some wooden steps and let him go. I followed as he raced down the shingle towards the sand where lugworm fishermen worked slowly beyond the encrusted groynes. The air was pungent with sulphur. Mussel shells strewn among coils of lugworm excrement. I hopped over mini-estuaries of running water in the sand as Hendrix gambolled in the breakers. Further out, a half-naked angler, waist deep, wrestled with his rod. On the horizon, the silhouette of the Sovereign Lighthouse on its platform beyond Beachy Head. To the east I looked though the legs of the pier to Hastings Castle and Pelham Beach, the outfall pipe and the mass of East Hill, where an Edwardian railway carriage moved up the cliff as if floating on a cushion of air.

I had an urge to go up there and walk in the sky.

*

Back in the Old Town again for a pint in The Dolphin pub at the foot of East Hill's cliffs. The humidity had broken and a wind whipped off Stade Beach, seasoned with fish guts. Instead of my usual ascent up the hill via the Minnis Rock, I walked the steps alongside the railway lift. There were memorial benches towards the summit: Jim & Trixie

Butchers 'A Wonderful Hastings couple' and 'OLLY "9 TOES" CAREY'. The epitaphs on East Hill were different in tone to those on West Hill. Looser, wittier, more irreverent. At the top of the steps was this:

Who on earth were you, Mad John? Why was your madness so uncertain?

I sat on his bench. It was positioned to take in the whole Hastings vista – the Old Town, the promenade, the castle, the pier and the coastline weaving towards Bexhill and Beachy Head beyond. Unlike the infrastructural arrangement of the benches on West Hill, this was the most natural location in which someone would stop to dwell. It was perfect, rooting me to the spot, possessing me with what I imagined John might have felt about life after death as a wooden resting place. I looked out with his gaze as if it were my own. I smirked on his behalf at the stuffy formality of those memorial benches over on West Hill, in their funny angles. Some of the people he knew when they were more than simply names carved into wood. There was Mrs Jenson who was apparently 'much beloved' – oh yes, beloved alright, snickered Mad John, she was known as the town bike back in the fifties. Yeah, yeah, say what you like about that, but everyone had a go, ask around they'll all tell you. Then there was Dicky Pierce. Big Dicky. Christ only knows why he'd been put up on the hill. The lazy fat sod barely left his bar stool at The Nelson. Oh, and there were Harry and Jill Michaels, too, 'a loving couple', so said the inscription. God, you should have heard Harry going on about Jill behind her back, right up until that day she whopped him with a saucepan and everyone down at the angling club laughed so hard at his black eye he ran right back out the door. Yet there they all are, laughed Mad John, dead and turned to benches instead of dust, arranged in neat rows, seething at each other for taking the superior spots. Oh, how they'd love to wrench their little metal legs from the ground and go clattering across the hill like crabs to get away from the tourists and find somewhere quiet to spend the next hundred years or so until the apocalypse. Ah, for shame, lamented Mad John, here on East Hill was the place to be, where the benches were wild and free with the most majestic views. East Hill was where the chaos happened.

No mistake, John's bench was in a good place. Better even than that of his namesake, John Coussens, who may have been mad too when he carved his Black Arches into the rock less than a hundred metres away. From where I sat, thinking of Johns, I could see a weather front approaching. An opaque twister darkened Beachy Head and moved along the coast, casting shadows on the ocean. Restless gulls spiralled up from the cliff like cinders rising from a fire, black against the blue sky, flipping to silver against the encroaching cloud. I envied them. Birds are the expression of the wind. They travel invisible paths in the sky, gone as soon as they are created, never to be repeated. These animals are free to live in the moment. But we humans are entrenched in the earth, doomed to follow in the footprints of others, mangling them with our own. Sometimes gravity was too much to bear.

Leaving Mad John behind, I walked to the highest crest of the hill and looked out at the English Channel. The rolling baize of grass around me was scarred with holes made by rabbits and metal detectorists. To the east ranged sandstone promontories and lush gullies spilling freshwater into coves. There was something about this view. Something eerily familiar. I couldn't . . .

Then it all came rushing back.

Two weeks before Mike fell from St Andrews Castle, I had this dream that I was flying on my bed, like Aladdin on his carpet, over rolling green cliff tops and a dazzled ocean. All of a sudden, the bed began to tilt. I gripped onto the sheets but they came away as big white blooms in my hands. Slowly I slid from the mattress and plummeted in a wide arc over the cliffs towards the sea. *I'm going to die,* I thought. *The water's coming up so fast—*

I woke up, sweating, to hear the ocean crashing, the ruins of the twelfth-century cathedral like black bones outside my window. I pulled on some clothes and went downstairs to empty wine bottles and overflowing ashtrays. A chicken carcass ringed by plates of congealed matter. Mike was sat in his dressing gown, ginger legs poking from the folds, pillow crinkles on his face. After eleven hours' sleep it took time for his face to realign itself. We were all like that at the time, really. Rubbery twenty-one-year-olds, malleable as candle wax. Drinking hard, smoking hard, sleeping hard, contorting ourselves into awkward shapes then bouncing back again. Our hallowed Alan Partridge VHS was playing on the television with the sound low, but Mike wasn't watching. He was staring out the window at the castle.

I didn't tell Mike about the dream. Why would I? It had

no significance. The only reason it stuck in my mind was because of what happened to him a fortnight later. Whenever I was drunk enough to talk about it in the passing years, I always referred to that dream as if it were a premonition of his death. But I ignored the obvious flaw that its rolling green cliff-top landscape was nothing like the coastline of St Andrews where the tragedy happened—those long ribbons of sand, golf courses, mediaeval ruins and university quadrants. This place was something *other*: a territory I had invented, or was yet to visit. As time passed the memory of this dream receded down a spiralling tunnel of events: my first job writing for radio in Cardiff, my move to London, marriage to Emily, two baby girls, a dog, mortgage, booms, crashes, debts, grey hairs. Eventually it became a pinprick in the canopy of my past, almost forgotten.

Until now.

If I could look down upon myself from a magic flying bed, I would be on that coastline I dreamed in 1996. I was sure of it. This was the place, this spot on East Hill. It felt like a fulcrum upon which the cosmos balanced: equal parts sky, sea and earth, east and west falling symmetrically away to either side. Time and space commensurate. And I was not the only one who felt its significance. I was flanked by memorial benches that marked where others liked to rest here and look out to sea. There was Mr George Fillerton, 'he loved this place'. Susan Harper, 'much missed'. Elizabeth Marchant, 'Mother Grandmother Wife'. Finally, Geoff 'Never a Dull Moment' Lanes, positioned a little bit further away from the others, as if he'd annoyed them somehow.

An elderly couple came and rested on the bench of Susan Harper. I remained for a while in their company, breathing ostentatiously. Unusually, I was in the mood for a random conversation, but they didn't seem to notice me so I left them to it, walking further along the promontory until I reached the path that stooped into woodland towards Ecclesbourne Glen. This was where struggling inventor John Logie Baird walked to recuperate from illness. At some point on one of these walks he resolved to develop a televisual transmission device, the likes of which spiritualists had intended for use in communication with the dead or phantoms from the otherworld. After its invention in 1923, Baird was forever changed. Despite his youthful assertions that humans were merely organic machines, he began to attend séances, including one in which he communicated with the spirit of Thomas Edison. He wrote: 'I am convinced that discoveries of far reaching importance remain waiting along these shadowy and discredited paths.' I wondered where precisely this epiphany happened. What could possibly have turned him against his rational instincts?

It was hard to know for sure because much of the cliff from Baird's time had fallen into the sea, including the coastguard cottages overlooking Ecclesbourne Glen. The nearby caravan park had cut down trees to give holidaymakers unspoiled sea views, leaving the rootless land vulnerable to heavy rains. In my first year in Hastings there was a path down from East Hill into the glen. After a series of landslips, it was cluttered with fallen trees and mounds of churned earth. Authorities had sealed off the route but people found their way through, ignoring the danger signs, clambering over concrete posts and broken fencing.

As Hendrix and I descended, we passed a man with his young son and their basset hound. They ducked under a NO ENTRY barrier and picked their way down a gully towards the sea. I assumed they knew what they were doing but it was long past low tide and a squall was rising. It seemed foolhardy. I climbed up the other side towards a farmed crest beyond the trees. As I checked behind me, I could see traces of old cottages on the cliff. Stone steps truncated by vertical drops. The remains of foundations on a crumbling ledge. A shrub on the edge, roots dangling in the air like a child's legs.

The path took me onto a precipice, bushy with gorse, its edge fenced off for safety. Behind me the sky was bruising over East Hill. I could hear voices in the wind. Shouts and calls drifting from far below. They sounded alarmed. Was it that boy and man I saw earlier with the dog? Were they in trouble?

Hooking Hendrix's lead to a bench, I climbed onto a fence post and tried to catch a view of the beach. In a cove I saw a man, tiny at the foot of the cliff, picking his way over the rocks, knee-deep in water, clutching onto sandstone to steady himself. A frenzy of dog barks. Someone shouting out. A child's high-pitched cry. Then I saw it—a shape darkening the blue swell, moving quickly towards the man. The shiny hump of a giant eel broke the water's surface, momentarily, before waves folded upon it. I didn't know what happened next. The man was now out of view. All I could see was bare rock and jets of spume as the surf pounded. It might have been an innocent scene, or something terrible was happening. But I was too remote, too alone, too afraid to step beyond the barrier and peer directly down on the beach.

It wasn't the height that frightened me, it was the edge. That being on the threshold between existence and obliteration. I feared that moment when I might suddenly be in the air, the cliff edge falling upwards at speed, and nothing I could do about it. That split second in which I would be alive and dead at the same time. That moment Mike must have experienced when he slipped off the castle wall.

It was an agony I couldn't get out of my head.

So many questions.

When your fingers came away from stone, did it come as a surprise, Mike? Did you really believe it was happening? Were you frightened? Confused? Did you feel free for that moment? Resigned to your fate? Did your life flash before your eyes? Did you hear our voices, your friends all jabbering and yelling in the castle grounds? Did you cry out? Or did your pineal gland instantly protect you, flooding your brain with DMT, so that you never really fell, but soared upwards into another dimension from which you looked down one last time upon the castle, wet with drizzle, the brutal surf, and our tiny human forms, before dissolving into eternity?

If I could bring you back to ask you now, here on the cliffs of my dream, what would you say?

'One day you'll know it yourself,' said Mike, stooped over Hendrix, ruffling his hair. He always did love dogs. Or did he? Come to think of it, I can't actually remember. 'That infinitesimal moment of death, which lasts for eternity, will be our greatest shared experience.'

'This doesn't sound like you talking,' I said.

'In that moment,' smiled Mike, 'we'll be friends again. You, me, and Mad John.'

But which Mad John?

XVI

The Cave

As he wheezed over East Hill in spring 1923, John Baird's body was a wreck. His biological engine was as flawed as his recent inventions. He had been in search of a breakthrough that would change the world and make his fortune but things had not gone well. He invented a glass razor blade which never needed sharpening, but it slashed his arm so badly he was hospitalised. Then his pneumatic balloon shoes burst underfoot during a live trial and sent him toppling like a clown. His revolutionary Speedy Cleaner soap—nothing more than regular bulk soap with a dash of outrageous marketing—did well until it was swallowed up in a takeover by its rival, Rapid Washer. He came away with £200 but the ensuing illness almost finished him off. The sea air in Hastings was his salvation.

When the doctor first urged him to take regular constitutionals, he felt it was a waste of time better spent working on a new project. But he became hooked on the oxygen rush he got from putting one foot in front of the other and those fresh ideas which flowed to his brain as he climbed high above the English Channel, wind in his hair and sun on his face. Today he felt strong enough to take the steep path down the back of East Hill towards the coastguard cottages.

Somewhere nearby he knew of a cave which had been occupied by an elderly hermit named Hancox, a well-educated fellow who ran a business in London before it fell on hard times. Broken in spirit, he came to Ecclesbourne Glen to live alone in a cave, for which he paid the landowner, the Reverend Milward, rent of twenty-two shillings. He kept his clothes in good order, cooked on a stove and read the copious books stacked around his abode. In 1918, the seventy-four-year-old was found dead of natural causes on the floor of the hermitage. This was precisely the fate Baird wished to avoid: a life of lonely failure. For all those platitudes about an impecunious life being a means to spiritual enlightenment, nobody would remember Hancox in a hundred years. Whatever insights he'd gleaned from his isolation died with his body. What difference had he made? He was a tree falling in a forest with nobody to hear it. If there was a choice between a solitary death in a cave at seventy-four or a famous death at fifty-four, Baird knew which he would choose. Still, it intrigued him that a person could cut themselves off from a world where everything was only just beginning to connect in wondrous new ways.

It took him a little while to locate the hermit's cave. A track of trodden grass took him away from the pathway. He followed it into a clearing of bluebells and gnarly tree roots at the foot of a steep incline, where he beheld the hermitage, a gaping eye socket in a brow of sandstone, shaggy with vegetation. Evidently it was still in use, for near the entrance was a pile of rags by a burnt-out fire. Baird poked about in the cave where he found etchings on the rock, the impetuous daubings of adolescent lovers to be expected in such places. Except there was this in Latin:

Nihil est verum, omnia licet.

'Nothing is true,' muttered Baird. 'Everything is permitted.'

Re-emerging from the cave, he heard sobbing. A little further ahead by some blackberry bushes a little girl in a blue coat and cloche hat was hunched with her back to him, gently shaking.

'Child! What is wrong?'

As he touched her shoulder she bowed forward, weeping. 'My dolly, Hannah, my dolly Hannah's in there.'

'Where?'

The child's arm stuck out, pointing to a fresh parting in the brambles.

'Well then, don't fret, it's easily remedied.' Baird went over and peered through. He couldn't see a doll, but an opening to another cave, with an entrance no higher than his waist. He sighed. It looked a pain to get into and he was not one for tight spaces, but the girl was visibly upset and surely it was better he search for the wretched doll than risk her being trapped.

Baird laid his trilby on the grass and entered the cave on his elbows and knees, groping ahead of him for the doll. Glimpsing a flap of white material, he shuffled forward to reach it. It flipped further inside the tunnel like a wounded butterfly. Forward again he went, hand outstretched. As his fingers curled to close upon the material, a gust of air whipped it into his face as a woman's voice cried 'You!' from deep within the tunnel. Startled, Baird jerked back, striking his head hard on the rock.

There was no pain, only a tide of darkness that swelled through him until he felt as if he would drown. His panic dissolved into blissful submission as space unfolded from itself, over and over, and he was lifted into a viscous whiteness, floating free, layers of his personality peeling away like leaves from a bough until he was left with his supreme higher self, a Prometheus of gold and silver feathers, soaring through the universe. Ahead of him there emerged blurry figures with simian arms and bulbous craniums. On a spindle, they turned a series of metallic disks ringed with holes, like a child might spin the wheel of an upturned bicycle. At the rear of this apparatus the mouth of a ventriloquist's dummy opened. Light blasting from its mouth burned moving images on his consciousness: metallic machines hurtling over cities, a cloud like a giant mushroom, a humanoid figure in white bouncing on the pitted surface of the moon, a couple fornicating wildly on a velvet bed, two towers collapsing in the sunshine, planet Earth enmeshed by a phosphorescent green web. It was as if he was a receiver picking up signals from time and space, so rapid and multifarious he could not fix on any single one clearly. Then the signals stopped. Baird was suspended above an alien landscape. Below, hordes of people streamed through a plain of pyramids stretching towards a pyramid larger than the rest, with an eye at its apex, radiating light. As he rose higher above these structures they became brighter and brighter, smaller and smaller, until the land was a mass of sparkling diamonds, a billion suns, an infinity of universes. Then, with a high-pitched whistle, they faded into pinpricks before blinking out entirely.

When Baird came to, there was wet blood on the back of his head. Beyond his legs, he could see the mouth of the cave and light glittering through the brambles. Baird could not account for what happened, later writing:

'It may have been an hour of unconsciousness which I experienced that day, or a brief moment of disorientation, it is impossible to tell in retrospect.'

He emerged coughing into the light, chest thick with catarrh. One of his spectacle lenses was cracked and his shirt collar bloodied. The girl was sat by the bushes with her back to him, sobbing.

'I'm sorry child,' said Baird, touching her shoulder. 'I could not find your doll.'

At his touch, the girl tilted over, stiff as cardboard, crunching onto her back. Little balsa-wood legs with crocheted feet stuck up in the air. Her wooden face was painted with circular red cheeks. Glass bead eyes stared sightlessly. Crude woollen hair splayed on the grass. Baird span around, looking for the trickster, gripped with fear. Above him, the sky darkened at an unholy rate and rain began to fall.

There was no time for him to grapple with the hows and whys of this madness, not yet. Sensing that someone was approaching, a terrified John Baird stumbled away from the caves, onto the path, and didn't stop until he reached the top of East Hill, where golfers hurried into the clubhouse to escape the deluge. Hunched and shaking, Baird kept going, desperate to get back to his apartment and write down what he'd seen. He could not understand what had happened, for it was not of the rational world he presumed to know. Yet he also knew that one could not ignore inspiration when it came, no matter how frightening and strange.

That spinning mechanical apparatus in the vision: he knew what it might be, and what could be done with it.

*

Presently, a cloaked figure entered the clearing. A man in his late forties with pockmarked cheeks, unusually tanned for the time of year. He had left his abbey in Sicily to come to this spot. This was almost certainly the place depicted in his opium visions. Over the course of a week they had grown in intensity until he could no longer ignore those signals which the universe was sending him. This cave before him could be none other than that which he had foreseen. This was the place where was hidden the key to the Aeon of Horus, of which he was the gatekeeper.

But after an impatient search, tutting and harrumphing, he found nothing but a discarded trilby hat near brambles.

Someone had been here before him. Most probably that thin man he'd seen scrambling up the path moments earlier. He picked up the hat. Inside the rim, he could make out lettering, smudged by the rain but clear enough:

J. L. Baird

The name was unfamiliar. But it made him uneasy. Worse, he was aware that he was being watched. At the sound of a cracked twig, Aleister Crowley looked up to see a little girl in a cloche hat and blue coat standing among the bluebells, humming 'Jack and Jill Went Up the Hill' with a fiendish look in her eye.

'Hannah!' he said.

At first, she didn't smile. Then she did, and it was horrific.

Crowley knew then that he had been robbed.

XVII

The Fallers

What happened to Baird made sense when I thought about his uncanny change of fortune after his descent into Ecclesbourne Glen that day in 1923. He had stumbled unwittingly into Hastings' psychic vortex. As I had found out, to walk along this stretch of coast for any length of time with an open mind was to experience a series of possessions, to catch glimpses of other lives through other eyes across the aeons, future and past. Perhaps this was why they called this bit of ocean the Channel.

The channel of water. The channelling of spirits. The TV channel.

After his experience in the cave Baird understood that there was a reality beyond physical space and terrestrial time. If he could only work out a mechanical way to manifest its unseen forces, he would create a new world in which stories flowed through the atmosphere, much like Tesla's ambient electricity. These same forces haunted my every step through the town in the memories that came to me, of sad boys and submarines, of devious palaeontologists and unscrupulous authors, of me and Mike and what happened to us, back in St Andrews. They were all jumbled in my mind until I couldn't distinguish between fact and fiction, history and myth, or if there was ever a difference. At first I had sought out these stories and wrote them down, but now they were like a myriad blaring televisions I could not turn off.

I remember as a small child in Glasgow in the 1970s my favourite programme was *Glen Michael's Cartoon Cavalcade.* I watched it religiously every Sunday afternoon, eating Fruit Pastilles that my Nana and Papa brought round after they'd been to church. Glen was the middle-aged presenter. He sat at a desk with a wisecracking lamp named Paladin. For an hour, he and the lamp would introduce cartoons that became my founding myths: *Bugs Bunny* (the cross-dressing Discordian trickster), *Godzilla* (the incarnation of nuclear apocalypse) and *Spider-man* (a fledgling writer with a dark secret). After each cartoon it always came back to Glen Michael, like a kindly uncle, sat with his haunted lamp, a conduit for these insane animated tales. Then one day my mum took me to see Glen Michael on stage at a Glasgow shopping centre and I was astonished to find there was no talking lamp. It was just an old man on a stage next to a lady making dogs out of balloons. It had never occurred to me that the Glen I thought I knew was a fiction, a ghost in a box, and nothing could be trusted.

This was the psychosis which Baird had unleashed upon the world.

Upon me.

My other television obsession as a child was Emu. Rod Hull's creation was wild and unpredictable, undermining its master, attacking chat show celebrities and smashing up stage sets. My parents bought me an Emu puppet in 1978 and it rarely left my arm. With Emu I could do anything. Harass relatives. Make strangers laugh. Unleash frustrations. Emu was my animal familiar. It went wherever I went, a shaggy elbow-length glove with attitude. Photo albums show a six-year-old me with my brother and grandfather on the day we moved from Scotland to England. Emu was on my arm on the car journey all the way to our new home in Derbyshire, where the townsfolk talked strangely, yet laughed at me when I narrated the school nativity in a Glaswegian accent. Emu didn't care. Emu didn't have an accent. Emu communicated only through direct action. Emu was who I wished to be.

Emu was in all the photos of our holiday to Wales. Me and Emu watching Dad's cousin, the deputy coxswain of the Tenby Lifeboat, airlifted by helicopters from the Goskar Rock during a drill. Me with Emu on my Great-Uncle Con's fishing boat, heading from Tenby to Caldey Island, where the monks lived. Me and Emu beneath a T-rex and Iguanodon in the dinosaur park at the Dan-yr-Ogof caves. I have always been thrilled by the idea of monsters trapped in rock. Maybe this was the lure of the coast for me. The same fascination that drew Charles Dawson into his lifetime of palaeontological fantasies.

Like the legions of occultists, mavericks and artists before him, Rod Hull was also drawn to this coast in older age, moving to Winchelsea in 1994. Five years later, he was watching Champion's League football on the telly with his son Oliver, but the reception was terrible. He climbed onto the roof to adjust the aerial. Oliver heard a light thud then a heavier thud as his father tumbled from the roof and crashed to the ground. The entertainer was dead. Poor Rod. He had been both a beneficiary and a victim of the television age to which John Baird had given birth only nine miles west. With his death died his creation. In the darkness of its box, Emu's beak hung open in a silent scream.

Curious to see the site of Rod's demise, I took a train to

Winchelsea one afternoon, only a ten-minute chug from Hastings. The train stopped at a level crossing in an East Sussex field, seemingly in the middle of nowhere. I was left on a tiny platform beside a sign which read:

Winchelsea town is ½ mile south east of the station

A country road wound me through freshly cropped fields, criss-crossed with telegraph poles, broody with crows. Rising above was the wooded hillock upon which New Winchelsea was built in 1288 on the orders of Edward I, after the great storm destroyed Old Winchelsea and turned the flatland into a tidal estuary. For a while it thrived as an important naval outpost and a bustling trading port. Vast wine cellars were built to contain the delicious imports from abroad. But while the first town was deluged by water, the second version was ruined by drainage as the upper reaches of the estuary were reclaimed as farmland, silting up the lower reaches, leaving Winchelsea stranded inland, a sleepy artists' retreat, pretty and purposeless.

Taking a steep curving road, I entered the town through a ruined mediaeval gateway by a house called 'One Moneysellers', harking back to its seaport days when foreign coins were exchanged upon entry. In 1297, King Edward

I came to this spot to inspect his fleet, which had amassed in preparation for a campaign in Flanders, and could be seen from the walls of his new town. Edward was a gangly man, over six feet tall, with greying hair and a fiery temper, undermined somewhat by a severe lisp. He was obsessed with the legend of King Arthur and liked to organise round table events, where feasting went on for days, and guests assumed the names and identities of characters from Arthur's court. That day Edward felt at his most Arthurian, come to inspect his kingdom on the back of a noble steed. Nose in the air, he trotted through the Pipewell Gate and approached the wall at the top of the cliff edge looking over the estuary. Suddenly, the horse was spooked by the sails of a windmill. The beast reared up, whinnying, and before Edward had a chance to cry out, it vaulted over the wall with the King on its back.

*

Plummeting over the edge, Edward's heart stung with fear. He gripped the reins tight and braced himself for death. As he fell he saw the sea glisten and the sails of his glorious fleet, silver in the sun. He felt the pull of the earth below and the walls of his beloved Winchelsea fall up and away from him. He closed his eyes for impact.

But the moment lingered.

Time slowed to a stop.

A great liquid sickness washed through him from his bowels to his brain, like he was drowning in his own humours. An aroma of decayed vegetation filled his nose. There followed a feeling of extraordinary lightness as if he were first rising from his horse, then rising from his own body, into a space without edges, an air without resistance, bright with light.

Was this death?

Was he to be carried away to Avalon, like his hero?

There was a clap of thunder. In the shimmering whiteness above, he saw emerge, like God Himself, the apparition of a monstrous bird with a long brown neck, yellow beak and blue feathers, the likes of which he had never seen on earth. The bird arched down to him and opened its beak as if to shriek into his face. But no sound came out.

Instead, a big-haired man came tumbling from the bird's gaping backside, falling until he was level with Edward.

The two of them hung in the air opposite each other, limbs flailing.

This man Edward instinctively knew as Rod of the Pink Windmill, and Rod knew also that this was the king they called Edward I.

Rod said to the king: 'Oh bugger, Sire, I'm falling!'

The king replied, 'Yea, thith is true. Likewithe I fall.'

At this the man they called Rod waggled his eyebrows. 'Total chaos!' He flashed a smile that struck fear into Edward.

Then the man known as Rod of the Pink Windmill began to move his right arm in a jerky motion, hand snapping like a beak, as if it were a creature alive and apart from himself!

But after a few seconds, upon looking at his naked arm, Rod fell to sadness and let the arm drop to his side, a tear in his eye.

The king felt a moment of pity for this man, undoubtedly a jester or deranged simpleton. Then it dawned on him that this might be a second chance. There could not be a death of a king today, not with the life of England at stake. It was no coincidence that a windmill had caused his horse to bolt.

This jester, Rod of the Pink Windmill, was surely sent for the salvation of the kingdom. It was a sign!

Knowing what must be done, Edward reached out with a cry of, 'Alath, thith ith what mutht be done!' and placed his hands on the shoulders of Rod of the Pink Windmill. 'Godthpeed!'

The king pushed him downwards with all his might. In doing so he propelled himself up towards the light as Rod's cry faded to silence below.

When he came to, he was in the material world again, on the back of his horse, wind in his hair, falling, falling, falling.

The crowd gasped and rushed to the edge, looking over the wall to see their king plummet down a thirty-foot drop. The horse hit a sloping bank, slid through a torrent of mud, and staggered to a halt with Edward still on its back.

They gasped again, this time in utter disbelief.

For a few seconds, Edward lay slumped forward over the horse's neck, breathing heavily. Then he sat bolt upright in his saddle, turned the horse around, and cantered back up the road and through the Pipewell Gate, defiance in his eyes.

The people cheered to see their king. In feverish whispers, they wondered at the miracle which had saved him. They felt a surge of hope and joy for the future. For truly Edward was God's appointed, and the England he ruled a promised land.

*

So the story went in my head anyway, wandering the neat grid-form streets from the Pipewell Gate, hearing phantom whinnies, smelling the mediaeval ghost horseshit on the ancient cobbled road. I wondered how it was that Edward cheated death and got a second chance. Why him? Why not Rod Hull? Why not Mike? Why not any of these poor souls in the Church of Thomas à Becket? Built in the middle of the town, nine years before Edward's miracle, its churchyard was the resting place of Spike Milligan, who was buried there beneath a headstone with the epitaph 'I told you I was ill' in Gaelic. Inspired by Milligan, I once said to Emily that I wanted this on my headstone:

Typical.

But she laughed and said there would be no stone and no casket. It wasn't ecological. Whatever my intentions she would fling me in a pit with a bunch of other corpses so I could fertilise an orchard and do something useful for a change. Standing in the graveyard of St Thomas, I agreed with her. Headstones were painful to look at, especially on the coast where they were exposed to the elements. Stone was not permanent. It was alive and it was dying slowly, atom by atom. There were grave markers from as recently as the 1980s and 1990s that were cracked and worn, green with lichen. Here was the era of my own lifetime, tumbledown at my feet.

I read the text on the headstone of Philip Ritchie, who died in 1927 at the age of twenty-eight. His could equally have been Mike's epitaph:

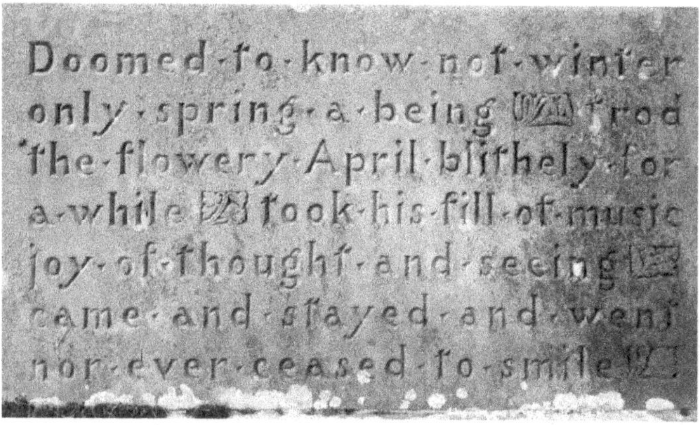

Doomed to know not winter
only spring a being trod
the flowery April blithely for
a while took his fill of music
joy of thought and seeing
came and stayed and went
nor ever ceased to smile.

What would Mike's headstone look like now?

I remembered the fresh soil in a tidy mound beside the grave and that I was crying because of that fucking bagpiper and because I'd helped lay Mike's coffin beside the pit, with the family around it and people from the Officer Training Corps in their uniforms, with my flatmates and faces from school who I'd not seen in over three years, weirdly out of context, like figments of my imagination. It was all too much. There was no way I could put him in the ground. I had let him down once already. I handed someone my rope and pushed my way to the back of the mourning crowd.

Hard to believe that only two months before that day we sat in my Peugeot in Morecambe, eating chips and staring out to sea like a couple of pensioners. Our former English teacher had invited us to come down from St Andrews and give a presentation for his lower sixth form class in his new school near Lancaster. The idea was to talk about life studying English Literature at university, inspiring them to apply, or letting them know what they were in for. He told us he'd pay expenses and put us up for the night. We leapt at the chance for a road trip. It was The English Teacher who got us into B. S. Johnson, Vonnegut and Banks, David Lynch and *Viz*, and we felt we owed him.

Mike and I spent a night writing a two-header talk, filling it with as many insults and slurs against each other as we thought we could get away with. We lay on our fronts next to each other on my trashed blue carpet, typing on a laptop, laughing. We were up so late we barely slept. The next day we barrelled south on the M74, bellowing along to my mixtapes, Mike's feet on the dashboard. We were jubilant. In three years, we'd graduated from hapless hitchers to masters of the road.

Stood together in a classroom again, it was like the old days, but we were free men now. I don't know why, but I kept my printout of the transcript and it somehow survived the decades. Among the puerile jokes, Mike attempted to describe a day in my life at St Andrews:

> Gareth gets up bright and early to the *Neighbours* theme tune. Being a hunter-gatherer he forages in his skanky room for clothes, preferably including some form of trousers, then he whistles for his socks. He deconstructs the Australian soap opera, pointing out the pathetic fallacy in the setting of Ramsay Street, before his flatmates send him packing with comments about his pathetic phallus. Then it's off to the English department. A two-hour tutorial ensues, during which all the desperate worry about his failing health and horrific financial situation is lifted. Life becomes an ecstasy of reader theory and narrative devices, with lots of chest thumping.

Then I said:

> Mike thinks romanticism means climbing through his girlfriend's window dressed like the Milk Tray Man. Often he messes around with his other job—wearing

green and shooting people – but that doesn't stop him getting excited about W. B. Yeats.

That night we worked our way through The English Teacher's collection of single malt whiskies, continuing after he and his wife went to bed, marvelling that somebody could actually keep hold of expensive alcohol for longer than a day and not have a thirsty hoard of friends come to demolish it. But he was married, living in a village with two dogs and a collection of Frank Zappa records. We'd felt so adult whistling down the motorway in my hatchback, but in this tidy domicile we felt like scruffy, half-formed kids again. We wondered if one day we too would have houses with cupboards full of single malts. Mike joked that he would rise through the ranks to become a general and I'd be an unkempt writer come to visit him. Initially the guards at the gates of his compound would try stop me from entering, scanning my credentials in case I was a terrorist. But we'd still be friends, like in *The Fox and the Hound*. I told him this would only happen if he wasn't first shredded by gunfire in a phony foreign war. He replied that he had no fear of death. He was happy to go down in a hail of bullets. I never knew if he was joking. We often said things to shock each other as a cover for our emotions. No matter how much we thought we'd risen above our school's stiff upper lip anachronisms, this was how we were, and it was bollocks. I knew that he wanted a future as much as I did. In that future, I'd drive to his house with a copy of my latest book, *The Stone Tide,* full of tales about Aleister Crowley, John Logie Baird and Charles Dawson. As I pulled up in my battered old Peugeot, he'd welcome me on the doorstep.

'You've arrived,' Mike would say, grey-haired at the temples, with a slight paunch, his dogs barking in the hallway behind him. 'You've arrived.'

XVIII

Crossing Over

On the last school run one Friday before Easter, the lollipop lady's smile seemed strained and she looked at lot older and smaller, like she was shrinking into the road. She didn't say anything about the weather. It was so unsettling that I almost turned around to comment on the black cloud amassing over The Ridge and tell her there was going to be a storm but that it was okay because it wouldn't hit 'til late morning and we'd both be indoors by then. But I didn't say any of that. I just kept going, tugging my daughters along with a sharp 'Hurry up', even though I was clutching their hands and they had no control over the speed.

When I returned from the school gate the lollipop lady was gone. A van had arrived and men were laying out cones and bollards, cordoning off one side of the road, pulling equipment out of a truck. When the summer school term started, there was no more lollipop lady, only a zebra crossing with Belisha beacons. They reminded me of her blond head, cartoonised and stuck on poles. Initially, I felt relieved. No more small talk. From now on I would have a clear run to school without needing to speak at all. Of course, there was still the gauntlet of parents: the woman in boots who was always on the phone, the old man in the obnoxious stickered car, the two gossipers and the nodding Malaysian guy. They were always there.

The lollipop lady's absence didn't seem to change my apprehension as I approached the school each morning. I had the sensation that even the zebra crossing expected something from me, some friendly words, a nod or acknowledgement of some kind. The crossing was no wider than a human being lain down, and in the centre there was a humpiness to it, an undulation that gave it an organic, cuddly quality.

'Where do they get the electric from?' asked my youngest, pointing up at the Belisha beacon.

'They dig underground and lay cables that carry the electricity,' I said.

'Why do they call it a zebra crossing?' asked my eldest. 'Is it made from zebra meat?' She laughed. She was weird like that, my eldest; she got dark ideas.

'No,' I said, 'under the zebra is just road, more road, until there's rock and probably dinosaurs.'

'Oh.'

'Don't you miss the lollipop lady now she's gone?' I asked them.

'No,' they said.

It was sad. You could do a job for years, then vanish from the scene and the youngsters you'd protected for all that time wouldn't care a jot. They don't look back, only forwards. But perhaps this is a good thing.

When I got home, Emily was covered in dust. She was doing up the bathroom with Alejandro, who was a dab hand at plastering, as I was informed on many occasions, the subtext being that I was practically useless. I'd noticed that Emily had begun mutating into the brown and grey hues of the house, wearing a semi-permanent coating of its microscopic fragments. There was a graveyard musk in her hair. The scent of spaces between the walls. She was truly part of this building, whereas my sole contribution to the interior design had been a dinosaur skeleton and the decision to paint the bannister yellow. I was colour-blind so when Emily asked me what colour I thought something should be, I usually said yellow. I knew where I was with yellow. It stood out. It existed on its own terms. Just like the lollipop lady. Except the lollipop lady had been replaced with a set of black and white stripes. I explained my feelings about this to Emily as she stood there in a dusty haze but she didn't really care. 'As you can see, I'm really busy, I've got to finish the tiling. I'll talk about it later.' She donned her face mask and retreated into the bathroom.

This was how things had been lately. Emily and I had developed separate interests. I was usually writing or walking. She was sanding, drilling and painting. In between we'd take the girls to the park, to garish soft play nightmare chambers, to the arcades, to the ice cream parlour, to pubs in the Old Town where we'd drink ourselves silly. When our paths crossed at home we bickered about dry rot, dado rails, bin rotas and who was doing the school run. It irritated me that she was constantly tapping away at her phone, speaking loudly to carpenters or off somewhere with Alejandro and Marcela, who had filled her head with veganism, polytunnels and hippy optimism. She started running. She cooked with quinoa and added orange segments to savoury dishes. She bought large blue dungarees that made her look like a feminist Super Mario. She was no longer interested in my stories of dinosaur hunters, submarines and demonic birds. She said she understood what I was like when she married me, and that it was probably all because I was trying to write a book, but I could be painful to talk to. She was moving forward with her life but I dwelled on the past instead of dwelling in the home we were supposed to be making for ourselves, for our children.

'You've got this stare at the moment whenever you walk into a room,' she told me once. 'Like your eyes are made of glass.'

She was right. My mind was on other things. The next morning when my daughters and I walked over the zebra crossing to the school gates I swore I heard it say something about a cold snap, like a whisper in my ear, but most certainly emanating from the lollipop lady, or some remnant of her. The girls didn't hear it, but then they weren't yet attuned to the vibrations of the landscape. Even if they had heard the voice, they wouldn't have thought anything of it, so accepting were they of the supernatural. For them, existence itself was magic. When I once told them that the moon's gravity caused the ocean's tides they found the concept bizarre and far less believable than the myth of Father Christmas and his army of elf slaves. They had not yet erected a barrier between perceived reality and fantasy, if there were such a thing at all.

Of course, I could have imagined the voice of the zebra crossing. That was more than plausible. For the next few days I tried to slow my walking pace in the middle of the crossing, where it undulated slightly, feeling through my feet for a pulse or tremor, the girls pulling at my arms to get a move on, instead of the other way around, while waiting cars growled on either side of us.

'Are you taking the piss?' said a dough-faced man, winding down his window.

I shuffled from the crossing to the school gates, passing the high-booted woman with the phone, the two natterers with pushchairs, the hatchback man and the Malaysian guy who always nodded to me. I kissed the girls. 'You have a nice day.' And off they went. When I reached the junction again I couldn't help myself. I knelt at the zebra crossing, lowered my head and whispered, 'I think it might rain!' I meant it too, for I'd checked on my phone's weather app especially for the occasion.

That was when the Malaysian guy passed by. 'You lost something?' he said. It was the first time we'd ever spoken.

'Yes,' I said, 'but it doesn't matter.'

*

Later that week, Emily and I decided to watch a film. We had become so preoccupied with our projects that we hadn't sat in the living room together without our daughters for many months. Home was primarily a construction site and place of work. The living room had been the first to get decorated and was the only fully completed zone, but it was barely used and already in decay. Cobwebs had returned to the corners. The varnish on the floor was fading where work-boots had scuffed it. That odour of damp earth from the cellar was more pungent than ever. All we needed was Angela with her piles of books and her cats, and we would have been right back where we started.

I'm not sure why, but the film we chose was Ingmar Bergman's *Scenes from a Marriage*, originally a TV series but then condensed by the director into a three-hour opus. Emily wasn't really a big movie watcher. She disliked suspense of any kind, asking me what was going to happen next and, if I couldn't give her a clear enough explanation, leaving the room until the tension on screen was resolved. She found thriller plots confusing. Or rather, she would get bored and start thinking about something else entirely, like how best to arrange the mirrors above the fireplace or what shape the door knocker should be. 'It's because I struggle to recognise faces,' she claimed, 'these men, they all look the same with their chins and hair. Who's *that* again?' Her preference was for those relationship-based European films where terse sexual encounters and awkwardly slow discussions fill three hours before everyone dies in a random car crash. I was more into horrors and comedies, which was why we rarely watched films together.

As Emily poured the wine and I clicked play I knew we were heading for an intense experience. I'd seen this film before, when I was a twenty-five-year-old party-loving singleton living in London with my flatmate, Jason, a man who would happily watch a nine-hour holocaust documentary as entertainment. It was Mike who introduced me to Jason. They had been flatmates in St Andrews in 1995, when I travelled up from Sheffield to visit. The station was outside the town and Mike was on his way back from a training exercise, so Jason picked me up in his car and drove me to Castlegate, where we waited for Mike, drinking bottles of wine and smoking crumbly hashish. That was the night we climbed over the railings into the castle, as was customary when a visitor came, and Mike duly scaled the walls to show me what he was made of. 'He's always doing this,' muttered an unimpressed Jason, 'it's madness.'

Moving into a flat in London with Jason four years later continued my connection with Mike beyond his passing, for it felt like a maturation of a relationship he had instigated, that would never have existed without him. A legacy of sorts. Mike would have been amused and delighted by our co-habitation, albeit pissed off that he missed the fun. Or perhaps if that fateful night hadn't occurred then Jason, Mike and I might have lived together in London. Mike might have blown his opportunity to join the army, or more likely blown one of his toes off in some reckless rifle jape and been thrown onto Civvy Street with the rest of us.

Might have, but didn't.

Instead it was just me who was forced by Jason to watch *Scenes from a Marriage*. It was like spying on the lives of aliens from another dimension. Who were these embittered old Swedes with terrible dress sense and chintzy furnishings? Why should I care about their middle-aged marriage problems? This would never be my life. Never. But on this evening in Hastings it couldn't have been more apposite. When the couple appeared at the opening of the film, sat together on a sofa being interviewed, he was forty-two and she was thirty-five, as were Emily and I, who were similarly sat on a sofa watching them. The protagonists also had two daughters, although these offspring remained unseen throughout the film. Bergman made the directorial choice to discard conversations about wider life issues and telescope on the relationship between the two people only. In this artfully edited reality their conversations concerned only themselves in relation to each other. An understandable decision. The complexities of a relationship are vast enough to cram into three hours of screen time, never mind wrangles about children, work, money and health. A piece of fiction cannot depict life in all its intricacies. It is woefully inadequate. But we must make do.

Emily seemed edgy as she sipped her wine on the other end of the sofa. The dog lay between us like a safety barrier. On screen, the married couple were being interviewed for a magazine about their successful ten-year relationship, but their responses were forced and strained. Emily and I had undergone something similar when her interior design for our Hackney flat was photographed for a magazine. The crazy psychedelic orange and black designs were, according to the eventual write-up, an expression of our *sense of fun*. At the time, we were horrifically sleep deprived because our second daughter had colic and screamed day and night. Emily was angry with me because my solution to this problem was to escape from my responsibilities into the landscape of the marshes. Neither of us was coping well. Yet there we were, beaming on a leather sofa, fat with congratulatory chocolates.

As *Scenes from a Marriage* progressed, we saw the husband leave his wife for a twenty-three-year-old woman. When he admitted his affair, he claimed that he didn't love his wife and hadn't for years. At that moment, Emily glanced at me with an expression I couldn't fathom, her lips opening as if to say something, a tear in her eye. Our hands were grasped around the dog's fur, holding on to something warm, but not to each other. Suddenly I felt like leaving the room. There was something ominous about this fiction unfurling on the TV screen, filmed in the year of my birth, 1973, describing cataclysmic emotional events in a relationship between two people who were very like us: the man failing in his literary ambitions, expressing despair and nihilism; the woman smarter, pragmatic, looking to the future. Both were emotional illiterates, feeling their way through the unknown, failing to communicate, misreading the love that was there, buried deep between them.

Was this happening to us? Until this moment it had never occurred to me that there might be something wrong. That my marriage wasn't safe. That the tide could go out as quickly as it came in. But I didn't say anything. We sat there for the duration, our breathing shallow, eyes fixed on the screen, not daring to turn them upon each other in case we glimpsed an inconvenient truth. Better to stay focussed on the lies of the screen. Better escaping into the stories of others.

What a stupid bloody choice of film.

We should have watched *The Evil Dead*.

*

That summer the house was invaded by bluebottles. One or two at first, then dozens circling our bedroom at night. I couldn't work out where they were coming from. In the morning, we'd come downstairs to see them seething on the windows, blocking out the light, and I'd go at them with a spray can, until there were dozens of twitching bodies on the floor. Days passed with no sign of their origin. A rotting animal in the cellar, perhaps? But there was nothing there, only our accumulated fragments of furniture, half-used paint pots and planks of wood. We decided to try the loft in the ceiling of the girls' bedroom. As Emily opened the hatch a shower of black confetti fluttered down into the room, catching in her hair and littering the carpet. They were dead bluebottles, brittle and paper-dry. For a moment, a haunted look came over her face. It was rare to see her that vulnerable. I wanted to go to her, hold her, but disgust at the corpses in her hair stopped me. With swift efficiency, Emily swiped them away, drew down the ladder and clambered into the darkness.

I remained in the room, staring up at the ceiling, listening to her shift about among our junk. 'They all seem to be dead,' she called down. 'I can't smell anything. Have we ever been to the back of the loft? It's quite interesting really, I didn't realise it went to here ...'

I tracked her movements as she padded across the walk-boards, listening to her muffled words. Then she fell silent. Minutes passed without a sound.

'Emily?' I called once, then twice. Nothing.

The little Minnie Mouse clock on the mantelpiece tick-tocked. I began to panic a little. It was strange to feel dread in the room where I read *Where the Wild Things Are* to the girls, their pyjamas laid out, wisps of Matey bubble bath in their hair, in the days before they started reading their own books and asking me to get the hell out of their room.

What happened to those tiny children? Not so long ago, Emily and I had two babies, soft burbling creatures who we coochie-cooed at adoringly. Then those babies were gone, replaced by two screechy toddlers. Just as we were getting used to them, they were replaced by manic tweens who would soon turn into surly young adults. The idea of losing your baby is the worst kind of tragedy and yet to raise a child you must suffer a succession of losses. You can never mourn those leaps of consciousness nor weep over those skins which are shed. It's all in the name of progress. But then there's the horror of losing a child when he or she is an adult, a loss for which there can be no replacement, no next stage. It is final and permanent. For Mike's mum and dad his passing must have been like the end of time. That's what

I realised only now, as a father. I was appalled by the hurt which Mike and I had caused.

After a while I heard footsteps. Emily emerged through the hatch, holding something that looked like a lump of lava, brown and peppered with tiny holes. Nails protruded from its surface.

'I think it might be a heart,' she said quietly. 'Mummified – maybe. Or something. I hope it's a model. God …'

I felt sick. 'What the hell was it doing up there?'

'It was tucked away in a wall cavity near the chimney breast. I could point my torch right down, right down the side of the house, all the way down.'

As Emily solemnly took the heart downstairs I gazed into the darkness of the loft hatch, half-expecting yellow goblin eyes to blink back at me. Then I grabbed the hook and slammed it shut. We didn't talk about it again.

We didn't really talk much at all after that.

XIX

Flotsam

Summer was followed by an unseasonably warm autumn. The hills of the South Sussex Downs were dry enough for a dropped fag to enflame. The gorse became touchpaper. Scorch marks streaked Mount Idle. The ground was hard as bone, littered with mummified dog shits. It seemed the weather would never break.

One afternoon, elongated clouds like alien spaceships amassed over the Channel, with bulbous turrets and a metallic sheen. Slowly they moved towards the coast, sucking electricity from the sea and dousing the land with water. Thunder rocked the night. Spiralling holes opened up in the sky and lightning lasered the church spires of St Leonards, Hastings and Rye. Crimson fire crackled between the pylons of Dungeness. Above the grave of Old Winchelsea, the sea was whipped into a frenzy as biblical rains returned. It terrified me. For should Dungeness suffer the same fate, the bones of its reactors would burn for an eternity.

Day after day, the water kept falling until the baked mud became rivers. The path from East Hill into Ecclesbourne buckled and sank into itself, wooden steps and fence-posts crushed together higgledy-piggledy like a bulldozed cemetery, the whole mass swirling down a slope towards the sea. There was no scrambling that route any more. Not that I wanted to go to East Hill in the aftermath. The mud was knee-deep. Nowhere was safe. Even the path to Old Roar Gill was blocked by tree-fall. Every night the overflow pipes in our street gushed raucously, like that famed waterfall must once have done.

The only thing I wanted to do was get out of the house and walk, and the rain wasn't going to stop me. On damp afternoons I stuck to tarmac in the Old Town, photographing memorial benches. It was vampiric, this feeding off other people's memories, making digital copies of reality to manipulate for my own benefit. But it had been years since my debut book came out and I was getting desperate to create something exciting, something better than the last, and by hook or by crook I was going to dig up the raw material. Really, I was little better than Charles Dawson. But I couldn't help myself.

On the Stade, bedraggled workers in overalls hauled lobster pots into piles. Tractors dragged boats up the shingle after beleaguered nights out. Equipment was heaped under blue tarpaulin. Cigarette smoke coiled from hut doorways. On the wall outside the Fishermen's Museum, four plaques were testimony to the dangers of storms which had come before:

In Memory of Boy Ashore
JIMMY READ
Killed Tragically
In the Hurricane of
16th November 1987

In Memory of Hastings Fisherman
DARREN FOX
Lost at Sea
2nd February 1998
Aged 23

In Memory of Hastings Fisherman
RUSSELL STEWART
Who died tragically
6th November 1998
Aged 25

In memory of

STEVE WEATHERALL

Fisherman

Lost at Sea 21-3-2000

Aged 37

The memorials were positioned where fishermen passed every day on their way to work, facing peril to catch cod, plaice and sole. Despite the museum pieces inside, this was still a working fishing community. In the shadow of the newly-constructed Jerwood Gallery a line of shacks sold the latest catch every morning. Above one a UKIP flag flapped. Above another flew the Jolly Roger. Some of the shacks had white lettering painted on the sides:

I walked to the furthest edge of the Stade fishing beach and stood by the rails where the town fell into sand and stone, broken cliffs stretching east to Dungeness, and listened for a while to the sea endlessly taking things out and pushing them back in again. I thought about how on a Sunday morning in December 1881 a storm drove a German sailing brig called the *Sagitta* onto the rocks in Fairlight Cove, just beyond this headland. The crew scrambled into a rowing boat, but halfway to shore they realised their captain was missing. As they turned back, a wave capsized the boat. One crew member spluttered ashore but coastguards had to wait until the storm abated to search for other survivors. There were none. The captain and two crew members were found dead amidst the wreckage. The body of the remaining sailor was delivered onto the beach at Pett Level on the Monday, along with the contents of the *Sagitta*. Boxes of rifles lay smashed in rock pools. Wooden toys littered the beach. Casks of ale and perfume bottles rolled in the surf.

Locals began to drift onto the coast to sift through the booty. Among them was a gang of teenage friends from the Old Town who heard tell of the spill and wasted no time in marching up East Hill to get their hands on some free booze. At the coastguard cottages by the cliffs, they called on their friend Alma. She was always good for an adventure, said Harry Benton, though his best friend Walter Adams said it was because he loved her, he loved her, he la-la-la-la laaaaaaaaaarved her.

'That's true as the day is blue,' sang little Sammy, the youngest at fourteen.

'Shut your sauce box or I'll bash your arse,' laughed Alma.

They stopped for a break at Lovers' Seat, a sandstone crag on a high peak overlooking the sea, sheltered by a slab of rock jutting from the hill. They came here often to laugh at couples declaring their love—'kissy kissy kissy, up your drawers!' they'd yell from behind a bush.

There was a legend behind the name Lovers' Seat. A

romance depicted in poems and paintings. The story went that a woman known as Elizabeth Boys was forbidden by her parents to marry Charles Lamb, a naval captain. Undeterred, they rendezvoused in secret at what was to become known as Lovers' Seat whenever Lamb's ship was moored nearby. Their love deepened. Eventually they ran away to London to be married and were happy ever after.

'That's utter nonsense,' snapped Alma, slapping Sammy round the head. 'That's not the true story you dolt. Elizabeth Boys did *not* marry him. Truth be told is that silly Mr Charles Lamb was a-feared to anger her father with a marriage proposal and turned coward. He abandoned Elizabeth to a life of boredom, so as he could live on the high seas with only buggery to get him through the nights.'

'Eeew,' said Sammy.

'Yes, yes, yes,' said Alma. 'Then one day, stricken with grief, poor Elizabeth came to Lovers' Seat and saw his ship passing. That was when she flung herself into the ocean—from this very spot—and was swallowed by an eel the size of a schooner! The END!'

Sammy looked sulky as Harry and Walter guffawed. They were always laughing like that when Alma was around, like it was a competition. And besides, if Alma's version were true and the Lovers' Seat spelled unhappiness, why did lovers come here to get engaged? Anyway, they might pretend that romance was soppy but he'd seen Harry and Alma *doing the bear* by the Black Arches up Mount Idle.

By the time the gang reached Fairlight Cove where the ship was wrecked it was as if cargo had rained from the sky. The surf was awash with flotsam. A couple of Hastings fishermen hauled barrels onto their shoulders. Some ne'er-do-wells snatched rifles from a shattered crate, bickering over who got what. For a moment, Harry got a dose of the morbs at the thought of the sailors who died. His uncle had gone down with his fishing boat not two years previously. But Alma said there was no time to mope, for her father was probably around somewhere. He worked as a coastguard and had warned her not to come down. The coastguards were duty-bound to protect the cargo from looting and would be here soon. They grabbed what they could. It wasn't easy to tell what was in the bottles, so they threw any old thing into a cloth sack and headed across the rocks.

On the hillside near the Lovers' Seat they found a clearing in the bushes, safe from the view of any passer-by, and uncorked the first bottle. Dear Lord, some of it was foul stuff indeed. Soon they were roaring drunk and couldn't feel the cold at all, racing each other up and down the hill, tumbling and fumbling. They played dares, who could go nearest the edge. Walter fancied himself a climber. He went down beneath the ledge while the rest weren't looking and hung by his fingertips, flat against the rock. He laughed as he heard them crying out his name. They peered down to try and catch him but he was clung to stone like a limpet so all they could see was rocks and sand. Then with a roar he hoisted himself into view, delighted with Alma's worried expression and the way it made Harry look foolish.

Another bottle cracked open. This one was smaller than the others, blue glass, with contents like fiery lemons with flowery scents that burned the nose. They dared each other to drink it. As soon as it hit Sammy's tongue it came spraying out as if from a whale's blowhole. Instantly he fell to vomiting into the bushes.

Alma refused. 'That's not liquor you buffoons.'

'Course it is!' cried Walter. 'Girls can't take the strong booze, that's all!' He held his nose and glugged it back, trying not to weep for the stinging. It was as if all the moisture in his gullet was evaporating.

'Give me that! I'll show you how it's done.' Harry snatched the bottle, opened his mouth and let the liquid pour down his throat. Afterwards he roared like a lion, thumping his chest and dancing a jig. Alma laughed, which would have pleased him but for the burning, the burning, oh, the burning. All the moisture evaporated from his gullet, heat blistering inside him. Soon it wasn't only him on fire, but the gorse on the hill which burst into blame and belched purple smoke until that it became hard to breathe or see much that wasn't directly in front of his face. The flames turned frosty, suddenly, and hardened, refracting light like shards of ice. A cool wind blew through them, chilling his bones, making his teeth chatter.

None of this could be real. It must have been something in the drink, perhaps Alma was right and this was not liquor.

Walter was in front of him now, beetroot in colour, saying something, but his words were out of time with his lips and seemed to Harry more of a scent than a noise. Blue words, pink words, yellow words, they blossomed and bloomed. It was like nothing he'd experienced in his life before. Elatedly he grabbed Walter and whirled him around. Alma clapped her hands, 'You two kiss!' Then she began to dance widdershins around them, contrary to their spinning, so they all wheeled in counter-orbits, generating their own energy, lifting into the air like spinning dandelion spores until they were high above the bitten cliffs and the hard, grey wintry sea. Harry could see himself and the others below, as if he was in someone else's dream. Then the centre lost hold, and everything came apart, all those sounds, smells and colours fluttering away like leaves, and a sensation of falling.

When he came to, he felt vomit on his chin. Wet grass on his knees. Why was he on his knees? It was hard to see anything, his vision was wobbly, but he could make out Sammy walking in a meandering line through the sheep field towards the hill's brow. Sammy! Sammy! Sammy! Close by he could hear Alma singing that nursery rhyme she liked so much:

There was an old woman,
Her name it was Peg;
Her head was of wood and
She wore a cork leg.
The neighbours all pitched
Her into the water,
Her leg was drowned first,
And her head followed after.

Her voice grew fainter, farther away and smaller, smaller, smaller, as if she was disappearing down a long tunnel. He waved his arms frantically, hoping to catch hold of her. But she was gone. Harry shivered. Cold, cold, cold. Where was Walter? He called his name, 'Walter Adams, Walter Adams!' but it came out like a gull's cry, 'Gwwwwwarrrrrkkkk aaarrrrk, gwwwwwwaaarrrrrrrk, aaaaaarkkkk.' Next thing he knew, someone picked him up off his knees and he was running again, aware of Walter beside him, drunk and angry. His vision cleared a little. He could see Lovers' Seat ahead, framed against the dimming sky. It must be late afternoon. He had no idea where the time had gone.

They stopped, panting, on the ledge, the viewing bench below them. In between breaths Walter slurred something about Alma. 'You only care for her … the restshhh … the rests … oh to hell! My damned tongue … the rest … ha ha! Got it! … the rest of us can go to hell … she's playing you for a fool.'

Harry tried to focus hard on his friend's face, blurring ghostly before him. 'What rot!'

'She's a skilamalink!' said Walter.

'I don't feel well. I think we should go home now, the cold is awful biting … can you not feel it, Walter?'

Walter swayed, eyes rolling. '… Skilamalink!'

'Please … I can barely think … what is happening to us?'

The two friends circled each other on the stone, the sky darkening at speed, as if they were turning the wheel of time.

Walter's words came thick and heavy. 'You've abandoned … the lads.'

'Oh, no more, for the love of God.'

'For a girl, Harry … for a dirty wench!'

'Stick it up your arse,' said Harry.

Walter swung a fist at Harry's stomach, but he was so disorientated that he missed, staggering towards the edge of Lovers' Seat, only just righting himself in time.

'Enough of this!' Harry cried. 'I'm going home!' He walked away across the hill in what he hoped was the direction of Hastings, feeling weaker with each step. When he looked back, Walter was gone.

'Righto,' he cried out. 'You go and play your silly climbing games!'

No doubt Walter's intention was to surprise him by leaping out from under a rock, or some such prank. Well, he would not give him the satisfaction, the dolt!

But he wasn't sure. Despite himself, Harry went back to Lovers' Seat where Walter had been standing.

'Walter?' He peered down. If he had fallen off the edge he would be somewhere directly below, near the viewing bench, but there was no sign. He hoped his friend would reappear shortly, grinning from behind a bush, but he heard nothing but waves and the cry of gulls. Harry sat and waited. It would be easier to get home drunkenly in the dark as a duo. A pair of best friends. There was only so long Walter could play this foolish joke before he gave in. It was very cold, but would keep waiting until Walter came back up from the cliff. It was dark, very dark, but somehow he would make it home as long as Walter was with him.

You wait here, Harry, he's going to come back any minute. Walter's a good climber. Wait just a little longer.

He will be back. You wait and see.

He's always climbing and playing tricks. That's what he is like.

It's what makes him who he is, and with a bit of patience, you'll see him soon. Nothing bad can happen.

Mike is always climbing.

Mike is your friend.

Mike will be back.

You just have to wait, Gareth.

You'll see.

Mike will come back.

*

The next day they found Harry Benton's body on the hill near Lovers' Seat. He had died from exposure overnight. Walter Adams was never found. They presumed his body was washed out to sea.

In the Old Town, the people mourned for their foolhardy young.

XX

Lair of the Limpet

Harry Benton, Walter Adams, Mike and I, we were nothing unusual. So many stories have ended on the coast. Death by falling, drowning, suicide. People swept off boat decks and harbour walls, carried away by deadly currents. Really, we should stay well away from it. But the coast has a strange torsion. Families and friends swarm to these perilous outcrops every weekend, hungry to make new memories.

This was what it was like in St Andrews, where Mike and I lived opposite the castle. All year round, visitors strolled past our house on their way to the cathedral, stopping to take photographs, descending to the beach with blankets and flasks. In the road outside were the tiled initials 'GW', commemorating the spot where the Protestant preacher George Wishart was burned at the stake in 1564 for heresy.

Afterwards, Wishart's grieving allies snuck into the castle to seek revenge on Cardinal David Beaton, the man who ordered his death, and hung his corpse from the battlements.

The scene of Mike's tragedy had been a historical place of memorial for over five hundred years, so on the morning his body was found, when the police cars had gone, we were left with springtime tourists taking photographs, all smiles and thumbs-up, right where we had clambered over the railings the previous night with a bottle of whisky. Giggling children looked for crabs in the rock pools where Mike had lain only hours before. A Labrador splashed in the waves that had delivered him home. It was as if nothing bad had happened. And, of course, for them nothing significant had happened. They existed in that blissful world I'd known until that morning, before I was hurled into a parallel universe where there was no laughter, no light, no Mike. From the window I watched them, seething with envy.

At the edge of the Stade in Hastings, looking towards the cliffs of East Hill, I wondered if I was doing the same thing, obliviously gazing upon the sight of someone's worst nightmare. Bearing in mind Hastings' thousand-year history, most probably. An old winch drum could have been from a wrecked fishing boat. That plastic bottle, the last thing held to the lips of a drowned woman. A rusted metal bar, a remnant of a car that careered over the edge. The low-tide landscape reeked of catastrophe. I could still make out that statuesque rock shape I'd seen in the cliff face after the landslip in 2014. It had become even more humanoid in passing years. The wind continued the work the waters left unfinished, scouring the rough edges. The figure's back was flat against the rock, its torso rounded and bulbous with head on top, its face shorn of features, like an eroded Sphinx. It watched over an ancient domain beneath the sea, once a mighty forest through which a great river flowed and the monoliths of forgotten civilisations poked above the trees.

Why had nobody else seen this? Then again, why had I not shared my vision with anyone else? Perhaps everybody in the town was pretending not to see the statue and I was complicit in a cult of silence. A mass looking-away from the truth that John Coussens was trying to tell us with his Black Arches: that dark forces lurked behind the paper-thin membrane of reality on this exposed edge of Britain, this weak spot in the nation's facade, where William the Conqueror chose to invade, where television was born, and where Crowleyist witches gathered in ceremonies to usher in the Age of Horus, that transformation of humankind into gods through cataclysm and renewal. It was working too. Winter by winter, the seas were peeling back the cliffs, unleashing memories of climate disaster and invasion, chaos and upheaval. History had come full circle. A great ecological reckoning was ahead and Hastings was to be its locus. Yet people here were too busy drinking craft ales and eating prawns to notice.

Below the cliff, a woman watched her Yorkshire terrier skitter among the rock pools, unaware of the threat. Freshly exposed algae steamed in the sunshine. The sea was calm, biding its time before the next uprising. In the far distance, Dungeness Power Station shimmered like Avalon on a bed of radioactive mist. I felt a great yearning to go there. Not by car or foot but at the helm of a dragon-headed longship. Once landed I would go beyond the pylons to the wide sand flats at the end of the world, where there would be nothing but a rim of sea between me and outer space, and I wouldn't have to worry about any of this.

Soon, soon.

I walked beneath the row of fishing boats drying on their shingle shelf. Fish heads and crab claws littered the trenches left by keels dragged up from the sea. Gulls fought over a dogfish in a stringy tug of war. The surf had left a dead seabird on the sand, a crashed Icarus. The tide was low enough for me to access the farthest end of the harbour arm, the only surviving effort after centuries of failed attempts.

It was incomplete, formed from a few hundred metres of stone wall running through shingle, kinked where it hit the water, then a missing section filled in with lumps of stone. Its terminus, a detached block of concrete covered in barnacles, loomed in the shallows like a fossilised container ship.

Up close I saw that the wall was made from a rough concrete of pebbles and shells coated in a living layer of seaweed, molluscs and green slime. I followed the surface inch by inch, pushing my face close. I could see now that the wall was moving. Tiny crabs scuttled through a forest of mussels spread towards the sky in the black and brown hues of a Scottish mountain, where Mark and Mike huddled in a tent, teeth chattering with the cold, telling jokes to keep each other conscious, Mike doing his Hugh Grant impressions and singing Billy Bragg songs. They were both so tiny and innocent, unaware of their place in someone else's memory, a bundle of synapses firing in a middle-aged man's brain.

The longer I dwelled by the wall, the vaster it seemed, the more complex its layering and detail. Barnacles clustered over whelks squeezed within a hegemony of mussels. Water leached from cracks, glistering on feathery fronds hung from the mouths of molluscs. The seething mass lured me in, the fishing boats receding behind me as the wall became the world. I no longer heard quarrelling gulls but the trickle of infinitesimal subterranean streams and the creak of calcium carbonate. The patter of tiny feet. The exhalations of algae. The clenching of muscles against the wind.

I began to explore the wall in centimetre increments, scratching my fingers on the blistered tops of barnacles, like extinct volcanos, until I came upon a shiny black ball bulging from a mass of shells. I couldn't tell whether it was liquid or solid. What the hell was it? I stared at myself in its shark-eye mirror, horrified. I fled across the gap in the harbour arm, filled with pillars and A-shaped blocks, like the remnants of a Roman temple dumped on the shingle, to where a new stretch of wall began, its upper section made from smooth concrete, devoid of life, and a lower half made from that rough mix to which the beasts loved to cling. Keeping my face close and looking up I beheld a plain of pyramidal structures. I was in the lair of the limpets, hermaphrodite pharaohs of the overhang, permanent as stone, oozing trails of spunky sludge. At the sight of them I bowed down in admiration. They began life as male plankton spinning in the current until they clamped onto an area of rock known as their home scar, a rivet where they could grow hard and strong. At high tide, they moved in search for food but they always returned to their home scar when the waters turned, following their own mucus trail. In later life, they turned into females but it made no difference. They were defined not by their fluid identity but by their sense of place, and for that I envied them. At low tide, these regal snails remained clamped to the overhangs while gnats and sea slaters cruised the steaming crevices below.

Further up the wall, ribs of orange iron protruded from the crazy mass of pebbles and shells. Little bolts and rivets stuck out from the concrete. It was as if there had been a cataclysm in which the entire Stade – its workshops, shingle, shellfish and boats – had erupted like lava and cooled into this mutant morass. I half expected to find human teeth and jawbones sticking out. Actually, if I looked closely I –

A sound, suddenly. Then another.

Smash – smash – smash.

I turned in surprise to see little pockets of shingle exploding behind me. *Smash – smash – smash.* Large pebbles were raining down on the beach. Then laughter. A voice cried 'Walt! Walt! Watch this!' There was cheer as a stone narrowly missed a gull. I was about to move out from beneath the wall when something gripped my leg. In terror I watched a hand, warty with barnacles, push from the slimy mortar and coil its fingers around my jeans. At that moment, a massive stone slab crunched into the beach, right in front of me. I yelled out, looking towards the top of the wall for my attacker. I heard footsteps and laughter. 'Whoa Harry, mental!' When I looked down again, there was nothing holding my leg. I ran from the wall towards the fishing boats. When I turned, I saw a line of four teenagers ranging along the wall with bags of booze, hurling stones ahead without any care for what was beneath.

A girl led from the front, a boy calling out, 'Alma, did you see that, Alma?' and another punching his arm and saying, 'Sam you cunt, where are the skins?' The boy at the back pointed at me, laughing, then hurried to catch up with the others, jostling to be closest to the girl. As they reached the temple fragments between sections of wall, they hunkered down and stared across Pelham Beach towards the pier, watching for trouble. Far beneath them, the limpets and their subjects seemed vulnerable in a landscape exposed to air twice a day. A life spent clinging to the edge at the mercy of human gods. That is, if we were truly such, and it was not they who were the deities.

As my racing heart slowed, I dared look down. There was no mistaking it. The ankle of my left trouser leg was ringed with slime and beaded with the impressions of anxious fingertips.

I tried my best not to scream.

XXI

The Homecoming

After the teeming microverse of the sea wall, the town centre was a strangely gargantuan place, as if I had returned from adventures on an exotic planet to find my home world alien. The Poundstretcher towered over well-trimmed municipal hedgerows. Teens drifted from McDonald's with oversized Styrofoam cups. A shopkeeper wheeled in his display of novelty hats, 'I LOVE HASTINGS' T-shirts and sunglasses with dolphins on the rims. Men smoked outside The John Logie Baird Wetherspoons. The Priory Meadow shopping centre, prisonlike with iron grilles and watchtowers, menaced pedestrians at the bottom of a Victorian passage. As shutters clattered over Debenhams' frontage the last coffee drinkers shambled from Caffè Nero, meeting the last coffee drinkers from Costa, directly opposite.

Human life was all surface. Shopfronts glassy. The pedestrianised streets a concrete lid over a shingle bank, nailed fast by bollards. Beneath my feet, water echoed the roar of Old Gill and the fizz of Iguanodon piss as it filtered through the America Ground, but nobody was listening. You needed the senses of a limpet to understand the atavistic ebb and flow, to know when to stray and when to return to your home scar.

Horribly shaken by my vision on the Stade, I followed the route of the ancient river up Queens Road, through Morrisons' car park and onto my road. Our front garden was a mound of stone and weeds. We'd always meant to do something with it, but never got around to it. Emily had tried pickaxing some of the earth to break it up, but men stopped to make jokes about women with tools, or offer unwanted advice, so she gave up and ranted about mansplainers on Facebook instead.

As I stood by the front door, noticing how the crack in the lintel had returned already, I realised I had no key. Through the bay window I saw the shapes of my daughters dance and spin. How had they got so tall? They were like bloody giraffes. Hard to believe it was my family in there at all. Was this how it would be if I wasn't here? Would things simply carry on without me – the bickering about homework, the hunt for lost shoes and the whiff of chilli on the hob? They looked happy. Like I wasn't needed. Like I'd never really been there.

Like I wasn't here now.

Pressing my hands against the cold stone sill I felt trapped on the outside, as I did that day at the Black Arches, wishing I could enter John Coussen's secret world within the hill. I'd always felt this way, a stranger yearning for acceptance. Since I was a child I'd never been able to answer succinctly the question, 'Where are you from?' I was born in a British military hospital in Germany, a patch of land rented temporarily by the MoD, neither a UK location nor, technically, German. My dad was a Welsh soldier and my mum a Scottish schoolteacher, making me half one thing and half another, with some Irish thrown into the mix thanks to my immigrant great-grandfather. When I was six months old my parents moved to Glasgow and I became one of the rootless class, living in a sequence of incrementally southern locations, from Glasgow to Manchester to Shropshire to Dover, all before I was sixteen years old. Then I travelled back up the country, to Sheffield, to St Andrews, and down again – to Cardiff, London and finally to Hastings. The end of the line.

A biology teacher once told me that he considered the digestive tract to be on the *outside* of the body. In the same way that you could drive through a tunnel in a mountain without ever being inside the rock, a morsel of food could pass through you without truly entering you. It was only those nutrients absorbed through the stomach into the blood that were ever really *inside*. I don't know if he was teasing me, or plain wrong, but the idea stuck. That was my life summed up. I was a plastic bag of coke slipping towards the anus of a drug mule. Down, down I travelled, through the topography of Britain, always moving, never absorbed. A similar thing was true of our time in this house. Emily and I had lived temporarily in its cavernous guts but we'd never entered its lymphatic system, its pulsing network of wires, laths and pipes. Only its builder, Mr Marsden understood the secrets of its hidden recesses. He was the gatekeeper of its soul, sending his diabolical avian agents through the chimney to torment us with our transience.

Come to think of it, beyond the books, protest songs and scatological jokes this was what Mike and I had most in common. We went to a hilltop school that bore no relation to the rest of British society, a temporal community exiled on the edge of England. On a quantum level, it did not exist when we were not there and, whenever we looked at it, the place changed. When Mike and I hitchhiked from Sheffield to visit the school in Dover it was like entering our home town to find it populated by strangers. The place had been the people, and the people had since been scattered to the winds. Only the walls of the buildings remained, and they had never been ours, no matter how much Mike tried to scale them after dark and subvert them with his poems and cones.

My hand hovered over the doorbell. How could I go in there and explain what was happening to me? This confusion. This sense of detachment. Really, all I wanted to do was run away and keep running. I felt a yearning to rise through the Old Town, past the Minnis Rock and up East Hill. I wanted to stand on that highest point by the gorse on St George's Churchyard and gaze upon the widest possible ocean, see the fishing boats go out and my beloved mutant armchair-headed eels gambol in the spray. That's where I belonged—*on the way to somewhere*. I wanted to walk to Fairlight, like John Logie Baird, then go further, through the drowned forest of Pett Level, the marooned hillock of Winchelsea and the silted harbour of Rye. With the sun on my back I'd follow the longshore drift, churning up my past and leaving new forms behind me, destroying and creating, destroying and creating. There would be no stopping me. I'd leave Sussex for the great Kentish beyond, where I'd stride without obstacle across the desert of Dungeness and onto the sands of infinity, where at last I could let everything fall away.

One day, one day.

But not yet.

Feeling strangely nervous, I pressed the doorbell. The sound was faint, as if it was ringing in a parallel universe.

PART THREE

Departure

'For as this appalling ocean surrounds the verdant land, so in the soul of man there lies one insular Tahiti, full of peace and joy, but encompassed by all the horrors of the half-known life. God keep thee! Push not off from that isle, thou canst never return!'

Herman Melville, *Moby Dick*

XXII

Between Floors

Months passed and slowly some semblance of a family home came into being. Habitable rooms emerged from the grime, painted in the lilacs, peaches, greys and blacks that Emily liked. But there were still rooms of crumbled plaster and ragged wood, piles of junk on the front lawn and a rampaging jungle behind us. Eventually we ran out of money and everything stopped. There was no more help from Alejandro and Marcella. Emily became sullen and depressed, staring constantly at her phone as she hunted for work to help pay the bills. Logically we knew that finishing it could take another year or two, but we had only my freelance earnings and half an aborted book about Dawson, Crowley and Baird that I had no idea how to finish.

Each morning I took my daughters to school, passing

the stopped clock in the church tower, the same old faces at the school gates. The zebra crossing still unnerved me. It reminded me not only of the lollipop lady but of something from long ago, related to Mike, but I couldn't remember why or how a zebra crossing featured. After the girls were safely in the hands of the state I would write for a while then take the dog up the West Hill if I felt well enough. I was still in a lot of groin pain from sitting, lying down for too long, or walking too much. I had to vacillate between these states of being to dodge the discomfort, like changing positions in bed during a restless night. I took the hot baths as the urologist prescribed, and tried to get on with life.

I'd started to visit a new wine shop on Robertson Street in the old America Ground, where I'd befriended the owner, The Writer. I'd met him at a literary gig in London when I was reading pieces from my moderately successful book about Hackney Marshes, when I was under the impression there was a future for me writing about landscapes. That book had described a time shortly after Emily and I had two babies in quick succession, when I used to escape into the urban wilderness, roaming canals and football pitches, foraging for detritus beneath electricity pylons. The Writer had a similar obsession with place that formed the backbone of his two novels and documentary series for the BBC. But he and his girlfriend Jess had a new baby and a business selling wine, beer and books. Their shop had shelves full of beautifully crafted landscape works by authors who, unlike me, somehow managed to stick to the subject and get the job done: W. G. Sebald, Rebecca Solnit, Iain Sinclair. There were also books about Aleister Crowley, including one that The Writer kept at his home, a rare hardback account of Crowley's time in Netherwood by Antony Clayton, worth an eye-watering £120.

The Writer was generous and convivial, with a twinkle in his eyes and always a glass of something expensive on the go. He spoke with a Hartlepool drawl but he was a DFL, Down From London, just like I had been three years previously. Other drifters would come to the shop and we'd drink into the late afternoons and evenings and for a while I believed I had achieved a tentative form of stasis. A life lived largely in the present without flashbacks or flash-forwards.

Then the rat came to our house.

*

I could tell it was a rat from the volume of the gnawing. *Gnrrrk. Krrrrrrrrk. Gnnnrk. Krrrrk.* At night-time it skittered beneath the floorboards, back and forth, back and forth, like it was building something.

Emily tried to trace the rodent's route through the house. She reckoned it was coming up from the cellar through the cavities in the stairs, scampering beneath our bedroom and dropping down behind the kitchen cupboards. A pest controller came to lay down traps of poisonous sweets. Emily asked him if the rat would die inside the house. He smiled condescendingly. 'No love, you have to understand this about a rat. It'll find its way out and die in its nest, that's what they do.'

He was wrong. Within a couple of days, a rotten stench permeated our home. I suggested we get the pest controller back to search for its corpse, as this was his fault, but she pulled a face. 'There's no need. We can find it. This is our home and we know it better than anyone.' I wasn't sure Mr Marsden agreed with that. It was entirely possible that he was responsible for the rat, and the bluebottles, and the demented gulls, and Christ knows what else.

'Well I'm not doing it,' I said.

'No surprise there,' said Emily. 'You've never helped.'

'That's not fair. I've done things. Here and there. For instance ... I ... we painted the bedroom together.'

'No,' Emily looked at me with an expression I'd never seen before. A nothingness, as if all the emotion had drained from her. 'Actually, I brought in that decorator to help.

Remember? The Greek guy who turned up on a wobbly bike with a trailer?'

'I – don't –'

'He painted the whole lot. Well we thought so when we gave him the money – but then we discovered that he didn't bother moving the bed or radiator, he just painted around it. Did a terrible job. You were furious … you don't remember this?'

'No, I can't quite –'

'You came in after you'd been writing and yelled at me for hiring a shit decorator. You said it was all my fault and you weren't going to fucking do it and even when I started crying you said I had to sort it out, then you stormed off.'

'Was it … like that? I don't remember that.'

'I was up painting 'til midnight, crying my eyes out.'

'That wasn't me …'

'Who was it then?' said Emily. There was no glint in her eye. No giveaway twitch at the corner of her mouth. She was deadly serious. 'Someone who was not you – but looked like you – pretending to be you?'

I tried to think back. Suddenly I did remember the Greek guy and his wobbly bike, vaguely at least. Not his face but his general Greek-ness, and there being a trailer. Yes, yes, and I was really outraged by his shoddy work. He made a right pig's ear of it. God, I'd blocked the whole episode out of my mind. Emily telling it back to me, it felt like someone else's story. But it was mine. I knew that now. That was me shouting, being a bastard. That's the problem with memory. It's all about the edit. It's all about who tells the tale.

I wondered if that made me a liar or not. Recently I'd been reading about how Hastings was the birthplace of Grey Owl, the conservationist and writer, whom everybody believed was a North American indigenous native. He claimed to have an Apache mother who met his Scottish father while touring with Wild Bill Hickok's Western show. He penned books urging humankind to reconsider its relationship with nature, touring Canada and Britain, raising money for his causes. But after his death in 1938 it was discovered that he was Archibald Belaney, an English solicitor's son who grew up on St Mary's Terrace on West Hill. His identity was a fiction. Did this make his work any less true or useful? Perhaps his origin myth was necessary for him to get closer to nature, to spread his message to the world. Perhaps he simply couldn't write as himself. Perhaps lies allowed him to express the truth.

He was less of a fraud than the St Leonards taxidermist George Bristow, who shot, stuffed and sold an extraordinary number of rare birds between 1892 and 1930. They included the Glossy Ibis, Slender-Billed Curlew, Little Bittern, Ferruginous Duck, Sociable Plover and Ivory Gull. All killed within a twenty-mile radius of Hastings. Except that they weren't. Bristow imported frozen pre-shot birds from far-flung continents, then paid hunters to claim they'd done the job, intermingling their accounts with those of invented hunters returned from non-existent trips to places like Rye and Romney. He died an ornithological legend, but in the 1960s his scam was exposed and his finds dropped from the register of British birds. It was no coincidence that he was acquainted with fellow fame-hunter Charles Dawson, the rarities appearing as Dawson was commencing his archaeological manipulations, the two men most probably in cahoots.

Of course, the wheels of time kept turning, and thanks to the warming climate most of Bristow's phony specimens were eventually spotted in Britain and re-admitted to the register of British birds.

He faked something that later turned out to be true.

*

After months of despondence, Emily had been revitalised by the rat. She looked for its corpse with dedication, like Ahab hunting the white whale. To pinpoint the location of its demise she drafted a detailed floor-plan, concentrating on the spaces within the floors, wall cavities and cellar. Then she started to work through her map of the house within the house, peeling back its skin to expose the flesh. Aghast, I watched her wrecking much of the DIY she'd done since we moved in. It was as if she enjoyed the deconstruction of everything we'd achieved. Floor by floor she probed its nooks, looked up the chimney breast, crowbarred up the floorboards and slid beneath them, clutching a torch in her teeth. 'It's surprisingly deep!' she cried, as if this was exciting and not totally mortifying. I stared at the dust-encrusted pipes, trying to hide my revulsion. This was like watching the interior of my testicles squirm on a hospital monitor. There are some things you don't want to see.

I went to make some tea. When I returned she was no longer beneath the floorboards.

'Emily?'

'Over here!'

I was startled to hear her reply come echoing through the fireplace. I pressed my ear against the chimney breast. 'Emily, where are you?'

'I'm in the loft!'

Grumbling, I took the tea upstairs. But when I got to the kids' room, the loft hatch was closed and I could hear no movement above the ceiling.

'Where are you now?' I yelled.

'For God's sake, I'm busy. What do you want?' Her voice emanated from the opposite side of the landing, somewhere near the bathroom. Emily had become so proficient at navigating our home's peripheries she could switch floors without revealing herself.

'I have your tea. Have you found anything?'

'Lots!'

I moved slowly along the landing, trying to work out where she was, nervously asking her questions to keep her talking. As I tracked her she reported details of surprising items she had found from the house's past, her voice muffled by walls and floorboards. A bell wire from the days when servants worked in the house. A roll of pound notes in a cigar tube. A pentangle scratched into a brick. There were finds from our lives in the house too. A crayon picture shoved between the cracks in the floorboards. A gig ticket—The Fall at St Mary's in the Castle. A memory stick from a computer, cracked and obsolete.

After a while she fell silent. No scuffles or clatters. It was as if she'd lain down in the insulation foam and gone to sleep. I paced around the kitchen for a while, emptying the dishwasher and taking out the rubbish. I remembered that time when she found the heart, after the bluebottle infestation. She disappeared then too, briefly. So I was sure she would emerge soon enough—a head poking around a door, feet dangling from a hatch, a voice from the back of the airing cupboard. But hours passed and nothing. Where had she got to?

I went to our study and rifled through papers to look for Emily's floor-plan. See if I could locate her using her own map. Most of the crap in there was mine. The walls were covered in pictures of the Black Arches, Aleister Crowley, John Baird, Arthur Conan Doyle, Grey Owl and photos of myself on the cliffs, hair blowing crazily. There were arrows between the images and Post-it notes saying things like LIARS! and FAKERS! and INVENTORS! The desk was littered with coffee mugs, unpaid invoices and tattered draft printouts of my unfinished historical book about Hastings. The whole thing was a colossal failure. Nothing more than digressions and wild speculation. At best I could offer these half-baked tales at scrap value to someone else, perhaps a mystery writer, psychogeographer or comic book artist. Then I could move on.

Among this clutter I found Emily's floor-plan. Her detailing was rigorous, showing everything from the thickness of insulation materials to the routes of redundant wires beneath the floors. I used the map to follow Emily's possible trajectories through the house, rapping on the wall, gently calling her name. Sprinkles of soot fell into the fireplace, a sign that she might be in the chimney breast. I worked my way up to the loft hatch, which I opened, but couldn't bring myself to rummage among the boxes. How had we accumulated so many things in such a short space of time?

Downstairs I tried the cellar door. 'Are you down there?' I stepped into the stinking gloom, flicking the light switch. The strip light hummed, clunked and flickered but never fully came on. In sporadic flashes of light, I saw a mop handle. The frame of a bed. A stack of crates. A rack of paint pots. The floor piled with boxes and bags. I felt something touch my shoulder. Panicked, I lost my footing and fell down the steps, cracking my knee on the concrete. As I lay, bewildered, I could sense movement in the cellar, bin bags flexing, boxes rattling. Something diabolical seething towards me. I cried out in terror, scrabbling up the stairs and into the hall, panting and heaving, that old pain hammering my bladder and balls.

There was a jangle of keys in the front door. Voices.

'Emily? Is that you?'

The door swung open. A woman clutching keys and tall man with a bag walked in with two young boys. They came into the hallway and stopped right in front of me.

'Well, here we are,' said the man, dropping the bag.

'I'd almost forgotten what it looked like from the viewing,' said the woman, looking at our subsiding walls and peeling paint. 'God, it's going to need a lot of work.'

'Hello,' I said. 'What are you doing here?'

They turned their heads, but looked right through me.

'Let's show the boys their room,' said the woman.

'Yay,' shouted the boys.

I closed my eyes, hoping that the next time I looked they'd be gone and everything would go back to normal.

One ... two ... three ... four ... five ... six ... six ... six ...

I opened my eyes.

Emily was hunched down beside me with her arm on my shoulder. There was nobody else in the hall except my own children. They looked stricken.

'Are you alright?' she said.

I shook my head. These visions of mine were getting further ahead in time, and becoming frighteningly more elaborate.

Something was wrong. I knew that now.

As soon as I had recovered my senses, I rang the doctor and demanded another appointment.

XXIII

The Eye of Horus

The weekend before my MRI scan, Emily and I sat in the kitchen drinking wine. It was the only place we could escape the decaying rat, if it really was a rat at all. The odour had become mushroomy, sweet and cloying like DMT vapour. It was strongest in our hallway where the dead shore propped up the ceiling, kids' shoes scattered beneath. From there it seeped into the living room, returning the cornice I painted two years ago to the sepia of Angela's dead husband's lung effluence. The kitchen had a different smell, odourised by slime from the subterranean stream in our garden, which spread down the wall and across the yard in a slippery green film. On hot days it steamed with ozone, like that which came off the rocks at low tide, a scent I associated with Mike lying beneath the castle. But it didn't bother me so much these days. I'd grown so accustomed to the omnipresence of his memory I could no longer imagine life without it.

Emily was in an indignant mood. After the first bottle of wine, she told me she was sick of the house. Sick of living in it, never mind trying to keep it from sinking into the mire. I didn't think anything of this. She'd been saying it over and over since the failure of her rat hunt, but tonight she was really going for it, lip curled, voice belligerent and strained. It had all been a mistake, she was saying. It was too big. Too unwieldy. Too infested. And we'd run out of money to finish it. I wasn't bringing enough in from my writing. Instead I was caught up in a book about God knows what that was making me ill and taking me away from my responsibilities. She spent all her time fire-fighting structural problems instead of designing things, moving forward with her own work, which was surely the whole point of us being here. Instead we had become custodians of a derelict hotel in which the only two guests were our children, and they weren't exactly giving it the thumbs-up. Where was the Wendy house in the garden we'd promised? Where, for that matter, was the garden? The girls up the road had a trampoline. Where was their trampoline? Why were there always hammers, chisels and pots of paint outside their room? Why was there a hole in the bathroom floor?

We had no answers. This wasn't how our lives were supposed to be almost four years after London. We had tried to run away from all our stresses, but we had gone nowhere except south and there was no further to go. Hastings was the terminus. The final stop.

'Well, we still have each other,' I said, surprised at how hollow that sounded.

Emily looked at me oddly, as if searching for something in my face. Then her eyes dimmed from blue to grey to black. It was like a light went out. Just like that. It was frightening.

'Emily ... we've got each other, right?'

She drained her glass. Poured herself another one. Then slid the bottle across to me.

'I can't do this any more.'

'Do what?'

'It's just that ...' She took another slug. 'Oh, God, I didn't want to do this now.'

'Emily?'

Emily, Emily, Emily, Emily. Why did I keep repeating her name? Pull yourself together. Think of something else to say.

'This is hard ... but I don't want to lie to you ...'

'What do you mean, *lie*?' I poured out my drink, trying to smile and act casual. 'I know about lies.' I took a sip. 'They're my speciality.'

'The thing is, Gareth ...'

'Mmm?'

'I don't think I love you any more.' She said this slowly, with great deliberation. It was almost exactly how she had said it in one of my precognitive visions, along with seeing my dog fall off a cliff and my daughters drown in the bath. I already knew this script. It had been written in my head many months ago. Her words were straight out of a nightmare of my own imagination. All the same, I was shocked. I felt that same swell of panic as when I first heard the news about Mike, as if my stomach had burst and all the blood was rushing to my head. I tried to stand up but the room was spinning, breaking into shards. The ground trembled. I heard water gush beneath the floor. A sharpening of ozone. It took me back to the roar of the surf on the rocks of East Sands in St Andrews and the horror of sudden loss. To realise that in the breaking of a wave, someone I loved was gone forever and the world had irrevocably changed. Now felt like then. And then felt like now.

Pain as time travel.

It seemed an eternity that I swayed at the table, Emily staring at me with tears in her eyes, but it might have been only seconds before I reached for her hand, less out of compassion, more out of a worry she was about to slide back in her chair and vanish through the wall forever.

'Don't—don't say stuff like this, don't say it. Just because you're in a bad mood—'

'I've been feeling this a long time. Longer than you realise.'

'This is crazy. Whatever it is, I'll sort it out, I promise. It's the stress ... the house ... you know I have a scan on Monday. I'm not well—'

'I'm sorry you have to go into hospital again but what do you want me to say? You've been on the verge of dying since I met you. That's always been the way with you. You're never in the present. You're always looking past life into—God, Gareth, I don't know what it is you see or want to see—but you can't help looking over the edge. Even though it terrifies you. Even though it makes you unhappy. Makes *me* unhappy.'

'You never said.'

'I shouldn't need to say. You should notice, then react. But look, it's not your fault. That's how it is, you stomping about, dealing with invisible dramas in your head. I should have learned to cope with it. I thought I could, but I can't. Not any more.'

For a moment, her face came sharply back into focus and I realised she looked different, suddenly, to the woman I married, to the person I carried around in my mind. Older, more angular of jaw. Slimmer around the shoulders. It was as if I'd bumped into her after ten years' absence. She looked good, damn it. She looked good.

'I was only twenty-three when met ...' she was saying. 'You were thirty-one. I've changed. You just haven't noticed. This is what you're like. You see all sorts of weird things that aren't there and yet you miss what's happening right in front of you.'

'Is there someone else ...?'

'That's not the point of this.'

'Is there someone else ...?'

'I'm not going to get into –'

'Fucking tell me if –'

'No, there's nobody else. But I think I might want there to be.'

The surface of my world cracked then broke apart. I felt that onset of mental fog before a DMT trip takes hold, as the pineal gland secretes its dream serum and dimensions fall away. Where there had been my kitchen, my wife, my fridge, my daughters' paintings, my dog's basket was now a swirling chasm. Fragments of Emily flickered through spinning holes in my vision, her face hard as a ventriloquist's dummy's, words coming out as if from a badly tuned radio. Words about how I'd never listened. About how I never paid her any attention. About how she never felt loved. About she was tired of being a bit part in whatever quest I was on. About how she was tired of my gloomy catastrophism. About how she needed time to think about what to do. About blah blah blah blah.

I staggered blindly around the table to try and hug her, kiss her, plead with her to take it all back. Tell me she was kidding. But she had turned to stone, knuckles white around the stem of her wine glass.

'This isn't happening.' I stepped away from her and turned to our crumbling hallway. 'It's too much. I need to go outside.'

As the front door closed behind me I heard somebody say some words. The words might have been Emily's. They might have been Mr Marsden's. They might have been Angela's dead husband's. They might even have been my own.

The words were: 'Walking away won't change anything.'

*

The only place to go was the sea. The indifferent, angry, calm, fucked-up sea. The sea that began life on earth. The sea that would finish us all off. The sea that took Mike then brought him back again. The sea that took the life of little Alfie's dad and then washed him up as a U-boat on Pelham Beach. The sea that took Walter Adams from Lovers' Seat and kept him for itself. That capricious beast, the sea. On the shore, I could gaze at its infinite fickleness and understand that nothing really mattered. Tides rose and tides fell. Everything was in flux and nothing lasted for ever. In the end, annihilation would come to all in the Great Levelling and, with it, a blissful amnesia in which all tragedies would be forgotten.

Yes, the sea was the place to be.

But I was disappointed. By the time I reached the promenade, night had turned the Channel to a syrupy black mass, barely distinguishable from the sky, but for a line of frothing surf, electric blue in the glare of the street lamps. To sit and stare out into the blackness, the eternal blackness – well, I was not emotionally ready for that, not quite yet. Better to walk, to keep moving.

Usually I was compelled to head towards East Hill on my wanders, but tonight I resisted the pull of longshore drift and instead walked westward towards St Leonards, passing the restored pier, where folk sipped beers in the glow of the bar and a beacon blinked a warning to fishing boats. I remember seeing its charred ruin on my second day in Hastings and those memories of Mike that returned in the gusts of sea air. Now here I was, remembering the memory of having that memory, pining for the innocence of a time when Emily loved me and we faced a fresh start. Jesus Christ. This nostalgia for nostalgia was lunacy. Where would it end? Emily was right. I was always one step removed from the present. Perhaps two, three steps or more, and counting.

Fighting the desire to go home and have it out with her, afraid of what truths she might tell me, I continued along the upper promenade above Bottle Alley, avoiding the drunks below deck. On the shore, beads of torchlight bobbed where lugworm hunters prowled and drunk teenagers raced between the groynes. Coming at me from the other direction were a father and son with fishing rods, a gang of twentysomethings clutching lager cans, and joggers to God knows where. A speed camera winked at a car whooshing beneath the grand Victorian terraces, five floors high with big bay windows. Few residents closed their curtains at night, unwilling to give up the sea view, even when it had faded to black. I looked up to see an old woman hunkered in front of her television. She was transfixed. As was I. Other people's lives were so compelling when framed in a well-lit window. Standing there, watching her, she became my television. Her reality, my fiction.

I wondered what Baird would make of these rows of homes blaring with his invention, or a version of it anyway.

Or what would Aleister Crowley make of humankind's transcendent potential reduced to this? The Aeon of Horus defiled. Instead of communing with spirits from the otherworld we had become a nation of slumped slaves. No wonder he had a pop at Baird on Bexhill seafront in 1946. But Crowley also knew very well that Baird merely exploited that which had already been conceived. He was a profiteer, not a prophet.

When it became too uncomfortable to watch the old woman any longer, I continued towards Warrior Square Gardens. On the promenade was a memorial bench with dead flowers taped to the back-rest, red tinsel looped around a photo of a man in his early twenties. The inscription read, 'Taken from this earth too soon'. Only metres away, the wooden sea serpent of Charles Dawson's waking dream rose in loops from the mini-playground. Beyond, Marine Court was lit up like a party cruiser. Fake monsters, fake ships. The essence of Hastings & St Leonards, where nothing was as it seemed. As I moved beyond Marine Court and its pillared walkways to the Victorian Grand Hotel I passed three middle-aged men discussing the least disruptive ways to commit suicide, while a girl with a pit bull bought drugs from a couple of low-slung-trousered scallywags in an art deco concrete shelter. Then the pedestrians fizzled out entirely and I walked alone until I stopped at St Leonards Parish Church, a giant red-brick building set back from the seafront, a stone cross angled awkwardly on the wall.

Something caught my eye up on a small hill beside the church. A pyramid silhouetted against street lighting. I had never noticed it before. Intrigued, I crossed the street and took a steep curving terrace to reach a walled garden no bigger than a tennis court, looking out upon the church and the sea. At the far end was a six-foot-high stone pyramid, much like the one depicted on the Masonic gravestone in All Saints Church, below the Black Arches. As I approached, light from a street lamp winked through a hole at its apex. There was a name carved into a slab below:

James Burton Esq, Founder of St Leonards,
July 29th 1761
Died March 31st 1837

This was the man who built this town, entombed like an Illuminati priest beneath an All-Seeing Eye, or the Eye of Horus. Was Burton a Masonic agent, creating St Leonards as an occult lodestone on the south coast? If so, then forget Crowley's curse, *this thing right here* was what pulled in the magicians, visionaries and inventors. This pyramid and the one on the headstone beneath East Hill were two poles of a magnet. They charged those subterranean waters which seeped from Old Roar Gill through the cellar of my house and the America Ground, energising all that lay between. This was what I'd been searching for. A piece of the puzzle to unite the stories I'd uncovered and explain why dark things had happened since Emily and I arrived in that damned house. Not that it mattered now. My marriage was in ruins and there was no book, nothing that you could call one anyway. It had been warped out of shape by my obsessions and delusions, reflecting myself in the landscape, telling only the tale of my own failings. This was what happened if you poked around here. This was what became of fraudulent interlopers like myself, like Crowley, like Dawson. We all got our comeuppance in the end.

But perhaps there was a way out.

I left the tomb and hurried across the road and down the steps from the promenade to the beach, where I frantically dug about in the shingle, using my iPhone's torch to seek out a stone with a hole in the centre. Something to undo what had been done. It was stupid. I knew from my research that Crowley's curse was an unfounded legend. It was a lie, like my life was a lie, like all the crap I wrote was lies, even the material I based on truth. I scooped up a bunch of stones with absolutely no holes in them and stuffed them in my jacket pockets. Then I wandered down the beach to the dark zone by the water's edge, remembering that evening in Dover in 1990 when I'd been thrown out of the pub and fantasised about drowning myself like Virginia Woolf, just to spite all those who mocked me.

Aha—as if on cue, there it was—a splash and slap in the darkness! Something gigantic swelled the waves just beyond the limits of my night vision, where obsidian shadows danced with ghosts of foam. I sensed that it was out there, the eel with a head the size of an armchair, haunting the edges of my memory, waiting for me. And there was something else too. A scent. Aftershave and the smoke from a Marlboro Light.

'Listen!' Mike was beside me, looking out at the nothingness, gesturing with a lit cigarette. 'You hear the grating roar of pebbles which the waves draw back and fling, at their return, up the high strand, begin, and cease, and then again begin, with tremulous cadence slow, and bring the eternal note of sadness in.'

I knew those lines. They weren't Mike's. They were the words of 'Dover Beach', by Matthew Arnold. He used to recite it whenever we were on that eponymous shore, nice and loud so he could be heard over the hovercraft roaring towards France.

'This is not how we imagined the future, Mike,' I said.

'Let us be true to one another,' Mike continued, opening his arms out wide, voice booming. 'For the world, which seems to lie before us like a land of dreams, so various, so beautiful, so new, hath really neither joy, nor love, nor light, nor certitude, nor peace, nor help for pain.'

I always thought that he recited that poem primarily to impress people. To show his deep connection with the place in which our school was located, even though we would always be aliens from the prison on the white cliffs. But perhaps he was wise beyond his years and really did feel deeply the emotional truth of this poem, aged only seventeen. There was an older man's head on his shoulders, we always said that about him. But I don't think I understood 'Dover Beach'. Not really. It was only through the loss of Mike's life, and all that had happened in the aftermath, all that walking and searching, the failed dreams and disappointment, that I finally understood what it meant, here on the beach of St Leonards, aged forty-three, with fire in my bollocks and a broken heart.

XXIV

Blood on Netherwood

I awoke to an empty house. It was Saturday morning. Emily was off with the kids for the day, so she told me in a lengthy text message, to give me space. She was sorry for being so brutal in her confession. It was the drink, the drink, but she meant what she said. She was sorry and she meant what she said. We could talk later. Tomorrow maybe. Or after my scan on Monday. *See you later,* she wrote. There was no kiss at the end of her text. Then again, we rarely did that kind of thing anyway. The clichéd greetings-card romance kissy-kissy heart nonsense was not our bag. Perhaps it should have been. I didn't really know how other couples behaved, how deeply they felt their emotions, or how you were *supposed* to feel after twelve years together, in the same way as it's impossible to know how another person perceives the colour blue—the intensity, the richness, the effect on the soul. Our brains are entombed in pitch black silence, with only chemical and electrical signals to suggest what's happening outside. So how do we know we are all getting the same signals? How do we know, truly, where those signals are coming from?

These stupid questions rolled in my head, over and over. I felt nauseous. I'd not eaten since yesterday lunchtime, but I had no appetite for anything other than a drink of something stiff to take the pain away. I gathered some dirty clothes from the floor, brushed my teeth and wandered down to Robertson Street in the America Ground to visit the wine and book shop owned by The Writer, purveyor of landscape-heavy novels and occult tomes. He seemed pleased to see me, despite my dishevelled appearance.

'Have a bit of this,' he said, pouring me a glass of impossibly strong Belgian beer. 'It's bloody gorgeous.'

We worked our way through several more beers, talking about the Black Arches, Dawson's fake bones and Crowley's battle with John Baird. I made out like this material was all going into a book that I had mapped out and that was actually going to come together.

'Have you read *Netherwood* yet?' he asked. 'Loads of good stuff about Crowley's last years. It's hard to get hold of. But I have it at home ...'

I didn't know if there was any point to learning more factual details about Crowley and the other mavericks I was writing about, now that I'd messed around so much with the truth. It might be best to compile the fragments into a 'Tales of Weird Old Hastings' compendium of ghost stories and urban legends, with plenty of gory illustrations, then sell it to tourists in the summer. When I was drunk enough I admitted this much to The Writer. I told him that it had all gone wrong and Emily was going to leave me. The house had defeated us, my attempt at another book had ruined our relationship and for all I knew I was being consumed alive by a hideous flesh-eating groin phantom.

He gave me a hug and, in consolation, said he too felt constantly on the brink of disaster. He told me of the stress he was under as he and his girlfriend tried to run a fledgling business while bringing up their first child.

'I feel like I am falling,' he said, 'but with improbable grace. I don't know how, but I keep landing on my feet.'

He told me that when he was sixteen he liked to walk from his home in Hartlepool to a rugged stretch of coast by a mothballed magnesium works and an abandoned pier, where he could be alone to think and smoke weed. One day he decided to walk along the ridge of a high precipice made from rocks, slag and industrial detritus. As he stepped over rusty corkscrews and bent iron girders, a slab of earth beneath him cracked, broke away, and he began to fall down an almost vertical incline.

'Suddenly everything went into slow motion,' he said, 'I don't know what happened, it was like my brain switched off and kind of a *muscle memory* took over. I just put one foot forward, then the next one, each time getting a purchase, somehow, and I just sort of ... floated down.'

'Were you scared?'

'No, I felt exhilarated and empowered. It was like I was touched by the Hand of Grace!'

It struck me that there were two kinds of faller. There were the likes of Edward I and The Writer, touched by the miraculous, falling with grace, and the likes of Rod Hull and Mike, who were shown no mercy by a sudden, malignant gravity. Although perhaps, in truth, all of us were falling. It was just that some of us fell faster and harder than others. Ultimately, we all shared the same destination.

Later that night we ended up drunk in The Carlisle, where a local band was playing. It was the first time I had been there since the *Ragged-Trousered Philanthropists* event, when The Poet defeated a heckler and I was told of a secret tunnel in East Hill which drove its explorers insane. It was a far less politically charged evening. People were here for wordless noise. The Sine Waves were a four-piece who played frantic surf-rock instrumentals pierced with analogue electronics, backed by library film footage of mad scientists, atomic bombs and proto-computer technologies, like something out of John Logie Baird's cave hallucination. The guitarist wore a blond wig and a surgical mask. The keyboardist's face was concealed behind a helmet. The bassist was a tall blond woman with a fierce stare. Disguises, misdirection and madness. There couldn't be a more Hastings band.

Mates of The Writer turned up and after a few pints he passed me half an E while rounds of beers and Jagermeister chasers racked up on the bar. We stumbled to the America Ground where we drank more of The Writer's profits, then on to his home in St Leonards, close to the pyramid of James Burton where I'd been the previous night. I was wasted, so wasted, that it was as if my body and mind had separated. I heard myself jabber and laugh as someone else operated my bones and muscles, pointless information pouring out of my mouth like shit from a drainpipe. By the time I asked for a taxi The Writer told me I was in no fit state. It would better if I stayed the night. I slumped in a corner of the sofa and faded out of the conversation, letting myself drift. The room telescoped away from me, further and further, until I was at the end of a long dark tunnel and could not hear a thing but my heartbeat.

Beeeeeep! Beeeep! Beeeep!

TALES OF WEIRD OLD HASTINGS

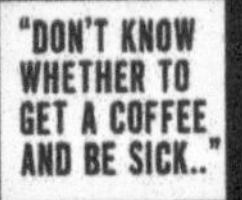

"MAYBE I'M ILL"

THE BOOK OF MAGICK
THE BOOK OF LIES
"SOMETHING WRONG WITH ME"

"OH THIS IS NOT GOOD..."

TIME FOR MY MEDICINE

I WAS ONCE
HEROIC

I HAD THE
STRENGTH OF
TEN MEN

I WALKED
WITH DEMONS

I TALKED WITH DEMONS

I WAS THE WORLDS
FIRST JUNKY
SUPERHERO

“OH GOD,
SHOULDN’T
HAVE STOOD UP’

NOW I JUST SHAKE
AND TREMBLE...

"OH GOD OH SHIT!"
MY BODY
IS WEAK
BUT MY MIND
IS AN INFINITE
UNIVERSE...
"I'M GONNA
BLEED TO DEATH!"

"AT LEAST THEY'LL KNOW
I'M NOT A HYPOCHONDRIAC"
I GO WHERE
THE HELL I LIKE
© VINCE RAY

Crowley awoke, astonished to see that the window of his room was awash with blood, casting a redness over the interior—the rumpled bedclothes, the opened books, the syringes and ashtrays, the desk covered in papers from last night's scribblings. He could not tell whether he was dreaming. Perhaps he had only just taken the heroin. Or perhaps he was dead. If so, it was about bloody time.

He tried to get up from the chair to inspect this strange phenomenon, but he found himself paralysed. His body had given up the ghost. Not that such trifling obstacles had ever stopped him. He had pioneered a route up K2, climbed the chalk cliffs of Beachy Head and stood atop Mexico's Popocatapetl volcano. If this was to be his next great journey then he would proceed fearlessly, as always. Crowley let his consciousness rise from its corporeal prison, leaving his frail old body beneath him, and drifted towards the blood-drenched window, effortlessly penetrating the glass and flowing down a long red tunnel wriggling with microbial tadpoles and Egyptian hieroglyphs. The symbols flickered past at exponential speeds until he burst through a membrane into a world where he was no longer Aleister Crowley but another being, sat at a cluttered desk in an unfamiliar room. On the walls were photographs of Arthur Conan Doyle, Charles Dawson, Teilhard de Chardin and a youthful image of himself, sun-ravaged and thin, bathing in a pool on K2. In front of him was a brightly illuminated screen full of words—a text that said, 'Blood on Netherwood'. Beneath was a strange, flattened typewriter without a cylinder, nor paper. Younger hands that were not his own began to clatter on the keys, conjuring new words to appear. As they streamed across the screen his consciousness was hoisted from the host body and propelled forth once more, through the glass into yet another world. In this one he huffed and puffed down a steep woodland path, zig-zagging through bluebells and nettles, until he came to a familiar clearing outside a cave. On the ground before him was a discarded trilby and a little girl in a cloche hat, except her face was that of a warty old lady and she said her name was Hannah. She lifted her arm and he was hoisted into the air at speed, rising high above bitten brown cliffs and a dazzling sea. Beyond was the castle and Hastings Pier. A man with a cocker spaniel on the crest of East Hill looked directly up at him, as if he alone could see him, watching him closely as he began to swoop like a gull over St Leonards, towards Bexhill, turning circles on the wing above the De La Warr Pavilion, where he beheld a man hunched on a promenade bench beneath a blanket, looking out to sea.

He knew that man to be John Logie Baird, the television

pioneer, chancer, thief of epochs, poisoner of humankind's spiritual well, and he knew instinctively that this was a vision of the future, for he could see himself on the promenade, walking towards Baird, his cloak billowing. At the shock of seeing his own avatar, Crowley lost his balance, tipped and tumbled in an arcing plummet towards the sea. *I'm going to die*, he thought. *The water's coming up so fast*—

Crowley awoke, breathing heavily. He was alive. The window was clear of blood. Sun streamed into the room, dazzling the dust particles. He leapt from his chair, stiff and wheezy, but full of ire.

What did his vision mean? And what was he to do with it?

He grabbed his I-Ching sticks from his desk. Trembling, he took the sticks and performed a divination rite, which revealed the Kwai Hexagram

KWAI: Cutting off; displeasure; front thy foe; but show reluctance due in acting so. Lay well thy plans before the march begins. Seek loyal friends and have no fear of gins. Fight on alone; persistent courage wins! Defeated, acquiesce—smiles conquer grins. Uproot small men like purslane—tan their skins; Cut off is he—and evil his end be!

Crowley knew right then what he must do that day. He must get Mrs Symonds to call for Watson to drive him from The Ridge to Bexhill—instantly! If both the dream vision and the sticks advised him to front his foe, then front his foe was what he would do. There was no need to have eggs this morning, he would eat Mr John Logie Bard for breakfast instead.

It was a matter of destiny!

XXV

Through a Scanner

Carefully, I pulled myself out of the wrecked coffee table in The Writer's living room and plucked the shard of glass from my hand. I checked myself for other lacerations. I was unscathed but for a bruised back and the flap of skin hanging from my knuckle. Blood from the gash had dripped onto the cover of The Writer's rare and expensive copy of *Netherwood*, depicting the ivy-clad guesthouse on The Ridge. A red splodge covered the window of the very bedroom in which Crowley had lived and died.

The Writer had already gone to open the shop but Jess helped me wash and bandage my wound and clear up the mess. I gibbered my apologies. Promised to pay for the damage and, once I had some spare cash, purchase the rare and expensive book that was now infused with my blood. Then I left as quickly as I could, walking down the promenade and through the America Ground where legions of mobility scooters forced their way through gangs of exchange students, pram-pushers scolded their snotty brats and drunks yelled threats at gulls. There was a deranged feel to the town. A tension. Like it could kick off at any moment. I sought solace in some chips but the first handful dried into a bolus in my mouth and I threw away the rest of the bag. I felt horrible. Truly horrible.

Once home, I clambered into bed, where I languished the rest of the day with the curtains closed, vaguely aware of Emily and the girls coming into the room to ask me how I was, gasping at the bloodstained bandage. Emily sat beside me for some of it, breathing softly in the gloom, smelling faintly of plaster dust and bonfires, wearing a geometric-patterned jumper I didn't recognise. She stroked my head and told me she was sorry. Her hands were cold. Eventually she left me alone and sleep gave me mercy. I have no idea if Emily came to bed that night. But she wasn't in it when I awoke the next day.

Drying myself after a shower I noticed that a scab was starting to form on my knuckle where the glass had slashed the flesh. It was triangular, in the shape of the Eye of Horus, with an orange pus-crust in the centre that formed the pupil. It reminded me of the eye I saw in my hand when I took that second blast of DMT in our living room beneath the haunted cornice. The scab might be a message of some kind, a mark of The Beast, or a complete coincidence, but I put it to the back of my mind. Today it was all about the MRI, not the DMT, and if I didn't rush I would be late for the scan.

I drove myself to Conquest Hospital, faint with hunger, and entered the radiology department where rows of elderly people sat in gowns, clutching their possessions. As I filled in a form at the reception desk, a man in a wheelchair – eroded by cancer to a thin, papery bundle of bones – stared at me in disbelief, like I was a ghost. His gaze pursued me as a nurse led me to a cubicle by the disabled toilets. As instructed on the sign, I stripped naked, threw my clothes into a green bin liner and donned a gown that showed off my white knobbly knees. I felt puny, suddenly, like I was back in my sixteen-year-old body, in the days when I was shunned by my schoolmates and lived in fear of an Eel with a Head the Size of an Armchair. Wracked with nerves, I sat down among the patients until I was called into the MRI chamber.

'So, you've taken off everything except your underwear?' asked the radiologist.

'I took *everything off.*' I blushed, aware suddenly of my genitals pressed against the flimsy cotton.

'Oh, well, it makes no difference,' she said. She was right about that, I supposed, nothing made a difference, not in the cosmic scheme of things. Seas would rise, civilisations would fall and new organisms would evolve. Pants or no pants, these things would transpire.

The scanner was bigger than I imagined, filling almost the entire room. But the hole into which I was going was not much larger than the doorway of our washing machine. The radiologist told me to lie on a narrow, flat bed. 'The machine is very noisy,' she said. 'We recommend you wear headphones. What music do you like?'

I couldn't imagine anything worse than listening to music right now, never mind whatever piped-in atrocity the hospital had on offer.

'It's okay,' I said, 'I'll not bother.'

She shrugged. 'The scan will take about forty minutes –'

'Forty minutes?' I had been thinking along the lines of five or ten. Perhaps I should have googled this before I arrived. As I began to slide towards the hole, I felt a sudden terror at being trapped in there alone. 'Actually, I'll have the music!'

The radiologist put the headphones on me, 'What would you like?'

There was no time to think. 'Bob Dylan,' I said instinctively. I don't know why. I suppose the music that saves you as a teenager becomes a default musical coda. Except that a large amount of life had happened since, from busking Dylan's songs in London with Mike, to singing 'One More Cup of Coffee' with The Rock Star in Clerkenwell, to a Dylan song being sung at my wedding to Emily, to this now – me in a giant scanning machine, wearing no pants, bowels twitching, the Eye of Horus on my knuckle. Barbed memories had entwined themselves around the voice and songs of Bob Dylan, making them jagged and painful. As the radiologist pushed buttons in the control centre and the scanner juddered into life, the Spotify playlist regaled me with a selection of Dylan's most painful break-up tracks, 'Tangled Up in Blue', 'Don't Think Twice it's Alright', 'I Don't Believe You', interspersed with the *THUDDER, THUNK, CLICK, BEEEP, THUDDER THUNK, CLICK, BEEEP* of the machine as it searched for radio frequencies emitted from the hydrogen atoms in the water and fat of my body, mapping me from chest to toe. This had to be the lowest point of my life, trapped in a white coffin, facing the end of my marriage and whatever it was in my bladder, balls and arse that had been causing so much pain for two years.

At the onset of 'Mr Tambourine Man', I recalled the time I made a harmonica holder out of a coat hanger, Sellotaping the instrument to it, so that Mike and I could play the song, me bleating tunelessly in the gaps between verses.

If you could see me now, Mike, I thought, *would you look at the state of me*?

But there was no reply. Not this time. Only a voice interrupting the song to say: 'Gareth, we're going to have to take you out and give you some injections.'

Out slid the bed, the machine shuddering irritably. The radiologist told me that spasms in my bowels were ruining the images. She had a drug that would calm my insides down. 'But you'll get blurred vision and a dry mouth,' she warned, strapping on the tourniquet. I couldn't see how that would make a difference. I was wracked with dehydration. My tongue was like leather already and my eyes were full of tears. She pushed the needle into my flesh and the plunger dropped. 'Now we'll have to start all over again,' she said, putting a plaster on my arm. Forty more minutes, forty more minutes of this.

'No music this time,' I begged as the bed began to slide in.

There was no music now to take me backwards in time. Instead I closed my eyes, listening only to the *THUDDER, THUNK, CLICK, BEEP* of the mechanisms, until I could detect rhythms in the scanner as it blasted magnetic waves into my body, yanking my protons in one direction, then pinging them in another so that they emitted radio signals. These signals were interpreted visually for the technician behind the screen. I had become the medium in a conversation between my atoms and a contraption built to detect that which the naked eye could not. I was the ghost in the machine. I was John Baird's dream. I was being broken down to my most miniscule parts and reassembled as an image in another place. I was both myself and version of myself.

THUDDER, THUNK, CLICK, BEEP.

Slowly, slowly, I was being broken down.

THUDDER, THUNK, CLICK, BEEP.

I was breaking down.

THUDDER, THUNK, CLICK, BEEP.

This was a

breakdown.

THUDDER, THUNK, CLICK, BEEP.

The noise of the scanner became overwhelming.

THUDDER, THUNK, CLICK, BEEP.

I had an urge to escape.

THUDDER, THUNK, CLICK, BEEP.

To go out into that landscape I loved.

THUDDER, THUNK, CLICK, BEEP.

To follow the longshore drift eastward.

THUDDER, THUNK, CLICK, BEEP.

To feel the wind on my skin, to see the sea flow all the way to the end of the world.

THUDDER, THUNK, CLICK, BEEP.

To walk and keep walking.

THUDDER, THUNK, CLICK, BEEP.

I dreamed I drifted from my rickety Victorian house across the park and up West Hill, high above the America Ground, a ghost of shingle in the dead harbour. I followed St Mary's Terrace towards the bones of the castle, framed against a sparkling English Channel, then down the slope, running my fingers over the inscriptions of memorial benches, to the steps beneath Rollo Ahmed's harpsichord house and down past John Martyn's place then deeper down to the Old Town. Past the skeleton-vending shops and antique streets, through Tudor twitterns beneath warped beams and overhangs. Past the doorway of The Stag with its smoke-dried witch's cats. Past the Masonic gravestone with its pyramid and all-seeing eye. Then up again, up, up, up. Past the Minnis Rock and the Black Arches, onto the crest of East Hill, where lush grass spilled around islands of golden gorse and I stood among the memorial benches, with my dead companions, 'never a dull moment' and 'sadly missed', and beheld the ocean—wide, blue and concave like the surface of an eye—the eye of the world staring out at the universe in wonder. It was as if planet Earth was the manifestation of a sublime universal consciousness, briefly enjoying its moment of self-awareness. The view was just like John Baird must have seen it, like Charles Dawson, like Madam Bodichon, like Aleister Crowley, like Teilhard de Chardin. No wonder that they all—

THUDDER, THUNK, CLICK, BEEEP.

No time. Keep moving, Gareth, keep moving.

I continued over the Neolithic hump of East Hill's earthworks and down a steep path to where the coastguard cottages once stood before the cliff fell into the sea, where the Old Town boys would come and pick up Alma for another adventure. On its distant spit of shingle, the power station of Dungeness was on fire. Tongues of red and yellow pulsed beneath an ebony corkscrew of smoke coiling into the heavens, turning the lid of the sky black. Helicopters buzzed over the pylons on the marshes as emergency ships sent up long arcs of water that made rainbows in the glare of a sun hung low in the sky. On the shore beneath the Dungeness lighthouse, the stricken fog horn sounded out:

THUDDER, THUNK, CLICK, BEEP!

Faster, more rhythmic came the noise—

THUDDER, THUNK, CLICK, BEEP.

THUDDER, THUNK, CLICK, BEEP!

THUDDER, THUNK, CLICK, BEEP.

A shamanic trance drum …

Drawing me into the otherworld …

THUDDER, THUNK, CLICK, BEEP.

As my body slid deeper inside the MRI scanner.

THUDDER, THUNK, CLICK, BEEP.

Deep, deep inside the plastic cave.

THUDDER, THUNK, CLICK, BEEP.

THUDDER, THUNK, CLICK, BEEP.

THUDDER, THUNK, CLICK, BEEP.

XXVI

The Great Convergence

At the end of the tunnel, sun dazzled through coils of brambles. I shuffled on my back until I was out of the cave and on soft earth, a breeze cool against my neck. Lurching upright, I found myself in a woody clearing, buzzing with insects, on the ledge of a slope. Below me was gorge of trees that were losing their leaves.

Had I fallen asleep? Quite how I got here was hazy. Apart from my clothes—clean black jeans and a white T-shirt—I had nothing with me. No bag. No iPhone. No wallet. No dog. I had no idea of the time or what day it was. But this was Ecclesbourne Glen, for I could see across to a familiar hill on the other side, bearing wooden steps that twisted up to the cliff top, the very vantage point from which I once saw a giant eel attack a man, boy and basset hound on the beach. Or at least I thought I did. Enough to write it down anyway. Not that I ever checked the newspaper the next day, or asked around about local deaths, washed-up limbs or recent disappearances, so absorbed was I in myself.

These same mistakes I make over and over. Woes befall the people I claim to love and yet I simply stand back and watch. Perhaps this was why I was here in Ecclesbourne Glen. Running away from home, from Emily, from Mike, from all those memories I'd stirred up with my meddling. Despite my cowardice, it felt good. A relief. The idea I could simply walk, and keep walking, all along the coast to Pett Level, to Rye, to the desert of Dungeness and into the wide blue yonder. But something was not right with my destination. Rumblings emanated from beyond the headland. Explosions and cracks like fireworks from the spit of Dungeness. Over the sea to the east, the sky purpled. Blood filling skin to make a bruise. The whirr of helicopter blades in the distance. Gulls in a mad flock across the Channel. A darkness in the water where the monstrous eel was stirring.

What was this place in which I found myself? And *when*?

The opening of the tunnel from which I'd crawled was so small it seemed impossible that I'd been within it only moments previously. Already the brambles had sprung back across the entrance, concealing it from view. I remembered those words outside The Carlisle ... 'A cave that has only been seen by three people. That's right, only three. The first one killed himself. The second one went mad. And the only reason I can tell you this is that the third one made it out alive to tell the story.'

There had been no Ouija board inside this tunnel though, so the story was probably bollocks. That was, unless you considered writing the stories of dead people a form of spirit summoning. In which case I had been in possession of a Ouija board all along. For I was the owner of a curved ergonomic computer keyboard with letters and punctuation for that nuanced communication with ghosts, so beloved by J. J. Williams and his British Society of Metaphysicians. My desktop computer keyboard was a twenty-first-century planchette and, like the original Ouija board, dangerous in the wrong hands. Notorious more for the way they play on the mind of the user than any supernatural forces they unleash. Strenuous bouts of invention could seriously disturb a person. Make them see things that weren't there. Make them fear for their sanity. Perhaps that was what the man outside The Carlisle meant, or whomever it was that told him the legend, and the person before that, and the person before that in the long chain that went back to the origin story.

I took a closer look my surroundings. Set into the hill

behind me was a much larger cave, a pile of dirty rags and a charred log in its mouth. I knew where I was. This was the hermit's cave in Ecclesbourne Glen. It couldn't be anywhere else. This clearing looked precisely as it did in my story about John Logie Baird's visionary trip down the tunnel, which I wrote without ever having visited. I'd tried to walk here a couple of times but after the landslip's destruction of the paths I figured the route was lost for now. I would return to it later. Instead I got caught up in all this craziness with Emily and hospitals and broken coffee tables so I cheated. I wrote the chapter as I believed the place might look.

Yet here it was, looking the very the same as I had imagined.

There was no girl in a cloche hat, of course, but that didn't mean I was alone. I could hear boots crunch on twigs. The deep *harrumph* of a man approaching, out of view but descending with purpose. I had seconds to decide whether to stay and talk, find out more about what was going on, or run. Everything inside me screamed leave now, so I took off towards the path down to the glen. As I reached the edge of the clearing I heard a voice cry: 'Hannah!' Despite myself, I turned momentarily to see a bald man around the same age as I, with pockmarked cheeks, unusually tanned for the time of year, eyes fiery.

'You!' I gasped. For it was he.

Without another look, I plunged into the woodland, running down overgrown paths damp with dew, leaping over brooks, heart in my mouth, hoping I wasn't being followed by The Great Beast. Once I reached the bottom of the glen, a muddy gully of rocks and fallen trees, I ascended the track up to the cliffs, where I paused on the outcrop by the viewing bench and looked back at East Hill and Hastings' harbour arm beyond. These landmarks had become so distant so quickly and for such little effort. I was hardly panting. I felt like Frankenstein's monster at the end of Mary Shelley's novel, bounding over Alpine glaciers in great strides, the world falling away at my feet as I fled my creator.

To the east, the Channel was growing moody and unsettled beneath the growing mass of black smoke amidst booms, rumbles and the tortured analogue noise of the Dungeness foghorn:

THUDDER, THUNK CLUNK, BEEP!

THUDDER THUNK CLUNK BLEEP!

THUDDER THUNK CLUNK BLEEP!

It was a warning to stay away but I felt compelled to walk towards it, to escape from all my failures. I pictured Emily and my daughters standing in the hallway beneath walls of cracked paint, where subsidence had wrecked our DIY efforts and the corners were dark with cobwebs we never kept at bay, the aroma of ancient water and dead rats wafting from the cellar. I could see Emily's face, frozen in the moment of her shocking revelation in the kitchen, eyes sorry and cold, but I couldn't get a grip on what my daughters looked like at all. Their faces were a blurred amalgam of features mutated over the years. Bah. There was no point in trying to hold an image in my mind. Nothing ever stayed the same. I had to push on towards the east and its implied futures, however catastrophic they might be.

I trudged over the brow of the hill and down a cliff-side track towards Fairlight Glen, passing a memorial bench with the epigraph 'She enjoyed her children', which made me think of cannibalism and tiny, roasted bones. On the peak ahead I could see Lovers' Seat jutting from a high ridge above. Odd, because Lovers' Seat had been destroyed by a spectacular landslip in 1980 and the celebrated meeting spot was long gone. The promontory flickered translucent, one minute clearly there, bold and angular, and the next minute horrendously truncated, a scree slope, empty and desolate. In the moments when it existed, figures walked around the big slab, dressed in Victorian and Edwardian garb, while grubby local tykes giggled and teased below. I thought of Elizabeth Boys and Charles Lamb, famous lovers, and

Harry Benton lying dead while the body of Walter Adams drifted out to sea, and all the other stories that had their beginning or ending at that stone. The private pledges made. Oaths sworn. All under the illusion of the Lovers' Seat's permanence, that no matter what happened, their sacred moment would remain forever engraved. But while these moments had lost their physical location, Lovers' Seat remained extant in stories told by the living. I could see it with my own eyes. Perhaps there was life after rock after all.

At the bottom of Fairlight Glen was a fence and a sign:

Due to the recent and
ongoing cliff falls the
access to the beach
is currently CLOSED

Should you choose to
make your own way
down to the beach
YOU DO SO
AT YOUR OWN RISK.

There was no point in worrying, not any more. I hopped over the fence, recalling the time I saw that man, child and basset hound do likewise, thinking them foolhardy. But I'd come to realise that imminent collapse was a state of being on the East Sussex coast. You learned to live with it. It became part of your psyche.

The path followed a stream bordered by ferns towards the sea, through banks where the land had been torn away. In the exposed hollows, roots dangled like the hair on skeletons in exhumed graves. This cove was a popular naturist beach. It was empty but for an old man prostrate on a towel, his arse a hairy moon. He didn't raise his head to look as I stepped past. Didn't move at all. Perhaps he was dead. This whole zone looked like the aftermath of an earthquake. The cliffs by the shore were broken into scree shelves and silty heaps, jumbled with uprooted trees. Stone slabs the size of tables were titled at angles, surfaces rippled with the contours, like topographical maps. Was one of these once Lovers' Seat?

I tripped through the rubble, finding a winch drum from a fishing boat, a packet of welder's electro rods and piece of A4 paper with the handwritten headline 'Probability Distributions' and this equation:

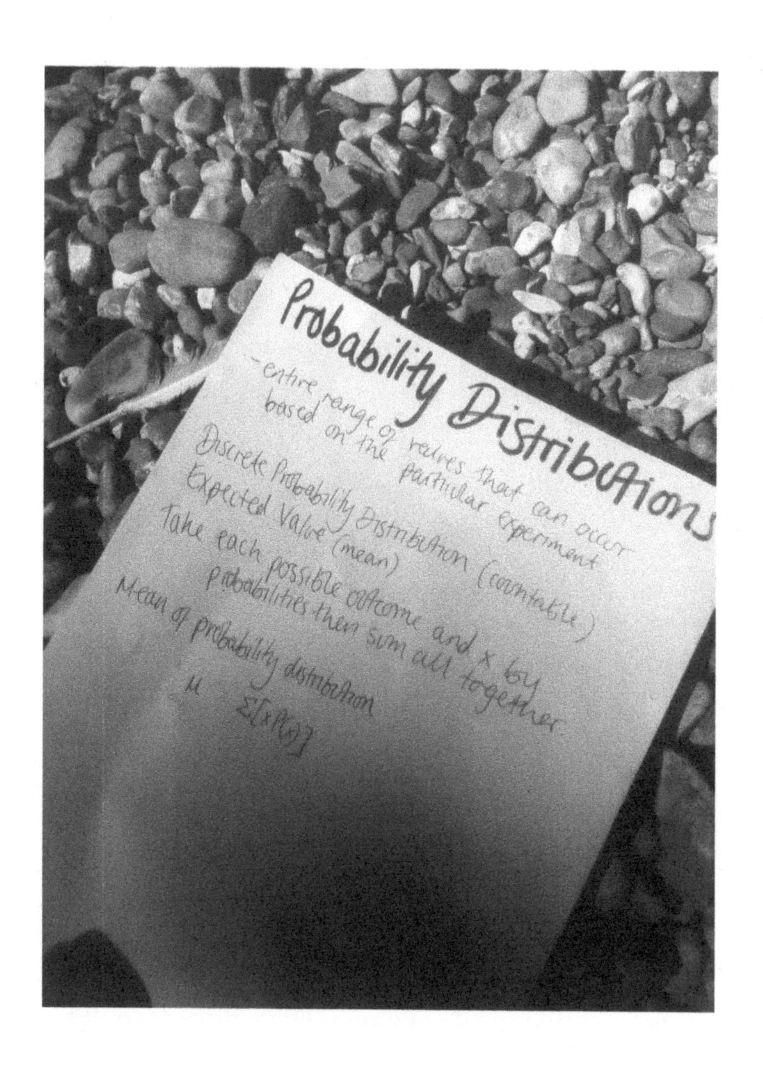
Probability Distributions
- entire range of values that can occur based on the particular experiment
Discrete Probability Distribution (countable)
Expected Value (mean)
Take each possible outcome and x by probabilities then sum all together.
Mean of probability distribution
μ Σ[x P(x)]

What did it mean? How could such a thing be here? How probable was it to find a probability distribution formula in a place like this?

The tide was far out and I hoped there was time to pass around the cliffs to the Pett Level. I had no idea how long it would take. The nudist beach had disappeared behind the headland and I was alone in a shattered world, beyond the point of no return. The sea screamed with gulls hunting rock pools as I wove through a smorgasbord of purple and orange boulders, swirling surfaces with Henry Moore curves, rocks with narrow white stems and bulbous green broccoli tops. Each stone was a map of time in flux. As I rounded the bluff, the shingle thinned into black sand, littered with golden pebbles, like the Tenerife beaches where they filmed *Planet of the Apes*. In the distance, Dungeness Power Station. I was in the final scene of the Charlton Heston film, except the Statue of Liberty was a nuclear reactor, and it was on fire, crimson tongues licking at the black canopy, the whole vista wobbling with heat.

There was a shout behind me. I turned to see Aleister Crowley prancing from rock to rock, surprisingly sure-footed on the slippery algae. He clambered onto a pyramid-shaped rock and stood at its apex, lifting the corners of his cloak in each hand like a cormorant fanning his wings. It was a ludicrous pose which I recognised only too well, for I had invented it. He was welcome to it. I would not let him intimidate me further. I had to keep moving quickly if I were to reach my destination, but now the shoreline had narrowed considerably and I was forced to clamber over rocks and squeeze through crevices directly beneath sodden cliffs that threatened imminent collapse. I couldn't trust them. This much I had learned. Nothing was safe. Not these cliffs. Not the ground we walked on. Not my house. Not the body which encased me. Not my marriage. The physical world was but a fleeting expression of something far greater, unknowable, and disinterested. It moved to its own mysterious, liquid rhythm. At any moment, the tide could change.

Rounding the next bluff, a row of white boulders was piled on the beach. Sea defences for the village of Fairlight, on a cliff which was collapsing at the rate of twenty-five metres a year. There were houses on the edge, fences dangling, paths to nothing, a garden wall in mid-air. Beyond was Cliff End, the fossil hunter's paradise of sandstone and clay deposits where I could see the young Jesuit priest Pierre Teilhard Chardin alongside the portly palaeontological hoaxer Charles Dawson. They were out where the sea lapped the rocks, on the hunt for dinosaur prints. Dawson was absorbed in what lay beneath his feet, eyes keen to find an anomalous fossil that might disrupt history and further his reputation. Teilhard's head was held high. He looked out beyond Dungeness to the future. This was the shoreline where he first understood that humankind was only one strand of a grand evolutionary process that had been ongoing for billions of years. Each step was a leap in consciousness, until consciousness itself had assumed the power to evolve. And so the world of information technology was born, helping us achieve in the physical world what witches and shamans had hitherto only been able to do in the spiritual world – to travel great distances in a split second, to communicate without physical boundaries, to manifest the unseen. Perhaps one day humanity would transcend its physical limitations completely and escape the catastrophe of terrestrial existence.

So absorbed were they in their thoughts, they didn't see me sidling by with my back against the cliff as I crossed from the rocks onto the beach of Pett Level, stepping over branches of oak, birch and hazel embedded in the sand. These were the remains of a 6,000-year-old forest that once stretched to France, revealed whenever the tide was low. Humans had hunted here, imbuing the forest with their origin myths. They worshipped gods. They called it home.

Then the sea levels rose and a mighty flood took away everything they thought was permanent and true. But these trees were no relic of a past calamity. They were an intimation of our future. The frozen water that encased the Earth's poles was liquefying at an unstoppable rate. Once unleashed, the seas would swell and drown coastal towns, sending refugees inland to fight over water, food and shelter. Millions would die. But if the likes of Teilhard de Chardin and J. J. Williamson were correct, this cataclysm would spark a revolution in consciousness. From the carnage might emerge a super-converged mind, forced to transcend its physical limitations and escape into the psychic realm.

Standing on the sunken forest, with the flaming concrete of Dungeness beyond, I thought about Teilhard de Chardin, Charles Dawson, Aleister Crowley, John Jacob Williamson, Alex Sanders, John Logie Baird, even my own father-in-law. I thought about their heresies and inventions, aura goggles, palaeontological tricks, seances, televisions, inter-dimensional communications and predictions of the Internet. I thought about their flawed, fantastic, narcissistic visions of new eras in which humans would be gods, immortal and transcendent, and how their storylines had connected on the East Sussex coastline. I realised suddenly what they had in common. They were all prophets of the Great Convergence and Hastings was their Jerusalem. A holy city. A place of pilgrimage. A hotbed of disputed claims and historical manipulations. A land that was as mythic as it was terrestrial.

The shore darkened. That noxious mixture of cloud and smoke from the east had reached me on a ridge of shingle that stretched towards New Winchelsea and Rye. Beside the path, something caught my eye. A stone inscribed with neatly inked letters:

I am a child of God
and He has sent me here

Was this the stone speaking or the writer? Perhaps there was no difference. Rock, plant or human, we are all carbon forms vibrating with the song of life. I put the stone in my pocket and continued along the ridge until the houses fizzled away into marshy fields, criss-crossed with drainage channels. The path seemed to go on forever, wind roaring in my ears, relentless and unchanging. To escape, I cut from the shore across the sheep fields, but the going was heavy. Rain began to fall. I could barely see a hundred metres ahead of me by the time I reached Rye Harbour Nature Reserve. A laminated map pinned to the entry gates depicted the reserve's triangle of shingle, saltmarsh and reedbeds. The ink was bleached. Paper warped. Yellow mould spread across its bottom half. The map had become the territory. Weathered, soaked and teeming with life. Next to it, another sign warned:

Please do not eat any of the fruits, berries, animals or plants from the area and do not touch or drink the water.

The Environment Agency has found that this land may be contaminated.

Water seeped up my jeans as I waded through poisoned grass, past Camber Castle, a squat compound sunk into the bog. A cry went up and geese flapped away from the path ahead of me. Where they'd been huddled was a severed sheep leg, gnawed to the bone. Dear God. Were they feasting on this? It had never been clearer. Dinosaurs lived amongst us, biding their time until humankind faltered, building up toxin resistance and an appetite for flesh. As Dungeness fell and the lights went out across our cities, Tyranno-geese would move in hungry legions from these floodlands to feed on the last survivors. One day humans would learn to fear the sound of honking.

Soaked and shivering, I reached the Rye Harbour Road, an industrial strip lined with factory blocks and silos behind steel fencing, bursting with weeds. The air was acrid with chemicals. I passed the Churchfields Industrial Estate then its namesake, The Church of the Holy Spirit, partly obscured from my view by the simulacrum of a church by the roadside—a graffitied concrete block sporting a telegraph-pole spire. In this place the arcane echoed the sublime. Everything was religious, and everything was ruined.

In the graveyard, the stone effigy of a man in a sou'wester overlooked a rectangle of engraved tablets. Each represented a crew member of the *Mary Stanford* lifeboat who died on 15 November 1928. It was a tragic tale. A ship called the *Alice of Riga* was foundering in gale force wind after a collision with the German ship *Smyrna*, when the crew of the Mary Stanford hauled their lifeboat from the hut on the beach of Rye Harbour. It took three attempts to launch before they rowed into darkness. Five minutes later the coastguards received a message that the *Alice of Riga*'s crew had been rescued by the *Smyrna*. A flare was fired to warn the lifeboat, but the crew of the *Mary Stanford* could not see it for the torrential rain and towering waves.

At midday, an upturned hull rolled in the surf and fifteen bodies were washed onto the beach. The sixteenth took three months to reach the beach at Eastbourne. The body of the youngest, only seventeen years old, never came home. His poor family. At least Mike was returned to us the morning after he fell from the castle, fully clothed and in a pose of peaceful sleep, so that it was almost as if we could call him to his feet. But unlike the crew of the *Mary Stanford*, Mike and I were not heroic, nor doomed by our sense of duty to save others. We were two idiots who drank ourselves into trouble.

It was Saturday, 11 April 1996, when the end began. In return for The English Teacher's hospitality during our road trip to Lancaster, Mike insisted he come up to St Andrews where we'd show him around the town and he could leave with a clutch of fancy new single malts. As soon as he arrived we hit The Castle Tavern, a dingy pub of plush velvet run by a burly barman who used to sell us mega-sized bottles of Stewart's Cream of the Barley after hours. A few pints later we emerged blinking into the mid-afternoon and walked to Ma Bells, a basement bar near the golf course.

That day we felt like friends again. We'd not hung out much since the trip to Lancaster. Mike had been away on his military antics, moving quickly over a terrain while carrying things, or telling other people to move quickly and carry things. That was how it seemed to me anyway. I'd fallen in love with Katy and spent a lot of time at her house, which irritated him hugely, or kept working on my terrible novel about a man addicted to climbing St Andrews Castle. While inspired by Mike's terrifying habit, the protagonist was a loose projection of what I thought I might become in my early forties, flung out from a failed marriage, drinking heavily, with a dog as my sole companion, seeking solace in the ruins on a wind-battered coast. It was an idea ruined by a convoluted plot and laziness. I was having too much fun to care about writing. What I really loved was walking down The Scores with Mike and The English Teacher, waves lapping in the distance and a warm pub waiting.

Here in Rye Harbour was the William the Conqueror pub, cold and empty. It stood between the River Rother and the Rye Harbour Holiday Park, guarded by a Martello Tower crawling with vines. The park gates were open but there was an eerie silence about the place. I passed by onto a wide saltmarsh left after the estuary silted up. An information board warned that such marshes were in decline because of rising sea levels. One day this sign itself would be under water, limpets clinging to the wood, starfish slithering over the text.

The path was crunchy with mussel shells, verged by sea kale and tile mosaics of hawk-moths, butterflies and weasels. In the thick, dirty mist I could see erratic objects scattered on the stones – broken buoys, fence posts, concrete boulders and blue piping. A hut with a red roof looked like it had crash-landed from Oz.

Close to the sea, the land thinned into a drenched desert. A man stared from a World War II pillbox. I didn't like the Nazi glint in his glasses, so I hurried towards the beach where I sheltered from the rain in another pillbox littered with cans, fag butts and Styrofoam containers. I peered through the gun slit at the harbour wall and Camber Sands beyond. There was no longer a horizon. Sea had fused with sky in a choking mass of smoke, thick as oil. The only proof that anything still existed beyond this obsidian veil was the *THUDDER, THUNK, CLICK, BEEEP* of the Dungeness foghorn.

That's when I saw them. The magician Aleister Crowley, the priest Teilhard de Chardin and the antiquarian Charles Dawson. They walked together from the water's edge towards the spectacled Nazi in the bunker, who had emerged onto the path, as if awaiting them. I could see now that he was not a Nazi at all but the famous inventor and coastal walker John Logie Baird, or at least someone who looked like him. They gathered together, talking. Then they turned and pointed at my bunker.

He's the one.

I slunk from the doorway and hurried between beach and saltmarsh, head bowed into the rain, passing burial mounds of shingle and steaming ditches, motifs of sheep and fence posts endlessly repeating themselves in the bleached monotony of the flatland. Whenever I turned to check, the four figures were always the same distance behind me, never closer, never further away.

I realised that they weren't chasing me. They were *observing* me.

Eventually a building emerged from the mist, flaked paint on doors hung with wreaths and a laminated poem beneath a crucifix:

Do not weep upon my grave
I am not there, I did not die
I am the seagull overhead
In the harbour here in Rye

This was the Mary Stanford Lifeboat House, unused since that fateful day in 1928. The atmosphere around the building was unseemly still. The water's edge bristled with wooden spikes, splintered and jagged with rusted nails. A milky sea lapped broken defences for a boat long gone, its seafarers departed this world, their memories trapped in this damned repository. I rattled the door, wondering if inside I'd find a cobweb-strewn nightmare of abandoned tea mugs and stubbed out cigarettes from almost a century ago. It was locked anyway.

I returned to the path where I saw something strange ahead. At first it seemed a trick of the light, but closer up I could see the unmistakable black and white stripes of a zebra crossing. The most inappropriately located zebra crossing I had ever seen. What the hell was it doing out here? The path was less than two metres wide, and so long and straight that, even in a mist like this, an approaching vehicle could see you from a mile away. It looked like the zebra crossing outside my daughters' school. Years of habit kicked in and

I was compelled to go to the verge of the road and await a suitable moment to step onto the stripes.

'Weather's terrible today,' I said to the zebra crossing.

'Someone'll catch their death,' it replied.

I looked to my right to check for cars. No traffic. Only a long straight path between the beach and the wetland. Then I looked to my left, where I could see the four figures approach in the near distance. To hell with them.

I stepped onto the crossing–

–crossing–

–crossing–

–crossing–

–crossing Market Street in the early evening darkness with Mike and The English Teacher, we bowed into the drizzle, car lights glancing in the puddles. There was one more pub on the way home, a last one or maybe two before last orders. The Central Bar was never a place to spend a whole evening but it was a convenient St Andrews watering hole. Mike and I were sparring good-naturedly, barking out one-liners and swigging with abandon. I remember he said something deliberately insulting and I slapped him lightly so his glasses fell crooked across his face. He was mock-angry, then laughed uproariously. *Ding ding*, the bell went and we staggered home where we grabbed a bottle of whisky, and asked our other flatmates to join us in the castle.

We hopped over the railings, down and up the grassy moat and across the lawn of the castle grounds. We climbed the steps to a raised platform beneath broken battlements where Mike and I continued our drunken bickering. I struggled to focus. I remember his face, pale and freckled, zooming in and out of a viscous darkness, his words muffled. He ribbed me about being under my girlfriend's thumb, about forgetting my mates. I said something back at him. Maybe it was funny, maybe it was cruel. Maybe it was both. I can't remember. He swung a half-hearted fist at my stomach. I told him I was going off to drink some whisky with the others, sat in a grilled portal on the other side of the grounds.

That's when he must have decided to climb the castle, most likely intending to surprise us from above, crying out some Shakespearean line, or looming up on the other side of the portal to scare the shit out of us. Ten minutes later, woozy and unable to make conversation, I walked back to where I'd left Mike and sat on the wall, staring down at the black waves. Then I returned to the flat to gather things to sleep at Katy's. On a whim, I went into Mike's room. He wasn't back yet. I grabbed his talcum powder and decided that the most hilarious thing would be to cover his entire bed in it, so that when he jumped in, he'd go up in a white cloud. I emptied the container onto his sheets, laughing at my ingenuity, tossed the canister aside and left.

The next morning, I was slumped on Katy's sofa with a pounding headache, reading a book, when the phone rang. One of Katy's housemates picked it up and passed it to me. I knew from the first word, just the way that Ben said 'Gareth …' that something terrible had happened. I knew what he was going to say before he said it and, when he did, the universe collapsed. I was turned inside out and sucked through a hole in myself. There was no air. No sound. Only a numb silent nothingness I wanted to hold onto forever, for fear of what would come next, that realisation which hit me like a fist. An explosion of pain. Then all the noise rushing back. I mumbled, 'I think Mike's dead', then I ran out of the house and across –

– across –

– across –

– across –

– across the zebra crossing to the shingle bank on the other side of the path, overlooking a beach sloping towards the sea's edge. It felt strange being in two places at once, the sounds and smells a portal across twenty years, flipping me between the mediaeval university town and the salt marsh by the lifeboat house. It was the same old sea after all. Taking things out, bringing them in again. I checked behind me. The black and white stripes of the crossing were still there, ludicrous in this no man's land, an Abbey Road for the afterlife. Across the water, through a fug of mist, the stricken nuclear power station of Dungeness blazed, smoke mass filling the sky, turning day to dusk. A row of pylons collapsed in a domino rally of brilliant explosions as the foghorn screamed.

THUDDER, THUNK CLUNK, BEEP!

A woman's spoke to me, crackly, as if through a tannoy system in my head.

'Gareth, are you okay?'

THUDDER THUNK CLUNK BLEEP!

'Gareth? Are you alright in there?'

THUDDER THUNK CLUNK BLEEP!

I ignored the voice. Instead I attuned my ears to the sound of low gravelly voices somewhere out on the water. They sang a song:

I'll be out in the lifeboat all night
For wrecks I'll be on the alert
I'll be out in the lifeboat all night
Dressed up in my waterproof shirt.

Closer, louder, more resonant became the song. A shape darkened the mist where the water eddied round a splintered wooden post. Finally, a large boat with two masts surged through the mist, oars turning in slow circles. Figures of maybe sixteen drenched men in sou'westers were hunched on board, water dripping from their noses. A hooded figure at the stern shouted, 'Oars!' and they duly lifted them, allowing the boat to drift to the water's edge. They stopped singing, turned in unison to stare at me as I trembled on the pebble ridge. The hooded figure gave me a solemn wave, beckoning me closer. Hypnotised, I began to walk towards the sea –

– where police constables were pacing on the sand. An ambulance on the road outside Castlegate. Medics with grave faces. There were some tourists too, asking the police what was happening. I recognised my flatmates by the railings, their eyes on the far end of the beach where the rocks stretched from the foot of the castle. They stopped me from going further. Nobody knew anything for sure, they said, but a body was lying out on the rock. A dog walker had found him and alerted the police.

I could see a human figure, tiny beneath the precipice, alone beneath the wall I knew Mike liked to climb, where I'd *seen* him climb that first time I visited St Andrews. Beneath that place, I'd left him drunk less than twelve hours ago without ever thinking to check if he was alright, to make sure he got home. None of the others had done so either. But it was me, I was the last to see him. I knew he was going to climb the castle. Where else would he have gone in that state, in that place, at that time of night? For good or bad, I had been his last chance of salvation. All it would have taken was for me to pay a bit of attention. To have a little bit of empathy for others. To think about someone else. To take action. There was a moment as I stared down into the waves from the wall of the castle when I could have called out for him, caught his attention and convinced him to come back to the flat with me. In that single act, I would have altered the fabric of reality. That is the godlike power we each have. We don't need Crowleys and Teilhards to unleash these on our behalf. They are within every human's capability. And yet I did nothing.

I did nothing.

I let him down.

Inebriation was no excuse. Billions of years of evolution had led from microbes to plants, fish and dinosaurs to humanity to me in that moment, blessed with the extraordinary powers of consciousness to understand there was a choice to be made between right and wrong, between love and selfishness, between intelligence and idiocy.

Yet in that pivotal moment, I walked away.

That moment would haunt my every step, no matter how far I ran. Like Jonah's flight from God's wrath, there was no escape. But finally, it was in East Sussex, with its cliffs and gulls, its castle and ocean, its salt air and memorials to the dead that the landscape revealed the true extent of my failure. For it wasn't inevitable that Mike should fall from the castle, no matter how often I tried to tell myself. Humanity is not locked into some ordained destiny. Consciousness is a force as powerful as time, strong as gravity. It moves through the universe, through the earth, through animals, vegetation and rocks. It mutates and evolves. It creates its own reality. The human mind, with its extraordinary imagination and capacity for invention, has unlimited potential, both to create catastrophe and avert it.

This is what Hastings taught me.

Yet despite these messages, the obvious bloody signs, I had made the same mistake again with my wife and my children. Our family was falling apart and I had failed to see it. I'd let it happen. I'd walked away from the truth.

But now I had no choice but to listen—

—to the song of the crew of the *Mary Stanford,* which struck up again, loud and clear as I clambered onto the boat among the crew and hunkered down at the bow, wrapping my arms around my knees, filled with dread and yet utterly accepting of wherever they might take me. As the surf slapped against us, almost tipping us over, I gripped the sides of the boat.

On the shore, the figures of Crowley, Baird, Dawson and de Chardin walked over the zebra crossing and down the beach to the water's edge where they stopped, ankle deep, and watched me depart. The self-serving occultist, the visionary priest, the fraudulent historian and the sickly inventor: four parts of myself shrinking into an amorphous blur as I floated away from Rye Harbour under a sky that was now pitch with smoke. The only light was from the fierce fires that raged on the disintegrating shingle spit of Dungeness. Deep beneath the mad, bucking hull of the *Mary Stanford*, the sunken town of Old Winchelsea was stirred by tremors from the exploding nuclear power station, fragments of timber, iron and crockery whirlpooling up from the seabed.

Not more than twenty metres away from my side of the boat, a shiny black hump broke the water's surface, formed a loop, then sank back into the waves. Another loop rose and fell. Then another. Finally, a long tail launched from the water, whiplashing foam into a phosphorescent shower, and followed the rest of the body into the depths. As we rocked in the wake of the giant armchair-headed eel the rain-soaked faces of the lifeboat men remained noble and expressionless, as if made of stone, their arms moving stiffly as they rowed me past the sand dunes of Camber to the end of the world.

Acknowledgements

Some of the text in Chapters II, VI and XV first appeared in my essay 'Wooden Stones' from *Walking Inside Out: Contemporary British Psychogeography,* edited by Tina Richardson and published by Rowman & Littlefield, 2015.

The account of Crowley's arrival at Netherwood in Chapter VIII is based on an article by Rodney Davies entitled 'The Last Days of Aleister Crowley, The Great Beast, At Hastings' on www.21stcenturyradio.com and also *Netherwood* by Antony Clayton (Accumulator Press, 2012).

The tale of Hannah Weller in Chapter X is based on an anecdote abstracted from the 'Recollections of James Anthony Gardner, Commander R.N' which appears in *Hastings Bygones Vol. 4* published by the Hastings Local History Group, 2001.

The comic strip in Chapter XXIV was conceived, scripted and illustrated by Vince Ray.

The Kwai Hexagram in Chapter XXIV is taken from *Liber 216: The I Ching* by Aleister Crowley

For my version of Charles Dawson, I'm indebted to the book *Piltdown Man: The Secret Life of Charles Dawson* and *The World's Greatest Archaeological Hoax* by Miles Russell (Tempus Publishing, 2003).

Special thanks to:

Gary Budden and Kit Caless for taking a risk with me (again).

Chris Wellbelove for his unfailing support and enthusiasm for this book.

Vince Ray for the illustration.

Hollis for the cover art.

The Hughes family, for giving me their blessing to write about their amazing son.

The people of Hastings for being so weird and welcoming.

Hendrix, for taking me on walks.

Mum and Dad, as always.

Thanks also to:

Michael Smith and Jessica Scarratt (sorry about the coffee table), Salena Godden, Emily, Dave Watkins, Tommy Orme, Matthew Clayton, Tina Richardson, Ben Thompson, David Southwell, Martin Fuller, Maxim Griffin, Mark Williamson, David Fyans and Broken20, Chris Russel, Katy Strange, Christina Lowe, Roland Lopez, Jason O'Flynn, Wendy Hurrell, Mychel Wayne Quinnell, Christopher Josiffe, Lee Brackstone, David Cowan and Ditte, Chris and Sadie Cragg, George and Sue Allison, Thilaka Hillman, Kelly Wilkinson, Simon Charterton and everyone involved in Weird Shit @ Borough Wines Beers & Books where I performed a great deal of this book to a wonderful crowd, James Wvr, Andrew Weatherall, Nina Walsh, The Fireflies, Vince Ray's Loser Machine, The Sine Waves, The Frat Cave, Lucas and the Slam Dunk Crew, Mandy, Naomi and the Hastings Storytelling Festival, The Hastings History House (thank you to everyone who works there, you're fantastically helpful) and Steve Peak's excellent Hastings Chronicle website http://hastingschronicle.net/

About the author

Gareth E. Rees is the founder and editor of the website *Unofficial Britain*, and author of *Marshland* (Influx Press, 2013). His work has featured in anthologies including *Unthology 10* (Unthank Books), *An Unreliable Guide to London* (Influx Press), *Mount London* (Penned in the Margins), *Acquired for Development By...* [Influx Press], *Walking Inside Out: Contemporary British Psychogeography* (Rowman & Littlefield), *The Ashgate Companion to Paranormal Cultures* (Ashgate), and the spoken word album with Jetsam, *A Dream Life of Hackney Marshes* (Clay Pipe Music). He lives in Hastings with his two daughters and a dog named Hendrix.

www.unofficialbritain.com

@hackneymarshman

This book was made possible thanks to the support of the following people

John Bateson

Anne Beech

Steve Birt

Owen Booth

Phil Brunner

Dana Bubulj

GS Catlin

Sarah Cleave

David Clelland

Emma Connolly

Katie Cooke

Simon Coppock

Anne Corden

Chris de Coulon Berthoud

David Cowan

Dan Coxon

Sadie Cragg

Detta Danford

Carolynne Donnelly

Dave Donnelly

Paul Dutton

Gerry Feehily

Sarah Garnham

Rob Gear

Matthew Gilbert

Hilary Hall

Thomas Hardy

Lucy Harrison

Francoise Harvey

Frank Hemsley

Kate Hodges

Steve Holden

Wendy Idel

Timothy Jarvis

Gareth Jenkinson

Jenny Kok

Sarah Law

Rebecca Lowe

Rowena Macdonald

Matt Morden

Ben Myers

Adam Neuman

Baz Nichols

Mark Nunn

Tommy Orme

Matt Petzny

Sean Powley

Richard Pye

Andrina Rees

Howard Rees

Simon Rees

George Sandison

Craig Scott

Kate Scott

Joe Skade

Michael Smith

Rob Spencer

Emma Strong

Charlotte Suckling

Carl Taylor

Ben Thompson

Martin Togher

Kerry Twyman

Justin Watson

Lynne Wilson

Rebecca Williamson

Julia

Influx Press lifetime supporters

Barbara Richards

Bob West

Influx Press is an independent publisher based in London, committed to publishing innovative and challenging fiction, poetry and creative non-fiction from across the UK and beyond. Formed in 2012, we have published titles ranging from award-nominated debuts and site-specific anthologies to squatting memoirs and radical poetry.

www.influxpress.com

@Influxpress